Pretty Souls

JULIE PARTICKA

A Paranormal Response Team Novel

ೞ

Decadent Publishing
www.decadentpublishing.com

Pretty Souls
Copyright 2011 by Julie Particka
ISBN: 978-1-936394-77-7
Cover design by Dara England and Razzle Dazzle Design

Published by Decadent Publishing Company

Look for us online at:
www.decadentpublishing.com

Printed in the United States of America

Praise for Pretty Souls

"Through the eyes of foster sisters Elle & Cass, we get a new look at what it's like to grow up being a paranormal. Even better, paranormal crime fighters. Loved it!"
Natasha~~Wicked Lil Pixie
(www.wickedlilpixie.com)

"This is a great debut novel from Julie Particka and it should be a big hit with the YA audience. I, for one, cannot wait to have an actual copy in my hand…It's awesome! Buy it and read it, you won't regret it."
Julie-Anne~~Thoughts of a Scot
(www. thoughtsofascot-nightshade.blogspot.com)

"Amazing debut by Julie Particka! A fun, fast-paced mystery mixed with the hidden world of the supernatural. Fans of urban fantasy won't want to miss this one. I need book two pronto!"
Andrea~~Aine's Realm
(www.ainesrealm.blogspot.com)

"Pretty Souls...has werewolves, vampires, demons and zombies, oh my! ... The ending makes it clear that there is another book to come. I look forward to reading it."

Bea~~Book Lovers Inc.
(www.bookloversinc.com)

"Elle has to stop a demon from raising an army of the living dead, decide if the hot boy she really likes wants her gorgeous half vampire sister instead and oh yeah .... try to keep her inner beast from taking over. All in a day's work!

Pretty Souls is filled with action, paranormal beasties, humor and mysteries that kept me second guessing myself until the very last page.

More please."

Karen~~For What It's Worth
(www.fwiwreviews.net)

~DEDICATION~

To my two wonderful children. You make me crazy, but it's a good kind of crazy. Much love always.

Chapter One

Tuesday, October 18, after midnight

Why couldn't tonight have just been a normal night? I had homework to do; so did Cass. We might've been able to swing giving a wayward vamp a slap on the wrist for getting a little too friendly with a homeless person or something. But we really didn't have time for anything weird.

Even with six years experience tracking scent trails, I still hadn't known what to expect at the end of this path. But even my best guess sure as hell wasn't to find Diego Martinez walking into the automatic doors at Sears. Especially since they'd been locked for hours.

Cass and I watched from the parking lot as Diego rebounded off the glass and stumbled back a few steps before striding up to the door again. "What do you think, Elle? Sleepwalking?" Cass tilted her head from one side to the other.

I pulled my lip between my teeth—thinking once more how I should really stop chewing on it—as Diego bounced against the glass again. "It'd seem like running into the door over and over would kind of disrupt his REM cycle."

Cass shrugged, the movement shifting her black duster so the wind caught the hem and fanned it out behind her. "Well, why don't we go see if we can wake him up? Unless that'll make you get all tongue-tied."

The breeze worked so much better for her than me. She got the avenging angel billowing coat. I looked like the victim of a tragic wind tunnel accident. I yanked loose strands of hair from my face with a grimace and snapped, "I'll be fine." It didn't help my demeanor at all that when I tugged my hair away, several pieces of fur flew right back into my face. Whoever concocted the whole werewolf thing really should have done away with shedding.

"You sure, Sis? Don't plan on drooling and falling all over yourself?" Cass moved toward Diego without waiting for a reply. *What Cassidy wants and all that.*

"Yeah. Completely over my Diego issues," I said to the night air as I jogged to catch up to her.

She reached Diego, grabbed his arm, and whipped him around. "Hey, Diego, old buddy, you have football practice tomorrow. Shouldn't you be in bed?" With his momentum toward the mall interrupted, Diego tried to walk forward in the new direction. Until he ran into the five-foot high, platinum blonde brick wall. Cass's body didn't repel him the way the door had, but she wasn't letting him leave either.

"Damn it, Diego, just stand still." I expected him to ignore me, too, but he stopped pushing against Cassidy and did the best impression of a statue I'd ever seen. A really hot statue with deep brown eyes, gently curling chestnut hair, bulging muscles, and….

Cass snapped her fingers in front of my face. "Yep, you're doing great." She rolled her eyes and turned back to him.

I snarled and squared my shoulders; my crush on Diego was a thing of the past. Not my fault he was still nice to look at. "His breathing isn't steady," I said, after listening for a few seconds. "How's his heart rate?"

"Too fast for sleeping." She parked her hands on her hips. "Drugs?"

A thin line of saliva formed at the corner of Diego's mouth and dripped toward his collar, building a shiny bridge of liquid. He also started bleeding. The impacts with the door had left a small gash on his forehead. My eyes darted to Cass, who glared at him, then back to the blood pooling in the cut.

"No way. Diego wouldn't do drugs; he's smarter than that." There was absolutely no reason at all to worry about the blood. It was just a little. Everything would be fine. I held my breath and watched as it dripped from the cut and ran down his face, mingling with the drool. "He actually looks kind of like a zombie."

"Hello? Heartbeat and breathing. Definitely not a zombie." Cass stood on tiptoe and waved her hand in front of his face. Without warning, she stilled and her nostrils flared. "Besides, his pupils are dilated. I vote for drugs." She dropped to her heels and backed away.

"But I don't smell anything...off about him." If he was high, it should have left some sort of scent—in his sweat, his blood, something.

"Yeah, well your nose isn't exactly in tiptop shape like this, is it? I told you not to shift back so soon. But no—you see Diego and poof." She made jazz hands. "Elle is human again."

"It wasn't like that." Actually it was, but not for the reason she thought. We'd reached the end of the trail. There was no reason for me not to shift back.

"Sure it wasn't."

I closed my eyes and counted to five—she didn't deserve the whole ten. "Whatever. I still don't buy drugs."

Cass turned on me and got right in my face. *Not good, not good at all.* "Use a little logic, Elle. Ockham's Razor says drugs."

"Who-ha's what?"

She shook her head. "Ockham's Razor. It's a scientific principle that basically says that all things being equal, the simplest answer is usually right. Drug abuser trumps living zombie." She turned and took a step away.

"Based on that theory, we shouldn't be what we are either."

Cass stopped and her shoulders tightened, stretching the coat across her back. When she finally spoke, it was through tightly clenched teeth. "No, we *are* the simplest explanation for us. We're just the ones no one wants to believe." She strode toward the edge of the parking lot.

"Drugs or not, we can't just leave him here!"

She spun around and glared at me with eyes that had

grown much darker than their normal cornflower blue. "Fine, then let's take the stupid, stoner jock home. Maybe in this state you can convince him you're the love of his life."

My teeth clamped down on my tongue. She'd avoided showing teeth when she spoke. If I'd had any doubts, that simple act confirmed my suspicions. We were in trouble. "Come on, Diego, let's get you home." I tugged on his arm and made sure to keep him downwind from Cassidy as much as I could.

❧

Cass didn't attack Diego on the way to his house, but she never dropped back to walk with us either. I hoped she was just irritated that we didn't find anything more interesting. Hoped, but doubted it.

We slunk through the shadows behind the Martinez's house until we had a clear view of their deck—and the sliding door with a bar across it. "Crap." I dug through Diego's pockets, searching for keys. Nothing. They probably had an alarm with coded doors.

"We could always break in." Cass stepped out of the shelter of a towering pine tree and moved toward the door.

I yanked her to a stop. "Are you nuts? I don't want to have to explain any of this when their security alarm goes off." I didn't want Diego's problems, whatever they were, to get any undue attention either. I might have been over my crush, but I wasn't a bitch.

"Fine. Then let's just dump him on the deck and be done with it. He can sleep it off with the mosquitoes until the sprinklers wake him up in the morning." Cass crossed her arms against her tiny frame and tapped her foot. Streetlights reflected off her eyes, making them look as black as oil.

I didn't have a better plan and unless there was something else waiting for him, Cass posed the biggest threat to Diego. I looked around the yard with its enormous flowerbeds and lush green lawn. A deep inhale told me that a family of deer lurked in the trees nearby, and they were more of a threat to the chrysanthemums and asters than to Diego. My sense of smell wasn't top notch in my present state, but it would have to do.

"Fine. The deck it is."

Cass tried to grab Diego's other arm, but I brushed her fingers from his leather jacket and pulled rank with a look. "Stay here."

I tried to lead him quietly up the wooden steps, but in his lumbering state, he tripped and made far more noise than I liked. And then the security lights went on. *I swear this house is out to get me.*

Luck must have decided to cut me a break though, since his parents didn't come running outside.

"That doesn't look very comfortable." I glanced around at the metal furniture. Very weather-resistant, but not great to sleep on. A storage box next to the door held some thick, flowered cushions that I spread on the glider. Diego sat without resistance when I pushed him. "Look, your parents are probably going to be pissed if these get wet in the morning, but I can't just—" I bit my lip to stop the babbling nonsense about to spew out of my mouth.

Diego stared at me blankly, and I willed him to say something. Anything. His silence hung heavy in the air.

Heaving a sigh, I started talking again. "Please just stay here. Your parents'll help you in the morning." Still no response, not even a blink. "Try to get some rest." With a gentle nudge from me, he lay down and closed his eyes.

I gave him one last concerned glance before joining Cassidy under the pine tree.

She didn't even bother trying to hide her toothy grin. "Is he all tucked in now? Snug as a bug in a—"

While she was busy mouthing off, I lunged for one of the fearless rabbits that live in our town. It must have decided we weren't a threat. It was wrong. With the bunny gripped in my left hand, I drove my right against Cass's throat, slamming her back against the tree trunk. Pine needles drifted around us as I glared at her and snarled, "Are you a freaking idiot?"

"What the hell? I was just kidding."

I wished I could believe her, but since she talked with her mouth mostly closed, I couldn't. Besides, she couldn't hide her eyes. Stark, inhuman blackness coated her irises. I hated those eyes. Covering the shudder that ran along my spine, I pulled her forward a few inches then slammed her back against the trunk. For a moment, as more pine needles drifted to the ground, the rabbit ceased struggling in my grip. The lack of scratching was an improvement, but I hoped I hadn't killed it by squeezing too hard.

"I'll ask you one more time. Are you a freaking idiot?" My voice hissed from between clenched teeth. When Cass didn't answer that time, I took a different approach. "When was the last time you ate?"

Her lips curved into a smile that didn't quite reach her eyes, and she spoke with deliberate slowness. "I ate dinner earlier tonight, Elle. You know that. You were there. Jen made tacos, and Eric told us all about his boring day at work."

My body trembled, but not with fear. Cass was so far gone she had the nerve to try to play with me. I supposed I had to count myself lucky that was all she was doing. I gritted my teeth and shoved the rabbit at her face. The movement must have made its shock wear off because it began thrashing around again, claws scraping at my forearm. "Eat it."

Her ebony eyes shifted to the rabbit then back to my face. "I'm not in the mood for rabbit tonight, Elle." Her fake grin slipped to something more condescending.

The expression came close to making my blood run cold. Not close enough though. I was furious enough to beat her senseless. "Too bad, because I'm beyond caring what you want. You were stupid enough to come out hungry. Patrolling without feeding? I can't trust you like this, and we aren't leaving until you eat the rabbit."

Cass crossed her arms and, leaning her body against the tree like she didn't have a care in the world, blinked at me. Long and slow.

I tried not to let my human instincts take over, but I felt my heartbeat speed up. The fear almost suffocated me, but I choked it down and shoved every inch of anger into my voice. "And really, I don't care if I have to force you."

Cassidy gave a tiny harrumph and raised her arm. "Fine. Whatever. Hand over poor, little, innocent Thumper." My hand still gripping her throat, I slapped the wriggling mass of bunny into her open palm. Her eyes narrowed to slits when I didn't let her go. "Don't you trust me, Sis?"

Exhausted with her stupid games, I sighed. "Just eat the damn rabbit so we can go home."

At long last she raised the animal to her face and opened her mouth, revealing canines that had extended to nearly an inch long. Without another word, she plunged her fangs into the bunny's quivering flesh. I held onto Cass until the sucking noises reached a nice steady rhythm, and the muscles that had locked into place finally loosened. Even though I let her go, her lips stayed glued to the small animal, whose struggles had long since ceased.

The drained body of the rabbit hit the ground with a quiet thump, and Cass raised an embarrassed blue gaze to me. "I'm sorry."

I simply shook my head—too tired to do anything else. "Don't you *ever* do that to me again. Neither of us may be happy with the hand life has dealt us, but whether you like it or not, you have to feed." I spun around, stalked into the woods, and headed toward home. "And I don't plan on ever being dinner."

Cass could follow me, or she could sulk until dawn. I didn't care. I still didn't think Diego's problem was drugs, and I just didn't have the energy to coddle a moping bloodsucker.

Chapter Two

Sleep didn't come easy for me. Cass did follow me home, and of course, she conked out as soon as her head hit the pillow. At least it meant she didn't hear me crying once all the tension finally drained from my body. Every night we went on patrol, I depended on Cassidy to have my back. And tonight my foster sister had betrayed that trust. She not only went out on patrol hungry, but vamped out as part of the bargain. We didn't have anyone else, and now I felt like I might be losing my only confidant and best friend in one fell swoop.

The only way for me to stop dwelling on Cass was to move on to the Diego problem.

I still didn't buy that he was on drugs. The University of Michigan had offered him a dual athletic/academic scholarship. His class clown act was just a way to deflect people from seeing how crazy smart he really was—bad for the image. The scholarship secured his future—as long as he didn't do anything stupid. I just couldn't believe he'd risk getting high.

But Cass wouldn't understand that. She'd just say I still had a thing for him, and I didn't. I'd spent my first year in Portage trying my best to blend in, to be normal, and normal at sixteen meant finding a boyfriend. He'd seemed like a great choice.

Even now, I couldn't deny that I found Diego attractive. Lucky for me, his love 'em and leave 'em reputation hit my ears hours before he finally asked me out. I'd never told Cass about it, or that I'd said no. Dating him would have put me on a different social path at school, but I didn't really desire membership in his conquest club. I just wasn't the notch-on-the-bedpost type.

My boyfriend dreams these days usually involved celebrities. No chance of getting a date there, but with the secrets I had to keep, I'd decided over the summer that I was okay with it. Visions of a certain tawny-haired, emerald-eyed guy who wasn't a college student, but played one on TV, managed to lull me to sleep—at the same instant the alarm shrieked to life.

I scrunched my eyes shut and buried my head under the pillow, pulling it tight against my ears. The noise had to be part of some horrific nightmare. Maybe the one where Cass tried to kill me. Yeah, that was it. The noise was part of a torture technique designed to weaken me so she could move in and finish me off.

Reality set in when I heard her feet hit the floor and pad across the carpet to silence the screaming bells. She whacked my pillow. "You want the shower first?"

"No," I groaned, tugging the fluffy softness closer around my head. Then I remembered my key part in tracking Diego the night before. Shifting in the alley. Shifting back inside the public toilet. Ripping the pillow off my face, I leapt out of bed. "Wait! I lied. I *will* go first; I feel pretty gross."

"Yeah. I wondered."

A quick glance at Cass made me smile inside. Morning was the one time she generally looked worse than me. Her pale, wispy locks that people fawned over? An oily, snarly mess. I didn't envy the guy who would eventually have to wake up to that every morning and still tell her he loved her. I had it easy. My job description meant I didn't even have to like her, and this morning I didn't.

"Go on, get your fuzzy butt in gear." She tossed some

clothes at me with a smile, her bubbly daylight persona coming out in its most annoying form.

Bundling them into a ball, I snarled at her, showing teeth. Then I froze. I hated when she shocked me into being irritable; I never failed to end up looking like an animal.

Cass didn't bother to notice my discomfort. With a cheeky grin, she wrinkled her nose and waved a hand back and forth through the air between our faces. "Jeez, Elle, I thought I was the one who sank my teeth into raw meat last night."

That did it. I might've loved her like a real sister, but making jokes about her idiocy was going too far. I opened my mouth to give her a much needed chewing out.

And she immediately clamped her hand over my lips. "Look, dog breath, I'm sorry, okay? It was stupid to try to wean off the blood. But, if you don't get moving, we're going to miss breakfast. I'm good with a granola bar on the bus. Can you say the same?"

I glared at her for a minute before spinning on my heel and storming down the hall to the bathroom. At least she apologized. She was right though—I needed to eat—but I certainly wasn't feeling generous enough to feed her ego this morning by saying so. After twisting on the shower, I let the familiar cadence of water on tile bathe me in blissful calm as I undressed.

I made the mistake of looking at myself in the mirror. Last night's wind had joined forces with the tossing and turning to make me look rougher than Cass. My hair twisted and swirled on the top of my head like some sort of honey-colored rats' nest, and the dark circles ringing pale blue eyes belonged to a raccoon, not me.

I spent more time than I would've liked combing the snarls from my hair before stepping under the beating water. The shower did more than loosen my knotted muscles and rinse the filthy soap bubbles from my skin. Much of my worry ran down the drain, too. Cass screwed up; she was smart enough not to do it again. Other than the gash he'd given himself, Diego hadn't appeared to have any injuries. We'd followed him from the park, where we'd sensed something supernatural. Cass had guessed magic, but our experience was a little limited, so we couldn't be sure. Maybe he'd just seen something that sent him into shock. *That could account for the blank stare and weird behavior. Right?*

I stepped out of the shower fully prepared to look up the symptoms of shock on the Internet, but the scent of bacon wafting up the stairs made Diego seem a lot less important. After all, he was alive and breathing, and unless it was a matter of life or death, my crazy metabolism dictated that food came before most other things.

I could do make-up on the bus, so I rushed downstairs to the sun-drenched table and breakfast. Jen, our foster mom, hummed while she messed with stuff in the kitchen, and I scooped up a second serving of bacon and eggs. It was about as good as my life got: food and quiet.

Then Cass bounded down the stairs, all sunny disposition and noise. One of these days she would wake up literally doing back flips. No matter how much I cared about her, if that happened, I would have to rip her throat out. Though Jen respected my need for quiet in the morning, Cass didn't require such tender handling at the butt-crack of dawn, or any other time for that matter. With her downstairs, the shiny, happy morning-people started prattling on about anything and everything.

I scarfed down what was left of my breakfast and dashed upstairs for my backpack.

ॐ

During the school day, Diego passed me in the hall a couple times, his presence reminding me too late that I'd meant to research symptoms of shock. The fact that he seemed to be managing his day all right made me decide I didn't need to. I mean, if he acted like the living dead here, I was sure the notorious school gossip mill would've been out in full force, and I hadn't heard a peep.

So, I walked to fourth period Mod Lit with my friend, Bailey, feeling much better about life. "No," I answered another stupid question about Cass and boys, "she's still acting like she doesn't know Trey exists."

"Is Cass nuts?" Bailey asked, her long, brown curls bobbing as she walked. "He's a hot commodity. If she doesn't scoop him up soon, someone else will. Hell, I might do it myself." She flashed me a slightly buck-toothed grin.

"Language, Bailey," our teacher reprimanded from just outside the door.

Bailey put a hand in front of her mouth like she actually cared. "Oops, sorry, Mrs. Feeny. Won't happen again." As soon as we were inside the room, we shared a quiet giggle.

"She has a pretty extreme definition of foul language," I said, sliding into my seat on the side of the room designated for juniors.

"No kidding. Now about Cassidy and Trey...." With a wink, Bailey moved across Feeny's "lecture" area to the senior side of the room.

I rolled my eyes. How could I possibly explain Cass to Bailey? She saw Cassidy, the cute little bubbly cheerleader. The dark, brilliant, haunted, emotionless half-vampire she knew nothing about. "I'll point it out to her," I promised. "I just think she is oblivious to guys."

Bailey stopped and spun around. "You mean she's a ...?"

"Oh, no. No." The last thing Cass and I needed was for one of us to be fodder for the rumor mill, and Bailey was a major player in that group. "She's just focused on school and cheerleading rather than dating. I think if she knew he liked her...." I shrugged, hoping it would be enough.

"Okay, well let her know before I decide to keep Trey Harper all to myself." Bailey tossed her books on the desk and started chatting up the friend who sat behind her. I could only hope they weren't talking about Cass.

While my human ears strained to hear their whispers over the louder chatter, Diego walked in. He looked good. Well, he always looked good, but he looked better than he had last night. The desk screeched across the floor as he sat down stiffly. Okay, so maybe sleeping on the deck hadn't been the brightest idea ever, but at least he wasn't drooling.

He caught me staring, so I smiled. He smiled back. Or at least he tried to. It looked more like a robot smiling, as if his brain had to search out what signals to send to which muscles.

My own expression slipped. *He's just screwing around. He remembers something from last night and is messing with me.* On any other day, I would have believed the lies I kept telling myself. He was the class clown after all. But I'd seen him the night before. I'd felt something at the park. He wasn't any better. Not by a long shot.

Chapter Three

Stragglers from the gym passed us by on their way to their respective practices without giving us a second glance. They'd grown used to Cass and me stretching on our own next to the track. People had tried to join us before, but sullen looks from me and a distinct lack of conversation sent them on their way. I don't know what people thought, and I'd never really cared. Cass and I preferred to have the few minutes to get our shit together away from our foster parents or anyone else.

I pushed against the fence, lunging into a stretch. "It's more than drugs, Cass. You didn't see his face today. He's still not all there."

"Doesn't mean it isn't drugs." She spread her legs wide on the ground and leaned to one side, grabbing her ankle. I growled at her, and she rolled her eyes. "Okay, let's just say you're right. He spent the night outside; that could make him less with it than normal."

I shoved away from the fence, lifted my right leg behind me, and grabbed it, stretching my quad. "Not like this."

Cass hopped to her feet. "It *could* still be drugs. I know you don't want to believe it, but it's not impossible." It was my turn to grace her with an exaggerated eye roll. "Okay, Elle, so what precisely do you want us to do? Follow him home tonight?

Make sure he doesn't start wandering the streets howling, 'brains…brains…'?"

I hated when she was right, and it happened altogether too often. "So what do you suggest we do then? Stay home and paint our nails?" With a snort, I jerked my head toward her newly pink fingertips.

Cass waved at a group of cheerleaders passing by, ignoring the wisecrack. "We could, but I found a new, more promising lead for us to follow."

"Really?" I straightened just as a pair of whistles blew. "What sort of lead?"

Cass edged toward me while we walked. "Apparently someone broke into Indian Fields Cemetery early this morning. Busted a car or something right through the gates." She paused, ruminating. "I never understood the need to lock the dead up anyway. I mean, if they are going to rise, a little metal gate isn't going to stop them from getting out."

My forehead creased both at her aside and her ridiculous idea of a lead. "I get why the cemetery is interesting and all, but a car accident doesn't sound like our kind of business."

Cassidy veered away from me and toward the cheerleaders, turning around so she could still talk to me. "Maybe the crash doesn't, but my source mentioned hearing screaming not long after it happened." With a wink and a mischievous grin, Cass turned and flounced over to the giggling gaggle of rah-rahs. Out of all the activities out there she could have joined to fit in, I'd never understand why Cass picked cheerleading.

An impatient gesture from my cross-country coach made me start jogging toward practice. As I ran, the tiny hairs on the back of my neck stood on end. Once I reached the rest of the team, I spun around, certain I'd find someone watching me. But only the cheerleaders were nearby, and they were facing the opposite direction. Nothing stared back at me from the bleachers—except shadows.

⚬⚭

"Why are we sneaking around like this again?"

"It's called detective work. What's the problem?" Cass's

22

voice was more snappish than necessary.

I tugged at the leotard stretched tight across my body. "The problem is your clothes are too small for me. This thing is riding up so high that I'm really wondering why women ever wear thongs."

"You didn't have a plain black shirt. I did the best I could on short notice." She shoved a branch out of her way as we picked our way through the trees toward the cemetery.

I ducked to avoid it hitting me in the head when she let go. "And that's the other thing. Why are we in head-to-toe black? We look ridiculous."

Cass turned around. She'd gone so far as to tuck her moon-glow hair up under a knit cap, and only her face was visible in the inky darkness. She reached up and yanked the cap on my head down further, likely frustrated with the fact that my ponytail streamed out from the back. "Because there's no moon tonight and black helps us blend in. Since we don't know what we're walking into, caution seemed smart."

"Did you forget what we are? Sneaking around is kind of part of our nature. And while the black might suit your sense of style, I just feel stupid." I should have shifted so I wouldn't have to deal with the idiotic outfit, scratches from brambles, or low hanging branches snagging my ponytail. As I freed my hair, or at least most of it from another tree intent on hanging me, I continued, "So what exactly did your friend say happened last night?"

Cass sighed, like I had no business knowing. "Bethany's brother works nights at the gas station on the corner. He heard the crash around one or two in the morning and ran out thinking something happened at the airport. When no cops showed up, he shrugged it off and went back inside. A little while later, he heard someone yelling, cursing like it was going out of style. He didn't put two and two together until he was driving home and saw the gates at the cemetery."

I jerked to a stop. "I thought you said there was screaming."

"Screaming. Yelling. What difference does it make?" She gave a noncommittal shrug and kept walking.

Was she serious? When she didn't turn around, I realized she hadn't even noticed that I'd stopped following her. "Cass? Screaming usually means trouble. Yelling could mean anything. One or two in the morning, it could have been some drunk thinking they parked at home only to get out of their busted up car and stub their toe on a tombstone."

An exasperated sigh escaped Cass's lips. "But most people don't plow through their garage doors, drunk or not. Something odd happened here, and it *might* be our kind of thing. So I want to check it out." She spun around and stomped off toward Indian Fields, finally calling over her shoulder. "Besides, we're less than two miles from the mall, with the park halfway in between."

Her words hit me like being slapped over the head with a steel pipe. I ran the few yards to catch up with her. "That's one hell of a coincidence."

"It could be, but based on what little information we have, it isn't likely."

Diego stumbling around like a zombie and someone gate-crashing a nearby cemetery afterwards? It would make a lot more sense if it had happened in the reverse order. And if Diego had been dead to start with.

I had to admit though, Cass was right. Again. "Okay, lead on. I'm sorry for doubting you."

"And so you should be. I might be younger than you, Elle, but it doesn't mean I'm stupid."

No, she wasn't; in fact, in some ways she was a lot smarter than me. Obsessed with numbers and computers, Cass believed in logic above everything else. I had more of a tendency to follow my emotions. She was the brain, I was the heart. All we needed was someone to play courage and we'd have our own little messed up *Wizard of Oz*.

Once we made it to Milham Road, we had to leave the shelter of the trees and cross the street. We could have taken a longer path and used the pedestrian bridge, but that involved passing through places where couples liked to hang out at odd hours. The few seconds we'd spend in the road was less of a risk.

While we stood, waiting for some late night traffic to clear, I felt a tingle run down my spine, not unlike the one I'd felt on my way to practice. As if someone had followed us through the woods and hung back, watching. I tried to brush it off as one of my random bouts of paranoia, but just because you're paranoid doesn't mean there isn't someone out to get you. So, I took a quick sniff, but the feeling came from behind us and downwind. I shook it off. *Can't fight what you can't see. Or smell.*

At last the taillights diminished to red dots. Cass and I bolted across the street to Indian Fields Cemetery. The brick walls didn't have a mark on them and no glass or other debris from the accident littered the ground, but the gate itself had seen better days. Like…yesterday. Someone had done one hell of a number on the ornamental aluminum.

The two halves of the gate were still held together in a lopsided embrace by a thick chain and padlock. But one side was completely pulled free from the brick wall. The other dangled by the top hinge.

Cass glanced at me and raised her eyebrows.

I didn't like it, but we needed a better look at the gate. Plus, hanging out on the side of the street didn't seem smart—black clothes or not. "I suppose they'll have to take it down anyway." I grabbed the metal near the last hinge and yanked. Had the accident not already jarred it loose, I wouldn't have been able to pull it free. I was stronger than a normal person, but not *that* strong. At least not like this. But there was so little holding the gate in place that my tug almost sent me falling on my butt.

"Nice. Been working out, have you?" Cass shook her head and picked up the other end of the gate.

"Hey, someone needs to be able to kick your ass when you're too stupid to feed before we go out." I lifted my end and we hauled the gate behind the wall. She didn't say anything. "Cass, you did feed tonight, right?"

She knelt down by the gate, flicked on a flashlight, and moved it slowly over the metal. "Yes, I took care of things." Since she had taken off on our way out of the neighborhood, I could only assume she was telling the truth and had paid a visit to the neighbor's dog.

"Stop." The light settled on a section that reflected its glow back. "That must be where it was hit. See how the paint is scraped away?" I pulled out my own flashlight, and we scanned the rest of the gate. "That's weird; I didn't find anywhere else that was missing paint. Did you?"

"No," she said, stretching the word out longer than necessary.

I shifted the light to my left hand and leaned in for a closer look at the damaged area. "There's no paint transfer, just what's missing from the gate." Something about the angle in the metal looked wrong, and I ran my gloved fingers over it trying to feel what I couldn't see. "Does this look dented to you?"

"A dent seems logical if a car hit it."

Thanks, Cass, I couldn't have figured that out on my own. I twisted the light back and forth, trying to get a better look. "It almost looks more twisted than dented to me." Sitting back on my heels, I glanced around the cemetery. "I still can't believe no one called the cops about this. I mean, the gate's been screwed up all day. People must have seen it."

"It's like they don't care about the dead." Her words were quiet and emotionless.

"Please." I rolled my eyes. "People don't care about the living, much less the dead." A stirring rose inside me as the beast woke. I tried to shove her back, but she bristled, instantly on guard. "I suppose even if someone had bothered to spare a glance at a tiny cemetery like this, they wouldn't waste their time or cell minutes calling about it." I played the light over the metal again. Something teased at the edge of my brain, but I couldn't quite put a finger on it. "Most people don't like to even think about death, and that silly fear makes them ignore innocent things like cemeteries."

"And you, Elle? Do you fear death?"

A snort escaped me as the beast growled inside my head. *What is your deal? Go back to sleep.* "No point in fearing it. Death is unavoidable; it comes for everyone eventually." I traced the gate with my fingers again. "It just isn't my time yet."

"Are you sure about that?"

Chapter Four

Cass had crept nearer to me during our exchange, and it wasn't until then that I noticed the tone in her voice. A sort of empty, sinister enunciation. The brisk fall air had nothing on that voice. Gooseflesh broke out across my body and the beast started snapping inside of me, searching for a way out. I raised the flashlight to the jet-black orbs where her eyes belonged. *Not again. She said she fed.* "Cass, back off. I don't know what's doing this to you, but you need to get a grip."

Cassidy blinked slowly. Too slowly for my taste. Then she ran her tongue in a languid trail across her lips as if savoring the taste of the air on them.

I stood and backed farther into the cemetery. She simply knelt by the wall. Watching me. The wind had shifted while we were examining the gate, and even though I'd done a sniff test when we arrived, something was wrong now. Not taking my eyes off her, I raised my nose to the wind and took a deep inhale. A faint coppery tang hung in the air. Blood. From the potency of the scent, it was nearby.

I should have checked things out more thoroughly when we arrived, but I had the scent now. Too bad it still controlled Cass. She stayed by the gate as I backed farther away, and I could only hope that, somewhere inside, she fought against the bloodlust. Cass was only half vampire, but once the need took hold of her, she had to battle her way out.

I stepped carefully over and around headstones, the flashlight beam dancing over names and dates that didn't even register in my brain. The metallic odor, which contained a hint of decay, led me to the fence on the western side of the cemetery. I stepped around a pair of tombstones that leaned to the side as if the inhabitants of the graves below tried to push their way out. Something beyond the wire fencing reflected the light, and my lips curled into a snarl. Metal? Maybe glass. Either way, it didn't belong in the tree and weed-filled land that circled Indian Fields.

A backward glance revealed Cass hadn't moved from where I left her. *Good.*

With the flashlight held between my teeth, I put my hands on the fencing, prepared to push it down and crawl over. As I put weight on it, the fence bowed. I pulled it toward me instead. Someone had cut it along the post and made sure to put it back in place. I had a feeling even in daylight it would hold up to a distant inspection. Whoever had done this hadn't planned on anyone looking for the trouble they'd caused in the field.

Leaves rustled behind me and I turned to find Cass meandering in my direction. Her slow stride told me two very important things: that her need was still strong and she was still fighting. I didn't wait. The blood would lure us both past the fence, but I hoped to get there before her and deal with it.

I kept the flashlight aimed at the ground, picking my way with caution, so as not to disturb anything, and letting my nose lead the way. The smell became cloying, filling my nostrils until I could taste it. I knew the source was close, but only when my light illuminated a line of reddish-brown on the weeds did I stop and lift my head.

The flashlight tumbled from my grip, and I covered my mouth with both hands. The beam landed so it lit up the sight in front of me, displaying it in all its horrible glory. Any hope this would be like things we had dealt with in the past disappeared.

No matter how hard I tried, I couldn't focus on any specific thing. My eyes kept darting from one image to the next, taking mental snapshots. The black cloth. The rough wood poking out underneath. The blood on the weeds. Splattered on the tree trunks. Soaking into the dirt around the makeshift altar.

I swallowed hard, trying not to choke on the lump of dread. "We are so out of our league here."

A sheen on the altar cloth drew me forward after I bent to retrieve my flashlight. I tried to avoid stepping on the bloody ground, but I didn't have a choice if I wanted to get close enough. And I had to know. I pressed my fingers to the cloth. Wet. Even though I knew, some perverse nature of either mine or the beast's made me look at my fingertips. Liquid red seeped into the crevices of my skin. Someone had bathed the altar—the entire altar from what I could see—in blood.

My gorge rose and, no longer concerned with whether or not anyone knew we'd been here, I leaned over to puke. I never got the chance because a tiny black figure flew past me. Cass threw herself at the altar, eyes closed but mouth open wide in an expression of complete rapture. Her tongue lolled out between fully extended fangs. I didn't think anything could disgust me more than the sight of all that blood. Then Cassidy pressed the soft, wet flesh of her tongue against the altar cloth.

I gagged and struggled to draw in a breath as I backed out of the circle. No matter how much I wanted to turn away, my gaze stayed glued to her mouth, covered in crimson. Memories flooded my brain, reminding me of all that I'd lost before I ended up here.

My family. And blood—so much blood.

Cass's eyes flashed open, and I stared into completely inhuman blackness. It jerked me from the past and dumped me back in the cemetery. I wasn't a little girl anymore. I didn't have to let myself or anyone else be a victim. This time I could do something.

I should have tried to draw her away before I searched for the source of the blood. It was stupid. As stupid as her not feeding last night, but now I had to deal and figure out a way to get her back to normal.

A small part of the Cass I knew gazed at me from behind those eyes. She didn't want to let her instincts have that kind of control over her any more than I wanted the beast controlling me. Forcing myself to re-enter the bloody circle, I called to her. "Cass. Cassidy Wegner. You don't want that blood." She lifted her head and cocked it sideways almost as if she hadn't noticed me before. I had one chance to get this right. If I couldn't find something to appeal to the vampire in her more than the bloody altar, she'd stay there until morning. Maybe later.

"Come on, Cass, that blood…isn't fresh." I winced. *Could I have given a more idiotic reason?*

No matter how stupid it sounded to me, it must have worked a little bit, because instead of licking the cloth again, Cass glanced at it with disgust on her face.

Okay. Good. Now to get her to leave. I waved at the altar and forced a laugh into my voice. "I mean, come on, what kind of vampire drinks old, rotten-smelling blood?"

Cassidy tilted her head to the other side and a slow smile spread across her features. Instead of feeling relieved, an icy chill ran down my spine. Her eyes were still black, and she ran the tip of her tongue over her fangs.

Shit.

Ignoring the snarling of the beast, I tried to slow my heartbeat. If Cass heard it going a mile a minute, it would only egg her on. The altar and the twenty feet separating the two of us provided absolutely no wiggle room. The beast raged inside me, but I didn't have time to shift. I edged my way outside the circle, holding my breath and watching Cass's every move.

She pushed off from the ground and stood, casually brushing away the dried leaves and twigs that had latched onto her clothes. One long but unhurried step and she reached the edge of the altar. I took an equally measured step backward. Without the altar and its offering in the way, she followed me without hesitation. Of course that also meant that I couldn't gain much distance from her with our careful movements.

I didn't trust her enough to look away, so I locked gazes

with her—waiting for the moment her blue eyes would shine through again. After passing the break in the fencing, I yanked it to cover the opening—hoping, praying, it would slow her down a step or two. She simply gave me that evil smile and did what any vamp high on power would do; she leaped over the fence in the airy way that probably prompted the comparison between vampires and bats. With her duster billowing out behind her, Cass looked like she could fly.

In a way, she did, because even though I took an extra step—maybe even two or three—she ended up a little closer to me than she had been. *So much for my brilliant plan.* We continued our little dance, with one change. She took a step. Then I took a slightly larger step. Anything to put distance between us. As long as it didn't look like I was running away.

I wanted to run though. Wanted it more than I'd wanted anything in a long time. Hell, I would have let the beast have control as long as it would've drawn Cass away from here, but I knew if I stopped to shift, she'd be on top of me. And her bloodlust high outweighed any extra strength I might have. Slow and steady would have to do. Too bad safe approaches never work for long.

Near the entrance to the cemetery, Cass's smile twisted to a sneer and her pace quickened. She'd grown tired of the game. Panicking, I tried to move backward at her increased speed. Then my ankle caught on a tree root sticking out of the dirt, and I fell to the ground, flailing and dropping my flashlight in the process.

The beam of light shone full on Cass's face as she flashed her fangs and leaped at my throat.

The beast must have taken over, because the next thing I knew, I had twisted in the dirt and rolled onto my hands and knees. Cass landed where my body had lain a second before. My one chance was to get her into the trees. The branches might hinder her movements so I could get enough distance to shift. I bolted across the street, not caring if anyone saw us.

Of course, maybe if someone did, they'd stop to help. Scratch that. Bad idea. But at the moment, I was desperate enough that it seemed the lesser evil.

I dove into the trees, thrusting limbs out of my path and ignoring those that hit me anyway. A branch snapped off to my left. Hope flared in my chest. Maybe I hadn't imagined someone watching us earlier. Even as a distraction they could help. But the sound didn't repeat, and I was forced to accept that I had to deal with Cass alone.

Without risking a glance behind, I didn't know where Cassidy was. *No time like the present.* I flung off the hat and kicked off my shoes. Running again to the rhythm of my jack hammering heart, I unbuttoned my jeans, prepared to shove them off along with the leotard. My hands slid under the fabric at my shoulders.

"Elle?" Cass's voice sounded small and tired, cracking as she struggled with her emotions. "I'm so sorry, Elle." A quiet sob reached through the trees and grabbed my heart in a fierce grip. My body sagged as the weight of fear fell from my shoulders. Somehow we'd made it far enough away. I had my sister back.

Righting the leotard and zipping my jeans, I retraced my steps in search of my shoes. I found them clutched in the hands of a tiny blonde with wide blue eyes. She sat on the ground, holding onto my sneakers as if her life depended on it.

I disengaged her fingers and slipped my shoes back on. I wrapped my arms around her exhausted frame and whispered, "It's okay, Cass. Just stay here; I'll be back as quick as I can." She nodded against my shoulder, and I headed back to grab the rest of our gear.

Once I had the flashlight in hand, I revisited the altar. Cassidy's activities showed, but I thought they'd pass a cursory inspection by anyone *not* looking for them. We'd trampled the weeds on the path, but I couldn't fix that. Instead, I contented myself with making certain the fence was put back the way I'd found it.

Too tired to do much else, I headed back into the trees, and snaked an arm around Cass. "Come on, let's get home."

Chapter Five

Wednesday, October 19 - early hours of morning

I can't stop screaming.

Tree branches sway and groan over my head as I curl in on myself.

Then the teeth rip into my flesh, tearing at my arms, my chest, my stomach.

Pain and blood and screams.

A gunshot.

I struggle to breathe as the teeth disappear.

A man holding a rifle says, "Little girl? Little girl...."

"Are you okay?"

I sat bolt upright in bed, the soft voice yanking me from the dream, and stared into the face of the person who would happily have sucked me dry of blood just hours earlier. The girl I called my sister. I threw my arms around Cass's neck and clung to her as I sobbed.

❧

Cass was kind enough not to bring up my dream the next day, and I certainly had no intention of mentioning it. The monotony of high school managed to bury the memory under a mountain of dates, facts, and figures.

I was still a little edgy as we made our way into the gym for the pep assembly after lunch. Before introducing the football team, our principal had to make us all suffer through his annual Homecoming tradition. He stepped up to the podium and tapped the microphone, blasting everyone's eardrums. "Hello, students, and welcome *home* for another great year. Once more we are honored to have some of our favorite alumni returning for the festivities." He waved a hand at one side of the bleachers behind him where about fifty people stood, most cheering like they were still in their heyday even though a lot of them had gray hairs I could see from across the gym. I yawned. "And we also want to welcome our newest Huskies into the fold. Please give them a round of applause and make them feel at home."

People in the stands clapped half-heartedly, and the group behind Principal Evans mainly looked like they'd just as soon disappear as have anyone recognize them as new kids. All except one. A dark-haired guy in the back drew my gaze like some sort of magnet. He didn't slouch, but somehow he managed to look casual, even standing in front of the entire school, like he had some invisible wall to lean against. Hair flopped over his brow on one side, shielding his eyes from view. His black T-shirt stretched across his chest, screaming of muscles, and plenty of them, underneath.

"See something you like, Jameson?" my friend Kris asked in a loud whisper.

I tore my eyes away from the new guy and looked Kris up and down. Spiky blond hair and blue eyes made him look more like my older brother than anything else. The thought brought to mind the little brothers I didn't have anymore and stabbed at my heart. I twisted my head, swallowing the memory along with the lump rising in my throat. To cover, I responded with exactly what he wanted. "Nothing close to what's right behind me, Benson."

"Yeah, I know, you've wanted me since the moment you walked into my life last year."

"Don't you know it."

Cass elbowed me. "Well even if you aren't interested, I saw something absolutely delicious down there." I followed her gaze right back to Mr. Tall, Dark, and Smirking. "Completely yummy."

Weird how we'd both hone in on the same guy. We'd never had similar taste in the past. Then as I sat up straighter, I noticed the guy in the alumni section right next to him. Much more Cass's type, all buttoned up and starched. Cute in his own way, but I wanted another look at....

When I turned back toward the other half of the bleachers, the new kids had dispersed, coming over to join the rest of us. Damn.

"That's my cue." Cass jumped to her feet. "See you after school!" The cheerleading squad erupted from their scattered places around the gym to jump and flip to their spots on the floor.

When the music blared to life and they started to dance, I leaned back against Kris as he rubbed my shoulders. Regardless of our flirting, Kris and I were nothing more than friends. He'd been in at least one of my classes since I started at Portage Northern the year before, and he'd never made a move. Probably for the best. I needed friends more than I needed a boyfriend. Besides, I didn't want to risk giving up his backrubs if we ever fell apart.

The assembly helped my mood. Even seeing Diego shuffling across the floor didn't drag me down too much. By the time the bell rang and we headed off to last period, I felt close to normal again.

At least until the substitute teacher in Biology put in a movie about predatory behavior. And because my luck always seems to follow the same path to misery, the lead hunters in the film were wolves. Watching the animals tearing into their prey yanked the dream right back.

I didn't know if it was the blood from the night before, Cass hunting me, the dream, the movie, or some combination of it all, but the dam in my mind that protected me from the memories burst and they all came flooding back.

Crimson stains clouding the view through my parents' tent.

The bodies of my little brothers lying at the wolves' paws.

The mouth of the wolf ripping into my side.

The screams that echoed in my head, so similar to the ones I bit my lip to keep from uttering again.

The moment I woke in the hospital, hooked up to machines that pulsed and beeped. Machines that my ten-year-old brain couldn't understand.

The doctor coming in and telling me my parents were dead. That there was no trace of my brothers. That I was alone.

The orphanage, where my wounds healed faster than normal and left no scars.

The first foster family who beat me for taking extra food.

The second who locked me in my room at night for the same reason.

The ambulance whisking me away to another hospital because of malnutrition.

The first change when I thought my body was tearing itself apart.

The change back, with a full belly for the first time in years. And the taste of blood and raw meat still in my mouth.

As the images in my head faded and those on the screen took their place, I dashed the tears from my eyes and shoved the memories back. I was a survivor, damn it. I'd learned how to hide what I'd become and fit in with the rest of the world. The beast kept me company, howling a melody in my head to mourn the loss of what should have been. But fitting in meant keeping her subdued, so I caged her in my mind, too.

The bell rang with the movie still playing. I released the death grip I had on my desk and gave the wolves on the screen one last glance. I wasn't a weak little girl anymore, and I wasn't an animal. I was a werewolf. And I had a new family, one I'd vowed to protect at all costs.

I choked down the pain, stood up, and walked out of the classroom in search of my sister.

❧

I shook off the last remnants of the bad memories on my way out to practice. Even though cross-country was a constant reminder of what I'd become—I ran for the sole purpose of keeping the beast at bay—I knew I could lose myself in the rhythmic pounding of feet on pavement. Feeling strong and surer of myself than I had in a few days, I walked out with almost as much of a spring in my step as Cass would normally show.

A movement visible from the corner of my eye made me skid to a stop. I turned and gaped. It was such a small thing. Just like with Diego. Inconsequential in the grand scheme of life, or even high school. If I hadn't already known something strange was going on in town, I might not have noticed it at all. Of course, the piercing yell would have caught my attention.

"Damn it, Alicia, what is wrong with you?"

Alicia was a senior and a national champion twirler. The girl had twirled in the last presidential inauguration parade. She was *good*. But today, she just stood there, baton in hand, her straight black hair blowing behind her in the breeze. She didn't say a word; just stared straight ahead.

The round little woman, who had to be her coach, spoke again in a frustrated tone that bordered on furious. "Do it again, and for God's sake, do it right this time." My ears twitched, and I barely picked up what she said under her breath. "You've been twirling for twelve years, and *now* you quit trying...."

Though she technically constituted part of the marching band, Alicia was a soloist, so she didn't take class with the rest of us. The familiar strains of the band playing "Johnny Be Good" roared to life, and Alicia began to move, dancing over a square of concrete marked off to the size of her performance space on the field. The baton twirled through her fingers.

For a moment I thought her coach was just bitchy. Then Alicia tossed the small metal rod into the air and bent to grab a second, preparing for some two-handed moves. I watched as the baton toppled end over end in the air, dropping toward her waiting fingers. Instead it clattered to the ground. She hadn't come close to making the catch.

My jaw slacked open. Alicia never dropped. Ever. I'd seen her juggle four batons on the field without a single fumble. But today her hands weren't in synch with the rest of her. She should have been throwing a bigger fit about the flubs than her coach. The lack of reaction from the biggest diva in school drew my attention to her face. Maybe the anger was building and she was about to explode...

Or maybe she just stood there—emotionless, empty.

"Oh crap," I whispered. "Not another one."

Chapter Six

Wednesday, October 19 - early evening

Cass tossed her backpack in the corner next to the closet. "Are you sure?"

I rolled my eyes as I sat down at the desk and pulled out homework. "Yes, Cass, I'm pretty damn sure. It isn't every day that I see a living zombie. Just almost every day this week." The pile of textbooks towered next to me. *There just aren't enough hours in the day. Ugh, I'm starting to sound old.* I ran my fingers down the spines, passing over history, which I hated, for algebra.

Cass perched on the corner of the desk, her butt pinning down the paper with my math assignment on it. "But you aren't absolutely positive?" She pulled an emery board out of the pencil cup and started filing her nails.

After opening my book to the right page, I tugged my papers from under her and spread them on the desk. "No, I'm not absolutely positive. How could I be?" I stared out the window for a minute, watching the red leaves of the maple tree outside flutter. One separated from its branch and began drifting slowly to the ground before I tried explaining what I'd seen. "Alicia had the same empty stare and, well, she just acted like Diego did. So, like I said, I'm pretty sure." I shook my head, turned to my paper, and started working where I'd left off in class.

"Okay, I get it." Cass sighed, stopping her inane filing at last. "But even if you're right, we still have no clue what happened to them. And we still don't know if it's connected to...." Her voice trailed off and she must have seen something really interesting on the floor, because she refused to meet my eyes.

"To the bloodbath at the cemetery? No we don't." I tapped my pencil on the desk, debating whether to drop the topic or plow ahead, knowing it would upset her. That whole "discretion is the better part of valor" thing? Never been a big fan. "Since you got a good taste of the leftovers, any chance you know if the blood was human?"

Cass's eyes went wide, and she turned from the interesting speck on the floor to glare at me. Pursing her lips, she brought the emery board to her mouth and blew fingernail dust directly into my face.

"Well?" I got out in between coughing fits.

She jumped off the desk and started pacing.

After about thirty seconds, I turned back to my homework. Cass hated admitting she'd fed off people in the past. And she couldn't avoid the fact that she'd tried to do it again as recently as last night. It could take her two minutes or twenty before she was ready to talk. I wasn't about to let the time go to waste.

I'd just managed to get into the math groove when Cass broke the silence, startling me so badly I snapped my pencil in half. "A human bled there. But not much."

"Cass, there was a lot of blood there." I turned around in my seat and threw the broken pencil into the trash. It clattered against the sides of the can, jarring my frayed nerves.

Still pacing, she nodded. "Yeah, but not a lot of it was human. I couldn't say for sure what kind, or even kinds, of animals the rest came from." She shrugged. "Honestly, other than some obvious differences between plant-eaters and meat-eaters, most animals taste the same to me."

I begged to differ, and so did the beast. For my money, different creatures taste, well, different. Maybe the blood just wasn't as flavorful as the meat. The more I thought about it, the less I wanted to, but I had to ask, "But not people?"

She shook her head. "Humans have...I don't know how to explain it. It's almost like you can taste their souls." She stopped pacing and avoided looking at me again, choosing to scuff the carpet with the toe of her shoe instead. "And every person has a unique flavor."

Yuck. How many people did she feed off over the years in order to say that? I squeezed my eyes shut, blocking out the image of Cass standing over a buffet of people. "So just one person? Diego? Alicia?"

Cass walked back to the desk and shrugged again. "Could have been one of them. Could have been the person who made the damn altar in the first place. Could be some poor schmuck lying in a morgue somewhere. Without doing a taste test to compare, there's no way for me to know."

A low rumbling penetrated the floor of our bedroom. Eric was home. "Okay, so what's our plan for tonight then? Something? Nothing? Sitting around twiddling our thumbs and pretending we are normal, good-for-nothing teenagers?" Since Cass had found the cemetery and I couldn't think of a good link between Diego and Alicia, I figured it best to defer to her logic.

Stretching like a cat, Cass headed for the bedroom door. "I don't know. Let's just go down and eat dinner. We'll figure the rest out later."

I jotted down the last answer and closed the first of the many books I needed to hit tonight. School paled in importance next to whatever was going on. "I'm not okay with sitting around doing nothing." Glancing at Cass's backpack, still zipped shut in the corner, I added, "Don't you have any homework to do?"

She waved a hand in the general direction of the bag. "If I can't get it done at school, it doesn't need to get done."

"They call it homework for a reason, Cass." But I was talking to her back; she'd already started down the stairs. I couldn't understand what part of her insanely rational brain thought skipping assignments was a good idea.

Dinner started like any other night. Jen played a modern

June Cleaver and set out a killer spread: pot roast with potatoes and carrots, salad, and bread. What more could a ravenous werewolf ask for? I dug into the meal, doing my best to forget about all the questions eating at my brain and our distinct lack of answers. The enticing scent of cooked meat just about took care of it, but a full belly would work wonders.

The Smiths believed in giving Cass and me as normal a life as two orphans could get, and I adored them for it. Sadly, however, that included dinner table conversation.

"How was work?" Jen asked Eric, before taking a bite of salad.

Eric stabbed a piece of meat with his fork. "Fine. How was school, girls?"

"Okay," Cass answered.

All eyes turned to me, and Cass kicked me under the table before I realized they expected me to say something. "Oh, yeah, school was…school." Jen and Eric stared at me for a minute like they were waiting for something more. Cass sighed, clearly unimpressed with my performance of "everything's normal." I shrugged, hoping nonchalance would come across as ordinary behavior.

Jen cleared her throat, intent on putting the conversation back on track. "Anything interesting happen today?"

I heard "no" in stereo as both Eric and Cass said it. Cass grinned, and Eric winked at her. I just shook my head.

"What about you, Jen?" Cass asked, toying with her food. "Anything interesting happen in your day?"

You know, in my life, I really like it when people answer that question with something silly. A story about the little kid at the grocery store dumping the display tower of apples, or some other goofiness that everyone gets a chuckle over, even though you know it would have been funnier if you'd been there. Either that or "no." Both of those answers mean nothing bad is going on in the world. It's just full steam ahead with the status quo.

Of course, the recent status quo was steeped in bad.

"Actually"—Jen tucked her shoulder-length brown hair behind an ear—"I stopped at the bank today. You know that young teller? The cute redhead?" Eric bobbed his head in a way that told us he'd noticed said cute redhead on more than one occasion. Jen laughed. "Of course you do. Anyway, she was acting really odd. It was almost like she couldn't remember how to make change. My first thought was drugs, but she didn't look high, just like she wasn't all there."

I don't know what anyone might have said after that, because as Jen spoke, I inhaled a little too sharply, forgetting about the piece of roast in my mouth. It lodged itself in my throat and I started to gag.

Before I'd even gotten over the wave of *déjà vu* and motioned to anyone I needed help, Eric rushed over, whipped the chair out from under me, wrapped his arms around my middle, and thrust his fist into my gut. On the third try, the piece of meat went flying. Jen and Cass stood on either side of me, worried expressions on their faces. The bank teller story forgotten by everyone except me. And maybe Cass.

"Are you okay, Elle honey?" Eric's strong arms held me up.

In that instant, everything seemed packed with meaning, and I remembered just how built Eric was. Way too built for your average IT manager. His business clothes hid most of the muscles, so it was easy to forget.

I almost shied away from him, wondering what secret he hid along with his biceps. Instead I choked down my paranoia—I wouldn't let myself think badly of him or Jen, I liked them too much to entertain the thought—and nodded. The movement managed to clear my thoughts, and I plopped back down into my chair. The wonderful meal called to me. God, I wanted the food, wanted it bad. Hell, I needed it. But would your average teenage girl start chowing down on the meal that she'd just choked on hard enough to warrant the Heimlich? I knew the answer was no, but I took a second searching for a way around it. "Can I be excused?" I asked, realizing I didn't have much choice. It took all my willpower not to reach for my fork and stuff another bite or ten in my mouth while Jen and Eric cast worried glances my way.

"Are you sure you're all right?" Jen chewed on her lip and stretched a hand toward me.

Um, no. Not at all. "Yeah, I just don't really feel very good now."

Eric nodded with a sympathetic smile. "That's fine, Elle. Let us know if you need anything."

I did my best not to drool all over my plate as I left the table and went upstairs, my stomach and the beast growling in frustration.

Less than a half-hour later, Cass burst through the bedroom door. "Are you nuts? I can't believe you just walked away from dinner!"

Jen had probably already put the leftovers away, but I could have sworn the scent of meat followed Cass into the room. I shrugged from my spot at the desk, but my stomach gave another one of its loud grumbles, arguing against my indifference. "It just seemed like the 'right' thing to do."

She snorted and strode over to the desk. "And I thought *this* was the right thing to do." A handful of beef jerky and a couple granola bars rained onto the desktop.

The jerky had barely hit the wood before I grabbed a piece, ripped off the wrapper, and tore into it like I hadn't eaten in weeks. "Oh my God, Cass, I'll never again doubt that you love me." I don't even remember really chewing the first strip, I think I just tore off chunks and swallowed them whole, hoping the food would be enough to keep the beast sleeping for a couple more hours.

"Consider it a peace offering." She caught my gaze and sighed, leaning against the wall. "You were right; I was wrong. We can't ignore what happened to Diego and Alicia."

I preened, enjoying the sensation of Cass being wrong for once. After opening the second package of jerky, I took a bite and chewed thoughtfully, savoring the salty taste almost as much as I enjoyed being right for a change. "Apology accepted. Even with your generous care package here, I still have to hunt tonight though. I don't want to, but I need more food, and I can't risk stealing from the kitchen."

"The Smiths won't care, Elle." Cass moved to the closet and opened the door.

I snorted, closing *The Secret Life of Bees* and watching her rifle through clothes. "They always care, Cass." It'd be so nice to believe the Smiths were different—I *wanted* them to be different—but I'd thought other families wouldn't care either. "I'm not willing to risk my life here on the chance you're right. This is the first place I've called home since my family died. I'm not going to give that up just because I don't want to chase a deer." Tired of watching her fashion hunt, and needing to get back to work, I turned to the desk. "Besides, people always complain about the deer population around here being too big. We can just consider tonight another one of my grand contributions to community clean-up."

Cass slid the closet door shut, walked over, and swung up onto the desk again, planting her feet on my book. "You know what? I think I'll tag along."

I raised my eyebrows, but didn't say anything. Instead, I just yanked the novel from under her feet. Why she wanted to watch me chase dinner had never made sense, but this wasn't the first time, and I doubted it would be the last.

"No worries, Elle. I promise to stay out of the way so you can eat. I just figured afterward we might head over and take a second look at Indian Fields. You know, really sniff things out."

Chapter Seven

A strip of jerky dropped from my fingers and hit the desk about the same time as my jaw. "You've got to be kidding me! You can't go back there after what happened last night. Blood doesn't just disappear; we might not be as lucky as we were yesterday."

Cass shrugged. "The blood will be dry by now. It shouldn't be a problem."

I blinked, trying to process her words and expression. She wasn't kidding. I flew from the chair and backed her against the closet door. My lip curled into a snarl that would have made the beast proud. "How much of the blood was dry last night? Did it matter? No." The urge to throttle her was almost too much to resist, my fingers itched with the desire to wrap around her neck. "You. Wanted. To. Kill. Me."

Every inch of my body shook. I shoved the rage as deep as it could go and managed to stop growling at her, even if the tension in my voice remained. "You don't get to go anywhere *near* that cemetery, or the altar. I don't care if you completely drain the neighbor's Rottweiler before going. That much blood makes you uncontrollable. I can't trust you like that."

Cass rolled her eyes but nodded. I backed away and stalked to the other side of the room to cool off. I definitely had to let the beast out tonight. The anger was letting her take hold of me. I grabbed the rail of Cass's bunk and leaned forward, taking deep breaths, but straining my shoulders in the process. The pain was worth it. A few minutes later I was calm again, if exhausted.

Cass must have sensed it, too. *Of course, idiot, she was probably listening to your heartbeat.* She padded up behind me and squeezed my shoulder. "Look, I won't go in. But you need to. You need to check things out better." She twisted around me and sat on my bed, presumably because I hadn't bothered to turn around and look at her. "I'm not sure if what's happening to people is connected to the altar, but Indian Fields our best lead. We need to know as much as we can about what we're dealing with."

My muscles started to clench again. "But you...."

"You're not going without backup, Elle. I'll stay across the street or something. Far enough away that the blood won't get to me, but close enough so I can try to help if you need it." Her eyes were wide, imploring. "Okay?"

Hell no, it wasn't okay at all. But I couldn't say that. If I did, she'd just follow me anyway, and end up getting too close. And, as much as I hated to admit it, I had to go because she was right; Indian Fields was the only lead we had.

"Yeah, fine."

༄

We left the house just after midnight and slunk to the nearest decent-sized patch of trees we could find.

"Are you sure about this, Cass? I could just hunt, check out the cemetery, and come right back here."

"Positive. I need to feed anyway, so while you are out hunting, I'll take care of business on my end then meet you across from the cemetery."

I tried to think of some argument that might change her mind. Homework. Police. Anything. But none of it would matter to her. I wondered if Cass was excited by the prospect of dealing with a bigger bad than we'd ever seen before.

Her hands pushed against my side. "Go. Standing here all night won't help us."

With Cass shoving me from outside and the beast tugging at me from within, I caved and walked deeper into the trees. It had been too many days of too much stress. The beast was starting to break free without me letting her go. I could smell not only the rich scent of pine needles, but the sap leaking from beneath the bark. Knowing she was coming out with or without my say-so, I yanked the sweater over my head and stashed it in the duffel bag I'd dropped by my feet. The rest of my clothes followed as quickly as I could take them off.

Shifting hurt more when I tried to hold back, so I took one last, deep breath to soothe my frayed nerves. I rolled my shoulders back and cracked my neck. Though I couldn't see the moon, its pull was strong. I closed my eyes, letting the sensation of bathing in silvery moonlight take hold of me. *Now or never.*

I let the bitch go.

Cold air caressed my body, raising all the tiny hairs on end, and my skin rippled as new, coarser hairs broke its surface. Tendons popped while my muscles bunched and changed shape. Pain coursed through me as my bones reformed, forcing me to all fours. My fingers tried to dig into the hard-packed dirt as the last of the change took me. A scream escaped my lips, the noise covered by the roar of the nearby highway. The sound ended in a howl of triumph. Standing there panting, I stared down at paws instead of fingers.

The gentle breeze whispered like music in my ears, carrying noise from the nearby houses with it. A baby crying cut through my brain like a knife. My ears twitched and I moved on. The crack of a twig off toward more trees. Prey. I sniffed the air. A raccoon burrowed in someone's trash. Far too many places for it to hide around the houses. Too dangerous, and not what I heard. I sniffed again. Deer. At least four, and close.

I grabbed the straps of the duffel bag in my teeth and bounded back out of the trees to Cass. She took the weight from my mouth and hung it over her shoulder. "Got something on your radar already, Furball?"

My tail wagged of its own volition and a whine came from

my throat. I cringed inside. I hated when the beast had control.

"Cool," Cass said, unaware of my discomfort. "I'll go get my own snack and find a spot in the woods by Indian Fields. I should be there by about twelve forty-five. Try to be at the cemetery by one, okay?"

I snorted and looked up at her with what I could only hope was the canine equivalent of irritation.

"Hey, you're the one who doesn't want me there." She laughed—the sound rang like a bell in my ears—and walked away. "Enjoy your hunt."

As soon as she stepped around a tree and out of sight, I tore off in the direction of the deer smell. Venison would have to make up for the roast I'd missed earlier.

I don't know if I managed to meet up with Cass before one or not, and the beast didn't care. She had a full belly and a long run. It didn't matter to her how long we'd taken.

Cass cared though. She threw the duffel bag at me. "Go, Elle."

Not in the mood for small talk? I snatched up the bag between my teeth and ran across to Indian Fields, dumping my clothes behind the brick wall at the entrance and scanning the scene. Graves three or four deep on either side of the driveway and not a car in sight. I sniffed the air. It was a good thing Cass had stayed across the street. There was more blood. It permeated the air. I had to search through it for danger.

Smelling no immediate threats, I did a more thorough circuit of the cemetery, stepping gingerly over broken pieces of ancient headstones that had fallen to the ground. Most were too worn to read, but I could make out a year on one: 1857. My fur ruffled as a shudder went through me at the thought of zombies. A quick estimate of the headstones numbered them right around a hundred, most as old as this one. I didn't want to consider the possibilities inherent in the dead rising and instead kept searching. No one—dead or alive—hid behind any of the headstones, waiting to attack me. Only the normal sounds of trees scraping against one another and dry weeds rustling came from past the fence.

Certain I could search without problem, I tamped down

the beast and her canine instincts. I pressed my nose to the dirt near the entrance. A lot of cars had come through here, but most of the scents were old. The dead who resided in Indian Fields didn't get a lot of visitors. I followed the vehicle path. Near the end, my nose twitched and I sneezed. Two cars had come this way recently. One old, the other a newer model. I didn't understand why, but just like old books smell different than new ones, old cars leave a very different scent trail than recent models. Like you can smell the years weighing on them.

The odor of the people who had come through proved more difficult to find. Unlike cars, which are wholly other, people smell natural, and their scents blend well with the outdoors. Finally, near the crooked headstones, I caught something. A scent that was almost human. Almost, but not quite.

As I breathed it in, I could taste things on the odor. *Meat,* the beast howled in my head. *Of course you smell meat, all animals smell like food to you. (Sniff.)* Curry? The scent mingled with everything else, but this time, it smelled like food to me. (*Sniff.*) Musk, something purely animal that made me want to hunt again. (*Sniff.*) Something metallic, but not coppery like blood. Hotter. It brought to mind a blacksmith's shop from some field trip I'd taken as a kid. (*Sniff.*) A minty pine-like odor that reminded me of cooking. Rosemary? (*Sniff.*) Cinnamon. Definitely cinnamon. The beast wanted to roll in the sweet, spicy aroma, coat ourselves with it, and carry it on our fur when we left.

I resisted the urge to roll in the dirt and instead followed the combination of scents to the cut in the fence. The trail continued on past the wire. I jumped over and followed it to the altar, but other than the new blood, nothing there had changed. And there was so much blood I couldn't differentiate the human Cass had tasted from the rest. It didn't matter. A scent was what I'd come for, and now I had what we needed.

Cass was pacing at the edge of the trees by the time I'd shifted back and dressed. She looked ready to rush across the street, regardless of what she'd agreed to. Since she didn't bother to hide from traffic, I dashed past the few late night cars as soon as the way was clear. I grabbed her shoulder as I passed, dragging her with me into the security of the trees.

"Well?" she asked, rubbing and scratching at her arms.

That's different. I pulled her farther from the cemetery. "I got his scent. At least I think it's a him. I couldn't really tell how much testosterone was there...."

My pause seemed to piss her off. "Great, so you didn't learn anything?"

I made a face. "Relax, the scent is pretty unique, and I'm almost positive the altar-builder isn't human." The beast rubbed against me inside, still reveling in the smell of our prey and the fact we'd turned the hunter into the hunted.

"So what is he then?" Cass stopped scratching and just held her arms in a death grip as she shifted her weight from foot to foot.

I shook my head, a few stray pieces of fur falling from my hair. "I'm not sure. Not werewolf, I don't think, but other than that...." I shrugged.

"Did he smell like me?" Her voice held a strange edge. It was tight, almost like her vampire had control, even though I knew better.

"I don't know." I took a subtle whiff. "I guess not, but I've never really given it much thought. You just smell like Cass to me."

She edged back toward the street. And Indian Fields.

I couldn't take it anymore; she'd started making me jumpy. "What is up with you?"

Worry lines cut across her forehead, and she turned away from the road. "Can we talk and walk?" Her gaze darted back toward the cemetery and its altar of blood. "Please."

I bit my lip and nodded, motioning for her to lead. We picked our way through the trees for a couple minutes before I broke the silence. "Are you going to explain what happened back there?"

"Even across the road it was bad. I could still smell all the blood. It kept pulling at me." Cass refused to look my way, but she sounded scared, which couldn't be right. Cass didn't feel emotion, not like a normal person at least. Fear wasn't part of her make-up. "How the hell am I supposed to help with this if I can't even get near the source of the problem?" Okay, anger made a lot more sense. She threw her hands in the air. "I don't want to hurt anyone. I sure as shit don't want to hurt you, and if I go in there, I'll turn into someone who would. And worse, I'd enjoy it."

Her words were meant to make me understand how she felt. Which they kind of did. Too bad they also scared the crap out of me. I reached for her hand and gave it a squeeze to steady us both. "We won't let that happen. We'll figure something out. Until we have to go back, we avoid the cemetery. Unless our brilliant plan involved staking it out until the bad guy comes back, we don't need to be there."

We left the shelter of the trees, stepping into an open field. The clouds parted and moonlight fell on Cass's face. The firm, angry line of her jaw weakened. "Staking it out would be the quickest way to end this."

I nodded. "You're right. But we don't even know what this thing is. I might be able to take it alone. Or I might not. Until we know more or figure out a way to keep you under control, we just stay away." I forced a brave smile onto my face. "It's that simple."

She flashed me a fake smile of her own. Her cheerleading smile. The one she put on to pretend to be normal. Cass's lie. "I hope so."

"Me, too."

By the time we climbed the maple tree and crawled back through our window, Cass had returned to normal. Without making a sound, she clambered onto the top bunk and shut her eyes. The history book lying open on the desk stared at me, taunting me about how I hadn't studied for tomorrow's exam. I sank into the wooden chair with a groan. The beast slept contentedly inside me while I clicked on the desk lamp and leaned over the pages, trying to soak up as many useless dates and names as I could.

Chapter Eight

Crazy thing about alarm clocks. If you don't set them, they don't go off. I peeled my face from a picture of the signing of the Declaration of Independence and blinked at my history book when I heard the pounding on the door. "What the...?"

"Girls?" Jen's voice came from the other side. "You have fifteen minutes before the bus gets here. You'd better move it."

I grabbed the clock and spun it around. We had fifteen minutes—if the bus was late. It looked like study time was over.

Cass was already out of bed and at the closet by the time I stood up. She tossed me a pair of jeans and my favorite hoodie. We dressed in record time, but still barely made it to the bus with our portable breakfast. No time for a shower. People would just have to deal with the fact that I smelled like a sweaty dog until after gym.

Our bus driver, Mrs. Crawford, gave us a dirty look when she noticed the food. "You two know that you can't eat that on the bus, right?"

"Aw, come on, Mrs. C. You know we won't make a mess." I gave her my most pleading tone and sweetest smile.

She narrowed her eyes at me and pointed to the first row of seats. "Right there. Where I can keep an eye on you. And if you make a mess, you get detention—cleaning the bus for a week."

"Deal." I slid into the seat, desperate to get some food and caffeine in my system. I'm sure Jen didn't approve, but she didn't say anything when I grabbed a Mountain Dew along with a water bottle.

Cass shook her head as she slipped in next to me. "I'm sitting with her, but I'll save my breakfast for school. If there's a mess, she cleans alone." Mrs. Crawford snorted and turned back to her driving.

"Jeez, thanks for the show of support there, Cass." I opened my bag. Jen had managed better than just a granola bar. I didn't know when she'd bought microwaveable breakfast burritos; I was just really glad she had, even if it kind of tasted a bit like egg-flavored rubber wrapped in cardboard.

Cass watched me devour my burrito with her nose wrinkled. "That doesn't even smell good. How about you get over my lack of sisterly support if I give you mine?"

I had to give her props for knowing the way to my heart. "Deal." They might have tasted lousy, but protein was protein.

She handed over the other burrito and whispered, "Do you think you might be able to sniff around school today? See if you pick up anything like what you found last night?"

I chewed and stared out the window at the cars racing past. Was the altar-builder in one of them? Shrugging, I said, "Not sure it'll work, but I can give it a try." My nose was way better than average, even in human form, but I didn't know if it was anywhere near that good.

"Cool." Cass transferred the apple Jen had given her to her backpack and forgot to keep her voice down. "Because the next best plan is me biting everyone, and I don't think that would go over so well."

"Hey, I can't speak for anyone else," said Michael, the greasy-haired sophomore sitting behind us, "but I don't mind if you bite me sometime."

"Good job, Cass," I muttered. "If you play your cards right, you'll have every guy in the school lined up for a shot at you by Saturday's dance."

❧

Cass and I never got a chance to talk during school. Someone from the dance committee joined us at lunch. And I spent my few spare moments after school begging Mr. Lialios, my history teacher, to let me re-take that morning's test. Turns out "I really needed a shower and didn't get one 'til gym" is not considered a valid reason for a re-take.

Cass slunk up next to me as I headed to Jen's car after practice. "Anything?"

I shook my head. "On the plus side, I didn't see anyone else acting weird today. How about you?"

"Nada." She smiled and waved at Jen. "So based on the sniff test, our culprit isn't in any of your classes. That's good to know."

"Uh, not exactly." I could feel Cass staring at me. "Hey, there's only so much I can do. Unless I get up close and personal with people, my nose just isn't that good. Hell, I'm not even sure getting closer would help, but not too many opportunities to test the theory popped up in my day."

She sighed, then her mood brightened, and she pulled me to a stop. "There is one option."

I waited, but she said it and just left it hanging there like a big piece of steak. I couldn't help myself. I bit. "And what would that be?"

"You said it was probably a guy, right?" She glanced at me and I nodded, unsure where she was going. "Perfect. So, you just become the school slut, and you can get up close and personal with as many guys as you want." She waggled her eyebrows at me and then took off running for the car.

I'm not sure what exactly it said about my state of mind that I stood there and contemplated her suggestion before what she'd said actually sunk in. Then I set my jaw and raced after the sound of her laughter.

The day had actually made me feel a little bit better about things though. Maybe our snooping around had managed to scare off the altar-builder. We hadn't seen any more people affected. Maybe it was all over. I piled into Jen's sedan after Cass, my heart feeling lighter than it had in days. I was almost happy.

As soon as I shut the door, Jen threw the car in gear and pulled out of the parking lot. "Hey, you girls remember the bank teller I told you about last night?"

My heart stopped floating, and I stared at Jen.

"Sure," Cass said, filling the silence as her eyes darted to my face, reminding me to act normal. "The one who forgot how to count change or something like that. Right?"

Jen nodded. "That's the one." She swerved to avoid a car trying to merge into her. "Something must be going around. People are turning into idiots around here all at once. I mean, crazy drivers I'm used to, but the teller and now the librarian at Waldo."

I blinked. "Where?"

"The library at Western. I went there today to do some research for an article, and the librarian had the same spacey look as the woman from the bank. Weird, huh?" She shook her head and chuckled nervously.

"Yeah, weird," Cass agreed, squeezing my hand.

Whatever was going on, it definitely wasn't just at school. I'd hoped the bank teller was a fluke. I mean, everyone else we knew of that had been attacked went to Northern. Now a librarian at the local university. Finding some association between Diego and Alicia seemed pretty pointless. There was no logical way all four victims were connected.

Unlike Jen, I didn't feel like laughing, not even faking it. In fact, I wondered for a brief second if I wasn't going a little crazy with the way my moods were shifting. Because that happy feeling? It flew right out the window, and neither the beast nor I felt like chasing it.

༶

As I lay in bed later that night, Cass's voice floated down in a whisper. "So it's not just school."

"Technically, we knew that yesterday." We were both exhausted, but clearly she hadn't settled in either. The wind outside whipped the trees around, sending the branches of the maple to flail against the house and scratch at our window.

"Elle, what are we going to do?"

This wasn't good. I was supposed to be the one asking

58

Cass for a logical plan of action. It meant things had gotten to her, probably because of her uncontrollable reactions to the cemetery. But it meant I had to take over as the planner. As the logical one.

Sometimes being the older sister sucked.

"For tonight, we rest." She started to protest, but I cut her off. "We're exhausted and not any good to anyone without some sleep. Tomorrow we start trying to figure out who the hell is doing this. And how to keep you sane around the altar for when the time comes. And what to do in case we can't figure that one out, because my gut says I can't take care of this alone."

"But what if we can't do it, even together?" Cass kept her voice even, but I could tell by the strain she worked at it. Whatever she felt, she was busy stuffing it deep inside some hidden mental well.

"Then I guess we get to discover just how deep that vampire blood of yours runs, or die finding out. Now go to sleep."

She didn't say anything to that. It was no secret Cass wondered on occasion if she could really die or if the vamp blood would save her. All I knew for sure was it wouldn't save me. I didn't exactly want her testing the theory either way.

After a long time, Cass's breathing evened out and I knew she was asleep. I wished I could say the same for myself. My thoughts were running a mile a minute on a mental hamster wheel. Finally, at around two in the morning, I gave up and flung off my blankets and clothes.

I slipped into a coat that barely covered my important bits, but it didn't matter, it'd be off soon enough. Climbing out the bedroom window, I watched the tree buck and sway in the wind. This was going to be ugly. Or a miracle. I jumped, and the branch I'd aimed for jerked up.

I managed to barely snag it with my left hand. I squeezed my eyes shut and grabbed the branch with my other hand. This was stupid. So, I couldn't sleep. Taking off by myself in the middle of the night was a rookie move. And now I was stuck dangling from a tree in a wind storm.

Then the beast woke up. The wind tangled through my hair and blew up the short coat. She howled with delight. I felt the beginnings of a change.

"Shit," I hissed between clenched teeth as I moved hand over hand toward the trunk. I shimmied my way down from there. By the time I made it to the ground, my options had disappeared. The beast took full advantage of my weakened mental state. She was coming out now, whether I liked it or not.

I threw off the coat, grateful for the darkness beneath the tree. Then I gave myself up to the pull of the moon. It had already set for the night, but it didn't matter to the beast. The moon called to her wherever it was. She could feel it all the time.

Tonight I just let go. I didn't force the change. Or fight it. I just let the moon take me. The change seemed to take longer, but it didn't hurt nearly as much as usual. Rather than incapacitating pain, the popping of bones and pulling of muscles felt like a reminder of being alive. And once I stood on the ground with four paws instead of two feet, the sensation flooded every inch of my body and mind.

My legs trembled as I reined in the need to stretch them. I slunk through shadows, past neighborhood dogs and security lighting. Past the houses with their lights still on, even at this hour. Past humanity.

When I came to the woods, I let myself forget for a moment that people existed at all.

And I ran.

My paws thrummed a soothing rhythm on the dirt. Trees caressed my fur as I dashed past. The wild wind sang in my ears.

A doe bounded into my path and froze. I skidded to a stop. I didn't need food. My belly was full, but my heart sped in anticipation anyway. My tongue lolled out of my mouth, savoring the young deer's scent. She tasted of forest and fear. A low, rumbling growl sounded from my throat, and she bolted.

Racing after her, I let myself come just close enough to nip at her ankles, and then let her leap ahead again. I toyed with her like that until she bounded across Portage Road and into a picnic area. When she jumped over some low brush and into the woods beyond, I let her go.

I trotted up the road until I reached the airport. Though the noise deafened me, I lay down against the fence, panting. Indian Fields lay a few hundred yards away, the area just visible from my vantage point.

The run left me feeling invincible. The beast wanted nothing more than to sneak across the road in hopes of catching the altar-builder at work. I held her back though. Something in the scent had made me nervous. I wouldn't do this without back-up, and that meant I needed Cass. I'd really hoped the run would clear my head so a solution to her problem would have space to pop up, but I had nothing. Laying my head between my paws, I stared at the cemetery.

I don't know how long I waited there before the coming of the sun brought me to my senses. Light bled into the midnight blue sky with the speed of a snail, but it wouldn't stay that way for long. I stood and shook leaves and dirt from my fur before turning toward home. The shifting of headlights across the street drew my attention back to Indian Fields.

Someone had just turned into the cemetery driveway.

The beast growled.

I had to agree with her. A little peek wouldn't hurt anything. I'd stay away from the altar, but if I could get into the cemetery and get a look at the car....

Any lead is a good lead.

I slunk across the road.

Of course, even in the wee hours of night, Portage Road had quite a few cars on it.

And my tunnel-vision blocked out everything but the cemetery. I never saw the van coming. Tires screeched, and I jumped out of the street just in time to avoid being clipped.

But my lousy luck made me land on my back leg wrong, twisting my ankle and then banging it against the curb. I yelped, and a beam of light swung my way from somewhere near the altar.

I took off running. The limp slowed me down until I caught the rhythm of running on three legs. Then I was gone and never looked back.

Chapter Nine

Cass was pacing back and forth by the bedroom window when I finally got home. The pain in my ankle made it hard to change back. I couldn't control how my weight shifted, and I ended up standing on it while it threatened to give way. A howl of pain escaped my lips as they altered from blackened wolf snout to my normal full, coral-pink mouth.

The window flew open. "Elle, where have you been?" Cass stage-whispered. I slipped on the coat and winced as my weight shifted. She must have decided that my whereabouts were no longer important. "Are you okay?"

I bit my lip and shook my head.

"Crap. Can you make it up here?"

Glancing up at the tree, I shifted to my good leg. I might be able to scale the tree. Maybe. But definitely not before people were up and about. Or quietly. I met Cass's eyes and shook my head again.

"Okay, be right there." She disappeared as she pushed the window shut. Seconds later, the sliding glass door opened and a fully dressed Cass urged me inside. Before I could utter any thanks, she ripped the coat off my back. I rushed to cover myself, but she made a face and thrust a bathrobe into my hands. "Get over yourself. I'm not checking out your furry butt, I'm saving it. Get upstairs and into the shower. No one except me knows you were gone, but they *are* awake. There isn't much time."

I hobbled up the stairs with Cass's help, but every step I took with my right foot ached. Cass ducked into our bedroom as soon as we hit the second floor. My hand landed on the doorknob to the bathroom just as Eric walked into the hall.

He treated me to one of his room-brightening grins. "Good morning! Nice of you to be awake to see me off for once."

It hadn't occurred to me how it would look for me to be up so early. My eyes went wide, and I probably looked way too much like the doe had right before I'd given chase last night. I tried to return his smile. "Um, I figured I should maybe say hi to you once in a while before dinner."

Eric laughed and ruffled my hair as he headed to the stairs. "Well, it's a big weekend for you and Cass. I'm not all that surprised you had a hard time staying in bed."

My breath caught, and my hand froze in the act of reaching for the doorknob again. "What?"

He twisted around and adjusted his tie while eyeing me. "Homecoming? Big game tonight. Dance tomorrow? It is this weekend, isn't it?"

My heart started beating and I could breathe again. With all that was going on, the trivialities of high school life had slipped my mind. And Homecoming was about as trivial as it got. "Oh, yeah. That. It's really more Cass's thing than mine." She was big on the social stuff. I had a hard enough time keeping my grades respectable and not coming across as a total outcast.

"Nonsense." After hugging me, he turned to head downstairs and called back up, "Your part in the halftime show is just as important as what Cass does on the sidelines."

I snorted, opening the door at last, and yelled back, "Thanks, but I don't think most people see it that way." Our school had a great marching band, but most people in the stands couldn't have cared less.

My ankle throbbed harder as I shifted my weight onto it and stepped into the bathroom. I shut the door before Jen came out and saw me. Leaning against the wall, I lifted my right foot onto the counter and looked at my ankle. *If this doesn't get better pretty quick, I won't be capable of doing halftime anyway.* Today was one of those days that I thanked my lucky stars for werewolf healing. My ankle had ballooned to twice its normal size and blazed red. The swelling and redness spread down my foot and up my calf. I don't know how Eric missed it, but maybe, just maybe, my luck was turning.

Though I feared my ability to stand in the slippery bathtub, the shower helped. The swelling was still there, but the redness had faded from my toes and below my knee. The French toast and sausage Jen made for breakfast gave me back the strength I'd lost making it home. And the nap on the bus made up for a little bit of the sleep I'd missed. By the time I showered again after gym, I felt almost human. The swelling had diminished to just my ankle, and I could put weight on it without too much pain.

Of course, even without the pain, going without much sleep the last several nights had taken its toll. I wandered through most of the day as much like a zombie as the people we were trying to help. The Homecoming parade came and went with me performing on auto-pilot. I could do my color guard routines in my sleep, so any brainpower I used went toward making sure I didn't step wrong and re-twist my ankle.

By the time I reached sixth period English, I'd started praying, to any deity that might care to listen, for the day to speed up so I could crash for a couple hours before the game. It must have been lunch hour for all the gods though, because Mrs. Peddington's class dragged on for what felt like twice as long as its scheduled fifty minutes.

Even though English was a strong subject for me, I hated her class. She was the type of teacher every teenage girl dreaded. For starters, she looked way too young for the job, and she was pretty. All the boys in class were entranced by her, regardless of her grading practices. I'd only heard of her giving a B once, and that was on a paper that went on to be published in the local paper. Those of us who regularly got C's from her counted ourselves lucky.

When the clock finally signaled the impending end of class, Peddington grabbed a stack of papers from her desk and started handing them back. I groaned. It had to be the short stories we'd turned in the other day. I'd been a little swamped with living zombies and had fictionalized this one time when Cass and I caught a vampire stealing rodents from local pet stores. It was pretty bad, even I was willing to admit it.

Her hand slammed my paper on the desk, and I made a face as I turned it over. *Just give me a D, okay? I'm really okay with a D.* My mouth gaped open like a fish as I stared at the large circled A marked at the top of my paper. Peddington never gave A's. There had to be some kind of mistake. But around the room, people were grinning from ear to ear, slapping high fives, and showing off their papers.

Then I looked at my teacher, really looked at her for the first time that day. Impeccably dressed in a black pantsuit, silky red top and killer shoes. Not a hair out of place or an inch of smudged make-up, as usual. But her eyes. Peddington rarely smiled around students, but her eyes always held this little glimmer of amusement—like she was in on some joke the rest of us just didn't get. Today her eyes were dead.

Just like Diego. Just like Alicia.

&

It's kind of funny. A glance at the packed bleachers and you knew the team had support. The fans were even willing to scream their encouragement with homemade banners and displays of our garish school colors of brown, orange, and white. *Who picks the school colors anyway? And what the hell were they smoking when they did it?*

But the outpouring of school spirit didn't make a bit of difference. The team was down twenty-eight to seven when the horn blew, signaling halftime. Diego had just blown another pass, and the team all seemed to breathe a collective sigh of relief when they jogged off the field. Their coach, on the other hand, fumed. I could have told him starting a zombie quarterback was a bad idea, but I didn't think he'd have listened to me.

I shook my head and glanced around as the players took

off for the locker rooms. There were a couple thousand people milling about. How many of them were like Diego? A handful? More? Portage barely existed as a dot on a map. What would happen if it spread? To the politicians in Lansing, or worse, D.C.? A shudder ran down my spine and I squeezed my eyes shut against the image of a living zombie as President. That prospect was even less appealing than the idiots who had recently occupied the office.

A sharp whistle blast yanked me from my thoughts, and I snapped to attention—shoulders back, chest out, chin up, and cheesy grin plastered in place. Every time I had to step onto the field like that, I wondered how on earth Cass could fake her perkiness all day, every day. Once the music started though, I fell into the job at hand, letting the monotony of drop spins and spatials settle me into a state of calm. Some real joy seeped into my expression. Color guard might not have the prestige of cheerleading, but I loved the power I felt holding the five foot pole and forcing it to do things it didn't want to do.

I only felt that way until we reached what would basically be the end of our part in the show for the night. We had to stop early for the presentation of the court. That meant we were ending at the pass off. The toss that never failed to make me look like an idiot because I couldn't catch it.

Actually that wasn't fair. Had my partner been anyone else there'd be no problem. But my partner was Lisa. And Lisa hated me. I don't know why; there never seemed to be a reason. Whatever her issue though, when she grabbed the end of her flag pole and pushed, instead of arching gently over the space between the lines, she sent hers soaring far over my head. We'd never performed where I didn't have to run after the damn thing.

Not tonight.

Lisa did what she always did, but this time, without any thought other than that I didn't want to look like a fool, I jumped for it. The metal slid into my grip, and my feet landed right back in my assigned spot. Lisa sneered, making it well worth the breaking of the line. The grin that split my face in that instant didn't have an ounce of fakery behind it.

But the expression faltered when I glanced at other members of the squad. I'd done something wrong, because a couple of them were staring at me with their jaws hanging wide open.

I swallowed hard. *Uh-oh. Too late for a do-over.*

Then Alicia took the field to finish out the song with her solo. What was left of our routine was just meant as a backdrop for her. The simple spins allowed me to watch every move she made. I saw every time she bobbled the baton. And every time she fumbled and dropped it completely.

The smile fell from my face. What was I doing out here? Cass and I shouldn't have even come to the game. We shouldn't have been pretending to be normal high school students. We needed to be out looking for the altar-builder. We had a job to do. I spent the presentation of the court willing people to move faster so we could get off the field.

But they filed between the lines of flags, soaking up the cheers—and scattered boos—like they had all the time in the world. I stared at the clock ticking down the seconds until the game would start again. Finally with only a minute left, the drum major blew a long note on his whistle, and the color guard led the parade off the field.

Needing to talk to Cass, I tried to break away from the group as soon as we were past the stands, but the guard captain, Edie, cornered me.

"Holy crap, Elle, that was amazing."

My eyes darted from one face to another, and a line of sweat broke out on the back of my neck. I tried to sound nonchalant. "Oh, come on, it wasn't a big deal."

"Are you kidding?" Bailey asked, laughing.

"Bai's right," Edie continued, curls breaking free from her ponytail as she nodded. "If it isn't a big deal, you need to do that every time."

I still couldn't figure out what I'd done that was so crazy. "Yeah, well, it's Homecoming. My catch isn't exactly the highlight of the show; I had to try something since it's..." I remembered Eric's words from that morning "...such a big night and all."

The group made a display of quiet laughter, nodding, and eye-rolling. Except Lisa, who still just glared at me. "Thanks for that," Edie said. "But seriously, try to do it from now on, okay? It'd be nice for that one toss to not ruin our performance every time." She shot a glance at Lisa.

Over Edie's shoulder, I saw Cass walk onto the track with the other cheerleaders. Any chance I had of talking to her before the second half disappeared. I forced a smile onto my face. "Will do, oh captain, my captain."

The color guard dispersed, most heading back to their seats, some veering off toward the bathrooms. I started to follow the group, when the only other straggler grabbed me and shoved me against the wall at the back of the bleachers. Lisa.

Why could I not escape this girl?

I wanted to throw her off me, and the beast she'd awakened snarled in fury. Too bad I had to pretend to be a normal girl. One who was about forty pounds lighter than Lisa. So, I tamped down the wolf and turned up the attitude. "What do you want, Mama Morton?"

She yanked me from the wall and slammed me back into the plywood. It reminded me so much of me and Cass under the pine tree at Diego's that I had to bite back a laugh at the absurdity. "You need to learn to show a little respect." Lisa grabbed a fistful of my uniform and tried to pull me up by it.

Silly human, Lycra stretches. "That's funny, Lisa, I always thought I was very respectful. Of my equals or better, at least." It was just too easy to bait her; I couldn't seem to help myself.

She shoved me into the wood again and raised her fist.

A voice of authority yelled from near the concession stand, and a tinge of fear colored Lisa's acne-spotted face. She slammed her fist into the wall and brought her mouth close to my cheek. "I don't know who or what you think you are, Ellery, but I'd watch my step if I were you."

I recoiled from the shocking odor of her breath wafting by my nose, forgetting for a second to be irritated with the use of my full name.

Lisa released me with a scowl and rounded the corner just

before Mr. Barker, the gym teacher, reached my side. "Are you all right, Elle?" he asked, glancing off the direction Lisa had gone. "What was her name so I can make sure she gets detention?"

My lips curled into a twist of a smile. Then I smoothed the front of my uniform and looked up at the big teddy bear of a man in front of me. "No names, Mr. B, I'm good."

He countered my smile with a stern frown, but the effect was ruined by the warmth in his tone. "I don't like it, Elle. You shouldn't have to put up with that. No one should. I will be talking to Mr. Gartner about this incident."

Great. "Do what you've got to do, Mr. B, but I'm not a snitch. Besides, she'll get hers." My eyes shifted in the direction she'd taken. "People like that always do."

He grunted something that sounded like "okay," and I walked away thinking of nothing but the unmistakable scent of curry on Lisa's breath.

Chapter Ten

The coach had replaced Diego with the second-string quarterback, but even though the tide on the field had shifted in a good way, I had a hard time celebrating. Inside me, the beast paced as I watched Cass cheering and felt Lisa staring at me. The entire situation made me nutty. Finally, I decided to at least quiet the beast and went in search of food.

I had the hot dog in my mouth when Cass found me. "There's a problem." She startled me badly enough that my mouth snapped shut. My teeth clacked together hard, even though slicing through the meat slowed them down.

While I chewed, I struggled to figure out what would have her in such a tizzy. Lisa had confronted me, not her. "What now?"

"Zoe's gone."

It took a minute for the name to register. "Your cheerleading captain?" Images of the bottle-blonde bimbo making out with a random guy somewhere flashed through my head. "And this concerns us…how exactly?"

Cass stared at me like I'd grown a third eye. I'd started reaching up to check by the time she responded. "I might not like her very much, but Zoe's dedicated to the squad; she'd never skip out during the middle of a game."

"You mean like you are now?" I snorted and took another bite of hot dog. She glared at me with more anger than even she could hide. "Come on, Cass. Did you check the bathroom?"

"Gee, no, Elle. You really think she might be taking a pee break?" She swatted the hot dog out of my hand. "Of course I checked the damn bathroom. I'm asking for your help here."

My shoulders slumped as I frowned at the now filthy hot dog. There was no point talking to her about Lisa right now; she wouldn't even listen to me. Instead, I put on my best "exasperated big sister" look in hopes that I could get her back on track. "I thought you and I were supposed to be trying to save the world. Do we really need to start with an annoying cheerleader?"

"Funny. Worrying about a certain football player landed pretty high on your priority list just a couple days ago." She planted her hands on her hips.

Her anger and words finally clicked. "Shit."

"Exactly."

"Lisa."

"What?" Cass glanced around, confused.

"Never mind. I'll tell you later." I grabbed her arm. "Let's go."

After searching the masses of people crowding the stands and sidelines, and re-checking the bathroom, we stopped on the side of the bleachers. I heaved a sigh. "Cass, I don't know where else to look. Maybe she just...." Shadows shifted under the bleachers. It might have been light filtering through as people moved in the stands, but as I turned for a better look, I glimpsed a small swath of white fabric.

"Maybe she just what? Went home? Locked herself in a car? I don't believe she'd—"

I slapped my hand over Cass's mouth and jerked my head towards the darkness under the bleachers. She raised her eyebrows but let me lead her into the shadows. Feet pounded on the wood overhead, muffling the accompanying cheers. It also dampened any noise we might have made.

Or maybe not so much. I didn't think we'd done anything,

but something spooked the person under the bleachers because the head in front of us shot up. Someone moved overhead and a sliver of light pierced the darkness, just bright enough to reflect off our prey's eyes. The way the person stared in our direction meant we'd been seen, too.

Any time for subtlety had passed. "Hey, you! What do you think you're doing?" It wasn't the best thing I could have come up with, but by pushing as much authority as I could manage into my voice, I hoped they might mistake me for a teacher.

One way or another, something made them run toward the other end of the stands. Cass and I started to follow, but she tugged me to a stop when she noticed the other person under the bleachers with us.

Someone standing stock still where our runner had been just a minute before. Cass touched the girl's arm lightly. "Zoe?" The head cheerleader turned toward Cass's voice, but her gaze traveled right past both of us. "Elle," Cass said through gritted teeth, "go after him."

I didn't bother correcting her on the gender thing. Lisa wouldn't get out of this. Curry might have covered the scent when she breathed on me, but I could smell a hint of the odor the beast had caught the other night. Even as a human, the rosemary and cinnamon tickled my nose. If I shifted, I could follow the scent with more certainty, but it would take time. Time I didn't think we had. Plus, someone could see me changing under here. With the scent already fading, I raced after it.

A crowd of people milled around at the end of the bleachers. I had to push and nudge my way through. Every step through sweaty bodies covered the scent a little bit more. With one last duck under someone's arms, I made it past the crowd and onto the path leading away from the stadium. The trail was still there. Barely. I trudged up the walkway, sniffing non-stop so I didn't lose the scent.

Cass caught up to me soon enough. "Please tell me you've got him."

The odor was dissipating out in the open where the breeze could catch it and whisk it away. "I think so." I led the way up the incline, sniffing about nervously until buildings blocked the wind, allowing me to pick up the scent again. I started jogging, trying to make up some of the time we'd lost with the crowd.

Then I stopped. Cass plowed into me from behind, her head slamming into my spine and making it crack. Tears stung my eyes. I didn't have time to worry about the pain though. My head twisted right, then left, then back to the right again. *This shit cannot be happening. Not now.* But it was.

"Um, Cass, we have a problem."

"Just follow the damn smell."

I glanced from left to right again, inhaling deeply. "Love to. Care to choose which one?" My voice dripped with sarcasm, but I couldn't help it. She liked to think my powers were infallible; I knew better.

"What? How can there be more than one?"

"I don't know, but I can tell you this, both trails are fading fast. Unless we move, we'll lose our chance." I turned around, ignoring the paths for a minute, and looked at her instead. "Got an opinion here, Logic-girl? For me it's a fifty-fifty shot. So what do you think: right or left?"

Cass chewed on her lip as her foot tapped out a nervous rhythm. "They both smell the same?"

"Close enough I can't tell you if the same person made them both or not." Cheers came from the stadium. We had to be cutting it close to the end of the game. People would begin pouring out of the stands soon and obliterate any trace of the scent. "Well?"

Her expression brightened for a moment. "Do you think they might have backtracked to throw us off?"

"It's not impossible." I had a hard time believing it though. Even more, I didn't *want* to believe it. If they doubled back, it meant they knew what Cass and I were—a prospect I didn't like one bit. Sad as it seemed, I preferred the idea that we had two people. It might mean double trouble, but at least it meant our secret was safe. "In human form, I just can't smell well enough. Let's choose a path and if the trail disappears, we'll come back and try to pick up the other one. We're wasting too much time trying to figure it out."

Cass gave a curt nod. "Then go right."

I followed the path leading up to the slope toward the school itself. The scents of cinnamon and sweet pine led all the way to the side door. The building lights blazed—a bright glow in the darkness away from the stadium.

"So," Cass said, "right or left around the building?"

A stiff breeze lifted my hair and chilled me through the thin material of my uniform. The sudden cold made me a tiny bit less apprehensive when I said, "Neither. They went inside."

"No way. The school's locked, isn't it?"

I shrugged. Of course, the school should be locked. I gave the door a fierce tug, nearly falling on top of Cass when it swung open. She caught me under my arms and thrust me forward again.

I raised an eyebrow at the door, waiting for it to do something else it shouldn't. Then again, it was Homecoming. Maybe there was some alumni function after the game. I supposed I couldn't really blame the door.

We stepped inside, and the aroma pulled me down the hall. I could tell by the way the beast writhed inside me that the end of the hunt neared. Our prey waited just around the corner. My lips twitched as my canines extended. Only my stubborn nature let me pull back from the change. It would be just my luck that Lisa would have a janitor around the corner with her and they'd catch me mid-shift.

Cass and I slunk down to the junction in the hallway. A quick sniff, then I nodded to Cass and jerked my head to the hall on our right. She returned the nod, and we rounded the corner. I opened my mouth, ready to lay into Lisa and call her out for the foul thing she was.

Except she wasn't there.

Less than five yards away, someone stood digging for something in a locker, face hidden by the open door. But the rest of them clearly didn't belong to Lisa. Yanking a book from the depths of the metal closet, he slammed the door and turned before he noticed us standing there staring at him.

Staring at every inch of tall, dark, and handsome that he

constituted. It was the guy from the assembly. Just like then, his dark hair fell forward, covering one of his gorgeous eyes. Eyes that stared back at me, looking like liquid amber. That gaze and his nearly irresistible scent were almost enough to draw a wolf in and hold her captive.

"Um, hello, ladies. I'd ask if you were lost, but judging by the uniforms, I'm guessing you two know your way around here better than I do." He raised an eyebrow, and I felt a tingle go all the way to my toes.

I couldn't say anything; my mouth didn't want to work. That's not really true, but inside me the beast had started drooling, and I was afraid if I opened my mouth, I might join her.

Cass broke the silence, startling me from my assessment of him. "Who are you and where were you about five or ten minutes ago?"

He tipped his head to the side and arched his eyebrow even higher, and my knees went a little wobbly. "I'm Jax, and five minutes ago, I stood right here fighting with my damn locker. It sticks." He turned to Cass, leaning up against the offending locker. "Who are you, and why do you care?"

She stood with her hands firmly on her hips and glared at him. As if a dirty look from a woodland sprite would make him spill the beans.

But once I shifted my gaze from her to him, I couldn't help but notice the way he stared at her. I let out a sigh. *I should have been a cheerleader.* "What did you do to them?"

His golden brown eyes met my own steady blue gaze. "Who?"

His apparent interest in Cass had put me out of drooling mode and back to all business. Or as close as I could get. "Diego. Alicia. Mrs. Peddington. Zoe...."

Jax cut me off with a laugh. "Peddington? While I'd love to say I had something to do with her sudden change in grading practices, I can't take credit. I don't know the other people you mentioned, but whatever happened to Peddington has made a lot of people in the Junior Class very happy."

This wasn't going according to plan at all. The bad guys are supposed to run, fight, or act all defiant when we confront them. They weren't supposed to laugh.

Cass put her hand on my arm. "Come on. Let's get out of here." She turned and started walking away.

Jax's eyes shifted back to her.

Great. What a way to cap off the night. Frustration bubbled up inside me, searching for release. I narrowed my eyes at Jax and let it out in my tone. "We'll be watching you."

He chuckled. Again. At least he met my gaze and stopped staring at Cass. "Glad to hear it. Will you at least let me know the identity of my stalker?"

Cassidy, the object of his affection, had already rounded the corner. I scowled and gave him a hand gesture to go with it. "She's my little sister, and she's out of your league."

His eyebrow shot up again. He looked like he wanted to say something more, but I didn't give him the chance. I spun on my heel and marched down the hall after Cass.

Walk away, Elle. Just walk away. Don't look back. You don't have to ever talk to him again.

Chapter Eleven

"What were you thinking, Cass? We had him cornered." I caught up to her as she stepped outside.

She shrugged, trudging across the grass to the path we hadn't taken. "Even if this Jax is our guy, he wasn't going to tell us anything."

"Oh really? And how'd you decide that?"

"Steady heart rate. We didn't hit a nerve at all."

"Really?" I'd been standing right next to Cass when he'd eyed her up and down. Maybe he wasn't as into her as I'd thought. "I figured there would have been at least one hiccup during our talk with him."

Cass smirked. "Okay, maybe one. But it had nothing to do with our half-assed interrogation." She caught my gaze, and then looked away, giggling.

What the hell? Cass doesn't giggle. Laughs, sure. Guffaws upon occasion. But giggle? Never. I tried not to think about what it meant. "So, I guess you don't think he's our guy."

"Maybe he is, but I don't think his shell is going to be all that easy to crack. We can't exactly pummel it out of him here at school." She waved at the air. "Can you still catch the other scent trail? Just to see where it goes?"

"It's going to take us right to Lisa, but I'll try."

"Lisa?"

"Never mind." Jax's scent had lingered in the air when we left the building, so I took a chance the other one hadn't disappeared and sniffed. My nose twitched, and I nodded. "It's really faint, but it's still here."

I risked a glance back toward the stadium. People weren't crowding the paths yet. We still had a couple minutes to follow this trail. It led us past the basketball arena and into the parking lot. All the way to a vacant parking space where the trail came to an abrupt end.

"Looks like we missed this one," Cass said.

"Unless you were right and Jax made it then doubled back."

She furrowed her brows and glanced at me. "I don't know. When I mentioned the backtracking, I didn't think the trail would go this far. Do you think he had time?"

Remembering his golden brown eyes, my heart sank. I didn't want it to be him, but I gave my best noncommittal shrug and told the truth. "Either one of us could have done it."

Cass fiddled with her hair like she chose her next words very deliberately. "Yeah, but we're…us. Did you happen to get a good enough whiff of him in there?"

Her voice made it clear she didn't want him to be our guy either. Crap. He wasn't her type. She preferred clean-cut and preppy. Besides she never showed any interest in dating before. I kicked at a loose piece of concrete as we turned back toward the stadium. Maybe she'd just realized she needed a boyfriend to really complete the persona she'd created. If that was the case, I could push her toward Trey. As for Jax, one way or another, at least I wouldn't have to deal with him dating my sister. "I told you, scent trails aren't exactly the same as the real thing." I waved my hand at the air around us. "Especially in human form, this is like a half-taste of someone. It only tells me the tiniest bit of what I could get from an up-close sniff in wolf-form."

"But you're sure one path or the other was made by the person who attacked Zoe, right?" Her voice sounded so hopeful, my heart broke a tiny bit hearing it. I didn't know if it was her anger over the attacks or if she did indeed like Jax.

I closed my eyes and sighed, trying not to think about the

second possibility. "No, Cass. I'm not sure. The scent trails could've been one of those crazy coincidences that plague us, and the person who attacked Zoe is back up in the stands, eating a plate of nachos and cheering on the Huskies." My brain went straight to our only other suspect who was probably doing exactly that—Lisa. The timer on the scoreboard showed less than five minutes left in an at-long-last tied game. We needed to get back—now. The breeze picked up again, blowing my hair behind me.

A sudden chill ran down the length of my spine. The beast went on alert, her low growl rumbling through my head. I froze but fought the urge to turn around and search for someone watching us. Cass kept walking, adopting the air of flouncy cheerleader with ease as we'd neared the game. She hadn't even noticed I'd stopped.

The beast raged against the sensation of being prey rather than predator, and I had no idea if she really sensed something or just fed off my paranoia. I tried to keep my breathing steady to calm us both. Still she pressed against me, urging me to spin around and confront whoever had the nerve to put us in their sights. The point came where I couldn't fight my fear and instincts any more. I turned, expecting to find someone right at my back, quite possibly with a weapon in hand.

But only some dried leaves skittered across the path. The breeze died again, leaving me standing alone as my breath came in little puffs of fog. *There's no one there. There's no one there.* My heartbeat started slowing back to normal.

A hand fell on my shoulder and I whipped around, ready to attack.

I stopped myself a half-second before I swung a fist at Edie's head. "Damn it, Elle," she said. "Mr. Gartner wants us ready to do the postgame parade. Where the hell have you been?"

I opened and closed my mouth, trying to think of an excuse, any excuse. I ended up blurting out, "Lisa was pissed after half-time. I was trying to find her so we could talk."

Edie sighed and grabbed my wrist, tugging me toward the crowd. "She said she wasn't feeling well and went home. If you wouldn't have taken off, anyone could have told you that. Now get your tail back to the band."

The unintentional pun made me blink. Lisa had left? Did that mean I was right? That she'd been the person under the bleachers? The path that led into the parking lot? "Yeah. Sorry, I'm coming." I followed Edie toward the stadium and the mass of people. Movement from the corner of my eye grabbed my attention and I turned back around. Edie sighed and yanked on my wrist. Craning my neck around, I saw a puff of condensed air rise from a patch of shadows farther up the trail.

My hair stood on end and the beast bristled. Neither one of us was the least bit happy. We had indeed been hunted, and for all intents and purposes, we'd been caught.

The conversation with Cass once we got home didn't go well. I couldn't tell where her brain was at. She didn't buy into my Lisa theory, and I couldn't tell if that meant she looked at Jax as our prime suspect or not. She went to bed before we'd decided who was the bigger threat.

I needed sleep so badly I could taste it. But between my after-school nap and everything that had happened at the game, I couldn't settle in.

My mind kept going back to whoever had stalked us outside the stadium. Who would've done that? And why? Was it Jax? Or Lisa? Maybe some wandering werewolf checking out the local competition. Hell, it could have been some weird guy who liked the way Cass's skirt swayed when she walked.

Of course, at the end, when I'd finally turned around and seen whomever lurking, Cass was already gone. It had just been me and Edie. I crossed cheerleader-obsessed creep off my mental list and realized that I might have to add the possibility that the person had been watching Edie all along.

All night, I lay there, filtering through theories and trying to figure out who, if anyone, was really in danger. The first rays of dawn were seeping through the window when I started drifting off. The last conscious thought I had was of Jax. The image of dark hair falling across his golden gaze seemed burned onto the inside of my eyelids when sleep claimed me at last.

"The two of you look gorgeous! I can't believe neither of you have dates for this thing." Eric beamed with parental pride when Cass and I walked into the family room in our Homecoming dresses.

Cass preened under his scrutiny, twirling around in her chiffon one-shouldered number. The full skirt flared around her legs, and she covered her mouth to hide a smile. It was all an act, and it killed me that she could pull it off so well. Even the choice of bright yellow was contrived because it made the dress "something special." Every decision Cass made had to fit the image she wanted people to see. She babbled on and on about how great the dance would be.

I, on the other hand, had a much harder time faking it. I liked dressing up and playing princess as much as the next girl, but we had more important things to do. Cass wouldn't relent and skip the dance though. She insisted it was a necessary part of us blending in. I didn't like it, but I didn't see much choice in the matter.

Especially when I looked at Jen and Eric's faces. I slid my hands down the silky fabric of the dress they'd bought for me. When I'd first seen how it clung to all my curves, I'd had to ask Cass if it looked slutty. She'd laughed and said no. Apparently I worried too much. And I did love the color; the royal blue made my eyes stand out. Thinking of how Cass had swept my hair up with jeweled pins into a cascade of curls made me wish I wasn't going stag. Even though I hadn't wanted to attend, it sucked that once we were at the dance, no one would really appreciate how good I looked.

I sighed. The moodiness had to go. Though they didn't show it, I'm sure the Smiths had started to feel like I took them for granted, and I didn't want that. I really truly liked them and didn't want to be the reason for the floor dropping out of our happy home. There had been nights I'd sat up listening to Jen and Eric talk about us. The things they said made it clear that, as much as they loved us, they were just waiting for something to go wrong. Neither Cass nor I wanted to risk ruining our life with them.

With the mental slap in the face, I managed to put on a smile for their benefit as Eric once again brought up our single status. "Hey, why have one date when you can dance with every guy there?"

"Ha-ha, that's a great attitude." He hugged me, doing his best not to wrinkle my dress in the process. Eric didn't seem to remember being a teenage guy. For the most part, if boys didn't have dates, they just didn't go to these things.

Then Jen pulled out the dreaded camera. "Okay, girls, I just want a couple pictures before you head out." She motioned us over to the fireplace.

We posed for over a dozen shots, eventually making goofy faces and succumbing to fits of laughter. Eric stepped in, chuckling, and laid a hand on the camera. "Jen, if you don't let them leave soon, the only memories they'll have of the Homecoming dance will be of you taking pictures."

Jen blushed and set the camera on the coffee table, stepping over to give us hugs before we left. Cass and I slipped into our coats then stood by the door, waiting for Eric to put on his jacket and take us to school. Instead, he gave Jen a questioning look, and they shared a smile at her nod. Then he pulled the keys from his pocket…and handed them to me. "Have fun."

I balked as Cass bounced up and down. "You're letting me drive?" I stared at the small pieces of metal in my hand, not believing what my eyes could clearly see.

"We added you to the insurance at the beginning of school. You've driven with us enough that we figured we could trust you for one night out." Jen wrapped her arm around a grinning Eric.

I didn't know what to say about the show of trust. Tears filled my eyes, threatening my carefully applied makeup. I blinked them away. *No more taking them for granted. Damn it, Elle, don't screw this one up.* "Thank you," I whispered, clutching the keys until they bit into my palm.

Eric stepped over and held open the door. "Home by midnight." I nodded mutely. "Oh, and try not to get a speeding ticket, okay?"

A grin split my face. "Yes, sir."

The night was looking better than I would have ever thought possible.

Chapter Twelve

Saturday, October 22 - evening

The dance sucked.

At least it did for me. I'm sure the couples had a lovely time in between chaperone interruptions to enforce the 'no sex on the dance floor' rule. And the social butterflies flitted happily about their bizarre high school network.

I spent most of my time cringing every time the DJ put on another one of the "approved" songs. The hands on the clock couldn't move fast enough for my taste. Eric trusting me with the car was the only thing keeping my spirits up enough that I didn't drag Cass out the door.

To be fair, she tried to keep me company whenever she took a break from her committee duties. She even dragged me out onto the dance floor for some of the faster songs in an effort to make me have a good time. Despite all that, I couldn't help but think about how different we were from everyone else. How they'd go off to parties or something later while we hunted for whoever was attacking our nice quiet town.

A glance at the smiling, happy faces around me made me suddenly claustrophobic, like there wasn't enough air in whole building to fill my lungs. I searched the crowd, my gaze passing over masses of people until the brilliant yellow of Cass's dress came into view. On the dance floor, of course.

She'd wanted me to go out again, but I'd dodged her and grabbed a glass of punch instead.

I paid for the mistake by having to wend my way through gyrating bodies until I reached her side. Tapping her on the shoulder, I said, "Hey, I'm going out for some air."

She turned to me, trying to mask her concern with a nervous smile. "Is everything all right?"

Her eyes and the viselike grip she had on my arm told me what her words didn't—she wanted to know if this was a werewolf problem, or if it had anything to do with the attacks. I opened my mouth to speak when another voice broke through the noise.

"Hey, Cass." Trey nodded at me, his tight corkscrew curls bobbing. "Elle."

"Hi, Trey," I said.

Cass smiled and said, "Hi," but she was still looking at me.

"I'm okay, Cass." I waved her concern away. "I'm just a little warm. I'll be right outside if you need me."

Her fingers dropped away from my arm, but she leaned in close and whispered, "Just stay by the doors, okay?"

I gave her my best I'm-not-an-idiot look. Turning to leave, I smiled at Trey. "Take care of her 'til I get back, would you?"

His grin lit up the darkness of the cafeteria. "My pleasure."

The edge of the dance floor was less than a dozen yards away. Freedom waited steps from where I stood. Then the music changed. For a split second I cheered inside that Trey had found Cass for a slow song. Then all the single girls deserted the floor en masse at the moment all the couples tried to push onto it. Bodies shoved and rocked me back and forth.

A path through the mess finally opened up, and I started to make a break for it when a hand wrapped around my wrist and pulled me back. The momentum spun me, and I fell against a dark-suited chest. Raising my head, I stared into the smirking face of Jax.

I glared at him, but he didn't let go of my wrist. Instead, he wrapped his other arm around my waist. Neither of us moved. Maybe he was waiting to see if I'd make a scene. I did consider it for a minute before biting my lip hard enough to draw blood and reminding myself to blend in. Besides, a part of me wanted to be right where he'd put me. Giving a gentle tug, I freed my wrist and wrapped both arms around his neck. His smirk widened into a full-fledged smile that put Trey's to shame and made something low in my belly flutter. He held me tighter, swaying to the music.

This close, the aroma of him almost overwhelmed my control of the beast. She wanted to rub up against him in ways that would get me detention—or worse. My breath came quick and shallow. I wanted to stay and wanted to run. Trying to cover my nerves, I went with the one thing I did well. Talking. "What are you doing, Jax?"

He tipped his head down so less than an inch separated his face from mine. "I'm dancing," he breathed. "What does it look like I'm doing?"

Where his fingers touched me, my skin blazed, even through the soft fabric of my dress. I swallowed hard. *He's into Cass. Remember.* I couldn't let him know how much his nearness affected me. I had more than enough embarrassment in my life without that. It was time to turn on the attitude. "Well, I wouldn't exactly call it dancing, but we both know that isn't what I meant."

His lips twitched to the side like he was trying not to laugh. Then he leaned in even closer and whispered in my ear, "You said you were planning to keep an eye on me. I just thought I'd make it as easy as possible for you."

The heat of his breath blowing tendrils of hair off my neck sent a shiver through my body and the beast howled in delight. I closed my eyes and tried to smother her. I'd seen the expression on Jax's face yesterday, and I knew this wasn't going anywhere good. "So why me? Why not Cass?"

"Cass?" He pulled back a few inches and gave me a look of complete confusion. Then a light went on. "Must be your sister's name. It seems to me she is otherwise occupied at the moment."

I turned and followed his gaze to where Cass and Trey danced. She cast me a wide-eyed look, her mouth forming a small "o".

Just perfect.

"You, on the other hand..." His voice drew my gaze back to the amber eyes I'd dreamt about the night before. "...looked a bit lonely."

The words fell like a blow to my face. I tipped my chin down so he wouldn't see when I clenched my jaw and pushed the hurt away. I gave my head a slow shake, chasing off the spell his eyes and scent had cast on me. Then I steeled myself to look at him again. "Gee, thanks a lot for the whole pity party thing. I appreciate it. Really. But I came alone by choice."

He actually had the nerve to stand there with his mouth dropped open like he didn't know why I'd said it. Typical.

The song ended just as I felt tears threatening. I managed to hold my head high long enough to say, "Go ahead and talk to Cass. I'm sure you can tear her away from Trey without too much trouble; it's her turn to babysit you anyway."

I plastered a smile on my face and walked off the dance floor before he had the chance to say whatever bullshit excuse popped into his head. On my way to the door, I caught sight of the one other person who could ruin my night. Lisa stood in the corner under the exit sign, a titanic vision of gothic horror in gauzy black. She glared at me like I'd stolen her puppy and beaten it to death.

Whatever.

My hands slammed against the bar on the door, pushing all my anger and frustration into the simple act of opening it, and I stepped out into the brisk night air. In that moment, I wanted nothing more than to rip the dress from my body and let the beast loose so I could run with her until we fell from exhaustion somewhere in the forest. But I couldn't.

Instead I thanked the heavens and earth for waterproof mascara as I stood with my face to the wind, letting it dry the tears as they fell.

⌀

Lying in bed later that night, I heard Cass's voice from overhead. "Elle?"

I curled into the fetal position and rolled over to face the wall, pulling the blanket up to my chin. My beautiful blue dress lay wadded in a ball on the floor near the closet, and I'd torn down the up-do as soon as we'd come home. What was the point in pretending to be a princess if all Prince Charming wanted from you was a date with your sister? Charming my ass. So instead of lying awake and letting Cass relive the night, I closed my eyes and tried to keep my breathing steady in hopes of feigning sleep.

"Elle, I can still hear your heartbeat. I know you're awake."

But obviously you don't know that when someone pretends to be asleep it probably means they want to be left alone. I sighed and tried to keep the tremor from my voice. "What is it, Cass?"

She didn't speak for a second and I had time to hope that she'd gotten the message. No such luck. "Are you okay? You sound funny." The bed creaked above my head, and I knew she was leaning over, trying to look at me.

I kept my back to her and clenched my fists around the blanket. "I'm fine. What do you need?" Please, let it be something simple like asking to borrow an extra pillow.

"I saw you dancing with the guy we trailed at the game last night. What was his name?"

Big surprise. I closed my eyes again, wishing she would just go to sleep. "Jax."

"Oh yeah. So?" She paused, but when I didn't answer she plowed ahead. "What was it like dancing with the enemy?"

I bristled as her words chased away a tiny bit of the depression that pressed on me and found myself leaping to his defense. "We don't know Jax is the one. There was the other trail, that could well have been from Lisa."

"Huh? Uh…okay…we'll look into Lisa versus Jax tomorrow…." Her voice trailed off, and then she blurted out, "I really just wanted to know what he was like. Is he a good dancer? That sort of thing."

Great. I wanted to cry, and she wanted girl talk. About the guy I had some messed up thing for. "I'm fairly sure he had ulterior motives for dancing with me. But as far as ability, he dances like almost every other guy I know—the old stand and sway. It's the new rumba, didn't you know? You really should try it some time. Can I please go to sleep now?"

"Um, sure. I guess." She sounded hurt. I hadn't wanted that, but I'd have to make it up to her some other time. "Do you think you'll see him again?"

Did I have a choice? Hell, even if I did, which answer would I give? "I don't know. Probably. He's still a suspect." The striped wallpaper blurred before my eyes as tears threatened again.

"Yeah. Okay." The bed creaked once more as she lay back down. "What's the plan for tomorrow anyway?"

Sleeping until I forget all about him. I swallowed the lump in my throat. "I don't know, Cass; we'll figure it out when tomorrow gets here."

At last she stopped talking. I let the tears fall and did my best not to notice that my skin still felt like it was on fire where he had held me.

Chapter Thirteen

Sunday, October 23 - around noon

A mass of kinetic energy flew onto my bed, making it bounce and jarring me awake. "What the...?" I started to roll over, intending to swat whoever, or whatever, had landed next to me off the mattress.

By the time I managed to untangle myself enough to turn toward the room, Cass had already hopped off the bed. As soon as she saw me, she said, "Oh, good, you're awake," and yanked the blinds open, flooding the room with sunshine.

I cringed away from the light. The glare was bright enough I briefly entertained the notion that an asteroid was about to hit the Earth right outside our bedroom window, wiping out humanity in some mass extinction. I wondered if Cass would survive that. Then decided it didn't matter, because if I lived, I'd kill her for waking me up in the first place.

Instead, I settled for throwing my pillow at her. "Shut those! Are you trying to blind me or what?"

She laughed and dropped the slats with a clatter. Then she flopped back onto my bed and hit me with the pillow I'd thrown at her. "Time to get up, sleepyhead."

I shoved her away and tugged the blankets over my head. "Go away. It's Sunday; I can sleep in if I feel like it."

"Sure you can, and you did. But if our goal is to look like

normal teenagers, you're ruining that by staying in bed this late. It's out of character, even for you." Cass tried to pull the blanket away and ended up yanking my hair in the process.

My eyes flew open and I flung the covers off, glaring at her. "Who cares?"

She stood, dragging the blanket off me. "The Smiths might. I mean, your standard ten o'clock would have been fine, but this could start raising suspicions of drugs, alcohol, depression, or who knows what else. And we can't really afford that."

Then I spied the alarm clock. *12:47.* A groan escaped my lips; I never slept this late. One of these days, Cass was going to be *really* wrong about something, and I just wanted to be there to see it.

Time to face the day—and the inevitable parental questions about the dance. I rolled to my feet and lurched to the closet where Cass stood, hanging up the dress I'd ditched the night before.

She shooed me away. "Go. Take your shower. I'll toss in some clothes for you in a minute."

"Thanks," I muttered, wanting nothing but to crawl back into bed.

The water pounding on my skin woke me up in a much more pleasant fashion than the blinding sunlight. I shook my head under the spray, sending droplets flying against the tile. I'd cried over a boy. A boy I just met. One who could be big time trouble. What was going on in my head?

Maybe the fact that—aside from the potentially evil thing—Jax was totally my type. Even crazier was how the beast reacted. We both wanted him—and we never agreed on anything.

I slammed the shampoo bottle down and scrubbed at my scalp. It didn't matter how much I liked him though. Didn't matter how much the beast was drawn to him. He liked Cass. I loved Cass. Those two things mattered more than anything, except for maybe that she seemed to like him back. Admitting it all hurt like hell but didn't change a thing.

I turned to rinse my hair and ended up clamping my teeth

on my tongue hard enough to draw blood when the water hit my back and tiny spots of pain flared to life. Once certain I wouldn't scream, I let the water spray on my skin again. Go me; I managed to not make a peep. Of course, my face scrunched up and I had to press my hand against the tile to keep from falling over, but hey, I didn't scream.

As soon as the water ran clear of bubbles, I twisted off the tap. I took a minute to stand in the shower and steady myself before stepping onto the rug. Then I spun around so I could see my back in the mirror. There, just above my waist, were ten small, bright red spots. My breath caught at the sight.

I didn't bother waiting for Cass to bring the promised clothes. I wrapped a towel around myself and dashed back to our room. She cast a curious glance my way, which I ignored as I rummaged in my dresser for a bra and panties. Cass laid a pair of jeans in easy reach, and I threw them on.

"Here, try this." She handed me a spaghetti-strap top in fuchsia.

I blinked at it. "I'm not wearing this."

She rolled her eyes. "Sure you are. You'll look great in it; we'll layer it with...."

I shoved the shirt back into her hands. "Nope. New plan. You stop playing fashion coordinator, put on your nurse's hat, and help me figure out what the hell is wrong with my back."

"Huh?" She gasped when I turned around. "Damn, what did you do?"

"Gee, Cass, do you really think if I knew, I'd be parading around almost topless for you?" I closed my eyes and took a deep breath. This wasn't her fault; at least I couldn't see how it would be. "I don't know what happened. They weren't there yesterday though." An image of big strong hands flashed through my mind. I closed my eyes, trying to forget it, but it came back even stronger.

"Do me a favor," I said, looking at Cass again. "Pretend you're a guy and we're dancing."

She raised an eyebrow, but wrapped her arms around me, reaching for my back. I craned my neck to see the image in the mirror on top of our dresser. My shoulders sagged and I felt like I couldn't breathe.

"What is it?"

"Take a look."

They weren't in the exact same position, maybe because Cass was shorter, but her fingers rested on my back right next to the red spots, and in the same pattern. I'd only danced with one guy the night before.

"What the hell did Jax do to you?"

I couldn't say anything, afraid my voice would betray the pain that screamed inside my head and heart.

I'm not sure how Cass and I managed to weather the storm of questions about the dance from Jen and Eric, but we both jumped at the opportunity when they suggested visiting a nearby apple orchard. We ran off with our basket and lost ourselves among the trees as soon as we could.

"So, with what he did to you last night, do you think Jax is our guy then?" Cass asked, plucking an apple from a tree and dropping it into our basket.

"Maybe." I shrugged, and she gave me a look that called me an idiot better than any words could have. "Hey, he's something, there's no doubt about that, but we're kind of grasping at straws right now. We don't really have a lot on him."

Cass glanced around before swinging into the tree in search of better apples higher up. "Please. He's new at school, turned up just in time for all this stuff to start. He left a scent trail that you followed from the game, and then look at what he did to you!"

I knew she was right, but I didn't want it to be him. Seeing Jax hook up with Cass was better than him being evil. "So, he's new and he's not quite human. Anyone in the know could say the same thing about us."

Cass tossed apples to me. "True, but people didn't become zombified when we moved to town. So who else do we have? Your ridiculous Lisa theory?"

As Cass dropped to the ground, I caught the last apple and took a bite. "It isn't ridiculous."

"You're basing your suspicion on the fact her breath

smelled like curry." I opened my mouth to protest, but she raised her hand. "I get the scent thing. You smelled curry at the cemetery, but the scent trail you followed was something else, right?"

I grabbed the basket in one hand and munched on my stolen apple, part of my mind already thinking about apple pie, among other things. "Yeah, mostly cinnamon and rosemary. There was something else, too, but it was more subtle."

"So, if the trail was rosemary and cinnamon, why didn't you smell that on Lisa if it was her?"

"I don't know. Maybe she eats curry to cover her supernatural aroma." I chucked the apple core. "Between the curry, her *threatening me,* and the fact she took off from the game right around when the attack on Zoe happened, we have just as many reasons to check into her as we do Jax."

"But who eats curry every day?"

"Hello? People who like something a lot eat it all the time—does 'pizza table' ring a bell?"

"Pizza isn't curry, Elle."

I snorted. "No, but if she's doing it to cover her scent, it makes sense to eat it like it is."

Cass stopped, maybe mulling it over. I didn't wait around. She jogged up to me a few yards down the row of trees, lowering her voice as a group of people passed us going the opposite direction. "What about the hormones? I thought you said it was a guy?"

This was getting silly. Did she want Jax to be the altar-builder? "I said it was probably a guy, but I wasn't sure. Besides, have you met Lisa? She isn't exactly the poster-girl for estrogen; she could probably out-butch half the wrestling team."

She shook her head, but chuckled anyway. "Okay, I give, we officially have two suspects." Cass waved across the parking lot at Jen, who sat outside the tiny store that serviced the orchard. "Which one do you want to check out tonight?"

"You mean after we get home and dive into the homework I didn't get the chance to even look at all weekend?" I pictured the stack of work I hadn't tackled, but she just waved it off. My mind left homework and went to the other thing I hadn't been able to escape all day—the ten little points of heat on my back. I ignored the pain, hoping if I pretended it wasn't there, it would go away. "Let's go after Lisa first."

"Really? Are you sure you wouldn't rather figure out what Jax's story is?"

I couldn't tell if the odd note in her voice meant she really was interested in him or not, and I tried desperately not to care. It didn't work so well. "No. I need my head on straight, and the simple fact he managed to mark me without my knowing has made me more than a little nervous." That sounded good. It was even a little bit true. I almost managed to convince myself it was the real reason.

The funny look Cass gave me said she didn't buy the excuse at all. "Uh huh. I'm sure that's it."

I hadn't told her anything. She couldn't know I liked him. And if she did, why wasn't she talking to me about the obvious issue of us both being into the same guy? Maybe for the same reason I hadn't brought it up to her. No, that was because she'd get him. Cass always won.

"Hey, Furball?"

"What?" I asked, shaking off the confusion.

"Race you to the store." She took off toward Jen, laughing.

I tore off after her, cursing the basket in my arms. Apples or no apples, I wasn't letting Cass win. Not this time.

Chapter Fourteen

Sunday, October 23 - before midnight

I wanted so bad to catch Lisa in the act. Not only did I want this mess over and done with, I wanted an ugly thorn in my side out of the way.

Unfortunately, the act we caught her doing was not the one I wanted to see. Some people should really make a point of closing their shades when they get undressed.

"Doesn't she ever shave?" Cass asked.

I tried not to laugh and ended up choking. "I didn't realize your eyesight was quite that good," I said once I could breathe.

"Sis, Lisa could compete with you for hairiness, and that's when you're a wolf. I don't need telescopic sight to see that." Leave it to Cass to lighten the mood and bring a smile to my face. Even though she drove me crazy with her whole "little Miss Perfect" act, she was still my best friend.

The lights clicked off, and we settled in to wait for Lisa to sneak out. And waited. I thought about shifting, but decided it was a bad idea in case I had to shift back—what with the nudity and all. Then we waited some more. Cass and I started testing each others' abilities. That lasted about half an hour before it became as boring as staring at Lisa's house.

A raccoon snuck into a nearby yard, making a beeline for the trashcan someone had left outside. I growled as loudly as I dared, and it skittered off before it woke anyone around here. Let the beggar forage elsewhere.

After resorting to sniffing the surrounding trees in an attempt to identify them by scent, I kicked the white oak we stood beneath. "I should have brought some homework." I nodded. "That's my new stakeout plan—finish all the crap I don't have time for the rest of the day."

"Could be hard to do without light," Cass argued, picking the bark off a fallen branch.

"It's also hard to stay on my toes without sleep, but I'm giving it the old college try."

"Can you really give something the 'old college try' when you're in high school?

I snarled and stalked away from her. "Go bite something, bloodsucker."

"Sorry, mongrel, you aren't my type."

My head whipped around. "That reminds me, did you stop by next door before we left?"

Cass fluffed her hair and smiled coyly. "Yes, Rex and I had a lovely evening."

An image of the one time I'd watched her sink fangs into the neck of the lovelorn Rottweiler settled into my brain, and I shuddered. Some things you just can't unsee. "That poor dog isn't going to last much longer if you don't find another blood donor."

"Oh, don't you worry your pretty little head." She walked over and mussed my hair, pulling more than a little of it from the ponytail holder. "We aren't exclusive. I have other friends with benefits."

Eww. I so didn't want to follow up on that particular cringe-inducing train of thought, even though I knew she didn't mean what it sounded like. She just wanted to get under my skin—as usual. Her other comment was a different story though. "You think I'm pretty?"

Cass rolled her eyes and gave me a gentle shove. "Of course, you dork, I think you're gorgeous." She batted my hair and plucked at my sweatshirt. "I just think you do yourself a major disservice by covering it up with ponytails and clothes that are two sizes too big." She shrugged and turned her eyes to Lisa's window.

I gaped at the back of her head. She sounded sincere, but she couldn't be. Could she? Cass was the beautiful one. The one everyone looked at. Wasn't she? I opened my mouth to protest, but at the same instant, a lamp clicked on in Lisa's room.

"Look sharp, Furball, she's up."

That was more like it. Furball, I understood.

Lisa stood at the window, gazing out into the darkness. The beast stopped pacing, her hackles rising, ready to spring the moment Lisa stepped from the house. My brow furrowed. "What is she doing?"

Cass leaped into the air, grabbed a branch of the oak, and swung up for a better vantage point. "It looks like she's sitting at her desk. Yeah, her computer screen just went on."

"Her computer?"

"That's what I said."

I leaned against the tree trunk and rubbed my neck. "Could she be making plans to meet people? Then when they show up, she attacks them?"

"Not likely. Even if I bought the idea that Diego and Alicia would meet up with Lisa in the dead of night, which I don't, what about the bank teller, or the librarian, or Mrs. Peddington?" Her weight shifted on the branch, making the leaves rustle and dislodging one, sending it drifting slowly to the ground.

I snatched it from the air and started tearing it into little pieces. "Fine. You're probably right. So what do you think?"

Cass jumped from the branch, landing feather-light on the ground in front of me. "She doesn't look like she's leaving any time soon, but I'm not really sure. Maybe she's hacking into some site with personal records of the people she's planning to attack. But honestly, she never struck me as smart enough for that sort of thing."

"Right again." I snorted. "She's about as smart as a bag of rocks. Any other ideas?"

Cass puffed out her cheeks and exhaled slowly, giving

herself time to think. "There's always the chance she's researching something to do with the altar or some kind of ritual." Cass shrugged. "Like everything else, we can't do much more than guess."

The shadows thrown by the lamp in Lisa's room shifted, but they didn't move toward the door or the window. So far, our experience with bad guys usually involved them being stupid. It was a lot easier to catch them when they weren't so good at hiding. Then again, we'd only teamed up and started patrolling a year ago. "Hey, there is something we can do. Or more specifically, you can do."

"Really? I'd love a better plan than hanging out watching her type all night, because I don't think she's going anywhere."

"Unless I'm mistaken, you can get into just about anything online, right?"

Cass nodded. "Of course. How dare you even question it?"

"Including her user history?" I jerked my head toward Lisa's window.

"Elle," Cass's voice took on a reprimanding tone, "are you suggesting that I hack into a fellow student's home computer?"

I bit my lip and did my best to look ashamed, but I couldn't quite manage it. "Yeah, kind of."

A grin split Cass's face and she mock-sniffled. "I'm so proud, and I thought you'd never ask."

About thirty minutes passed before Lisa's lamp clicked off. Another thirty minutes of waiting and she still hadn't come out. We decided to head for home and a few hours of sleep before the alarm roused us for school. I would just have to cram what homework I could into the bus ride and my time between classes.

⁂

Once we made it to school, I didn't see Cass until lunch, when she shrugged off her fellow cheerleaders and headed outside to eat with me. The day was chilly, but the risk of someone overhearing was a lot less than in the cafeteria. We settled on a bench away from the main gaggle of students.

"Everything seem okay today?" I asked, leaving the

question vague just in case someone heard.

"Yep, nothing new or different about anyone I've seen," Cass replied, taking a drink from her milk carton. "What about you?"

"All good." I shoved mystery meat from one side of my tray to the other as I glanced around. "Maybe we scared her…away…."

Bill Elwood walked out to join his circle of friends huddled in a corner of the building where they liked to imbibe in something that most definitely wasn't lunch. Some people just aren't meant to be messed with. Bill was one of those guys. Tall and muscular, he could be the nicest guy in the world when he wanted, but he had one hell of a temper. He'd spent a semester last year at the alternative high school after throwing a desk through a window. When someone pushed his buttons, it was wise to get as far out of the way as possible.

Today, something was different. His gait seemed off, like his leg was hurt, but not enough to really limp. While I stared at his non-limp, I caught motion out of the corner of my eye. A milk carton sailed through the air, smacking Bill on the side of his head and bursting open. Creamy white liquid streamed down the side of his face, into his long, unkempt hair, and marring the smoothness of his leather trench coat.

I gasped and glanced in the direction the projectile had come from. Bill's attacker grinned from ear to ear, too stupid to even hide his guilt. Derek. One of the school bullies, all of five foot tall with a major Napoleon complex. Bill would squash him like the little bug he was.

I waited for the thundering roar from Bill, but it never came. Turning back to him, I watched as he reached up and wiped the milk from his face, flicking droplets at the ground. He didn't even bother cleaning it off the trench; he just kept walking. When he reached his friends, he leaned against the wall, staring at those of us in the courtyard, but not seeing anyone.

Despair pushed my eyes closed. "Damn it, I take it back. Whoever it is, we haven't scared them in the least." And if they could get to Bill, was there anyone they couldn't hurt?

೪

It didn't take long after we got home for me to reach my breaking point. I hurled my history book across the room; papers that I had tucked carefully into its pages went flying. "How many more, Cass?"

She looked up from the computer. "Days of school?"

Tears burned unshed in my eyes, and I glared at her. "How many more people need to get hurt before we figure this out? Before we *do* something?"

Cass picked up my textbook from the floor and brought it over to where I sat on the bed. "I knew what you meant; I was kidding. And we're doing what we can."

In my mind, the Cass that handed me the book had empty eyes that stared right through me. I shuddered. "It isn't enough."

She turned around and started gathering the papers from the floor as I sulked. "Okay, what do you think is enough? Storming the altar?" Her voice took on a harsh tone and she started snatching at the papers. "I'm all for it. Too bad I can't guarantee your safety. Too bad I can't guarantee I won't get there and do this." She spun on me, her eyes black pools and her fangs exposed. I jumped to my feet, mouth hanging open. "In fact, I can pretty much promise this is exactly what I would do." Her eyes bled back to blue and her fangs retracted. "That's not a risk I'm willing to take. And last time you went near there alone you got hurt. Remember?" She kicked my ankle.

"No one attacked me, Cass, I tripped...."

"It doesn't matter. The point is we're doing the best we can, and we'll keep doing that until we figure out a better plan." She held out the papers like a peace offering.

My knuckles had turned white from gripping the book so hard. I forced my fingers to relax and saw nail impressions on the cover. Ten tiny marks, just like the ones on my back.

Ignoring the still warm spots on my skin and the stabbing in my heart, I said, "Then if you don't find anything on Lisa's computer, tonight we go after Jax."

Of course, as soon as I laid out the plan, I should have known someone would throw a wrench in it. Cass and I were about to head upstairs after a fabulous Italian meal, complete with cannoli, when Eric motioned us back to our seats. I shot a questioning glance at Cass, but she just shrugged. As my heart started racing, I inched my butt into the chair, feeling cornered and wanting nothing more than to make a break for it.

Jen came back from taking dishes to the kitchen and sat back down next to Eric. She took his hand with a soft smile, but when she turned to us, her expression was stern. "I received two calls from the school today."

Oh crap. Neither of us said a word. I wasn't sure what we'd done, but I had no plans to give them anything else to get mad at us about. I did my best to look remorseful. Whatever it was, I'd fix it.

Eric took up the parental line. "For some reason, both of your grades are slipping, and badly. Cassidy, we let you test into pre-calc, but right now you're close to failing. Your teacher kindly informed us it's too late for you to switch to a lower level class. You either tough it out and get the grade up, or you drop the math credit."

Cass's head snapped up. "I can't drop math! I need as much math as I—"

Jen cut her off. "That's all well and good, but failing this class isn't going to help any either."

I watched as Cass's dream of a career in cryptanalysis started to evaporate before her eyes. The urge to hug her almost crushed me. Then I felt the weight of two gazes shift my way, and Cass's problems suddenly seemed a lot less important.

"As for you, Ellery," Eric said, and I winced at the use of my full name, "we're well aware that history isn't your favorite subject, but the dismal score on your last exam pulled your grade right into the toilet."

Oh. That. I couldn't think of a single thing to say in my defense. Instead, like Cass, I just stared at my hands in my lap.

When Jen spoke, her voice was barely a whisper, but even that low, it cracked, "Don't you want to stay with us anymore?"

Cass and I jerked our heads up and shouted as one,

"What?" My panic to get out of the room had disappeared. Now my eyes darted from face to face, hoping the comment was meaningless, but knowing from their miserable expressions that it wasn't. This was my home. I had learned to love this crazy family of ours. Even if it weren't for what Cass and I did, this was the only place I'd felt close to welcome, close to loved.

Jen's body sagged in her chair, but Eric met my eyes. "When we became foster parents, they questioned our fitness to take in teenagers because of how young we are. If you two don't keep your grades up, it could give them a reason to take you away from us. We love you, girls. We want you to be part of our family, but you've got to help us out a little."

My heart pounded in my throat. Someone could take us away. Take me from a family that wanted me. Take me from Cass. "We'll do better. I promise."

"We need more than that." Jen wiped tears from her cheeks. I wanted to run around the table and hug her.

Cass squeezed my hand under the table. "Anything," I said, and Cass nodded in agreement.

Eric forced a smile and reached over to rest his hand on my shoulder. "Good. Then you'll both meet your new tutors tomorrow. Get back on track, okay?"

Chapter Fifteen

Monday, October 24 - just before midnight

"Tutors. We don't need no stinking tutors." Cass had been complaining about our situation ever since we'd snuck out of the house.

Normally, I might have agreed with her irritation, but we'd done this to ourselves. Summer had given us the luxury of staying out late every night to make sure the local supernaturals stayed in line. We hadn't bothered changing that schedule when school started back up, and now we didn't have much choice. "Hey, you're the idiot who signed up for advanced classes and didn't switch out when you had the chance. So suck it up and deal."

She put her hand between my shoulder blades and shoved with all her might. I stumbled but caught myself on the fence next to us. "You're just being pissy because I didn't dig up anything on Lisa's computer. Ugh. Except for that disturbing messenger conversation she had with that weirdo, DarkCore666. What kind of guy calls himself that?"

"The kind that would be into Lisa." I didn't bother looking back; I just kept on walking.

She laughed. "There is that, but now we have to check out Jax, and you're afraid of what we'll find."

I spun on her, words poised to leap from my mouth. But I

couldn't say them, not to her. *For all I know, we'll find pictures of you all over his walls, Cass. And yeah, that scares the hell out of me.* Instead, I lashed out logic. "What is with you? Checking out Jax tonight was my idea. If I really didn't want to find out he's behind this, I would have pushed Lisa again."

With a condescending smile firmly in place, Cass batted her eyelashes at me. "You just keep on telling yourself that. You might even believe it sometime."

She walked past me without looking back. She knew. I don't know how she figured it out, but she knew. And her continued interest in him meant she didn't care about how I felt. So much for being best friends.

Neither of us spoke again until we crouched behind a bush and stared into Jax's yard. He'd stuck to his word and made keeping an eye on him easy.

"What the heck is he doing?" Cass asked, her face twisted in confusion as we watched him.

"Roasting marshmallows? How am I supposed to know?" She ignored me, which was just as well because I only had eyes for the display before us.

Jax stood in his yard, a blaze in a metal fire bowl licking the sky in front of him. He held his hands toward it like he was trying to warm them, but I could see the light reflect off the sweat glistening on his forehead. Besides, if he was cold, he would have put on the jacket that was lying on the ground, rather than standing around in just his jeans and a T-shirt that clung to every one of his muscles. The fire danced like nothing I'd ever seen before. The flames would die down until all we could see was a faint glow, as if the blaze had gone out completely, then they'd leap into the air like someone had poured gasoline over them. They would caress the tips of Jax's outstretched fingers and then settle back down again.

The strange display continued for several minutes. Then Jax collapsed into a lawn chair and watched as the fire slowly died. He wore a small, proud smile, and leaned back as if completely content. His eyes drifted half-shut, and he looked like he might fall asleep right there.

I felt a tiny twinge of guilt about watching him but pushed

it away. We were here on business; it wasn't like I'd snuck into his bedroom to watch him sleep. "So, when you were digging around for information on our boy over there, what did you find? Besides his address, I mean?"

"Is this professional curiosity, Elle? Or personal?" She had the nerve to smirk. Why did she have to be a bitch about this?

"It's me trying to make sure that both predators know their prey." Something in my voice must have told her I wasn't in the mood for banter because she lost the smile and got down to business.

"Jaxson Espisito. Age sixteen and a half. Junior. He just moved here at the beginning of the school year. Excellent grades, especially in history and science. Single parent family. His mom works at a place that makes parts for trucks or something. No information available on his dad. Not much beyond that."

"What do you mean no information on his dad?"

"I mean even the spot on his birth records said 'unknown'."

"Weird. Nothing else? No details on his last school? Or the last town he lived in? Unexplained trouble there maybe?"

"Nothing yet. I didn't have a whole lot of time after the Lisa business."

I turned my gaze back to Jaxson. I didn't like it.

At least Lisa was a known entity. Her family had lived in the area her whole life, only moving in from a more rural area for her to attend high school. Anything we hadn't figured out about her from personal contact, we could find with very little digging.

With Jax we were running blind. I'd made some inquiries around school, most of them subtle. Nobody really knew the guy. The best I'd gotten from anyone was that Jax tended to keep to himself. He was never rude, but he didn't go out of his way to make friends either. I'd been told him dancing with me was the most social anyone had ever seen him. Fabulous. And now even his background told us little more than we already knew.

The fire had gone cold, and a few minutes later, Jax stood

and stretched. After a glance in the fire bowl, he picked up his jacket and wandered inside. A light—probably his bedroom—clicked on, but turned back off within seconds.

We waited again, expecting him to pop out any time. "What the hell? Did he go to bed?" Cass asked.

Did she suddenly think I read minds? "I don't know, Cass. Why don't you sneak over there and see if you can hear his heartbeat through the walls?"

She cocked her head to the side, staring at the now dark window. "I've never tried before. Do you think it might actually work?"

"No, but feel free to give it a go. Hell, if you get close enough and he's awake, it might even be a welcome intrusion."

She turned to me with a furrowed brow. "What is that supposed to mean?"

Oh, I don't know, that he might invite you in? Damn it, I'd tried so hard to suppress my frustration, but one stupid comment from her, and I blow it. "Nothing. I'm sorry. If you want to see if it works, go ahead. It's okay with me."

She cocked an eyebrow, shrugged, and took off in a crouched jog toward the house. There wasn't really much sneaking involved. Cass slunk straight up to his window and brazenly leaned her forehead against the glass. She stayed there for a couple minutes before coming back to where I was kneeling behind the bush.

"Didn't work, huh?" I asked, trying to patch up the damage I'd done.

"No, it worked fine through the glass—it's not like you where you have to filter other sounds, all I get is the heartbeat. Anyway, he's out cold. For a minute I thought I was picking up his mom or something because he hadn't been in there long, but"—she chuckled—"then he started snoring loud enough to rattle the window panes. He's dead to the world."

"This doesn't clear him though, does it?" I didn't want him to be the one we were after, but if he was evil, at least we wouldn't both be, well, after him.

Cass shrugged. "Not any more than last night cleared Lisa.

The only way to know for sure is if we watch him all night and something happens anyway. And we can't do that."

"No, especially not with the grade thing." I stood up and brushed the grass from my knees.

Once we were out of the neighborhood, Cass asked, "Do you really think they'd take us away from the Smiths? Just over failing one class? It doesn't make sense. Good foster homes aren't easy to come by."

"I don't know. Maybe Jen and Eric made it up to guilt us into shaping up, but maybe not." I thought about the tears Jen had shed and decided she was either a great actress or her concerns were genuine. "All I know is they're our family, and I don't want to chance losing that."

"Yeah, same here." Cass kicked at a small rock and sent it sailing into some weeds. "So, tutors huh?"

I stand next to the window, peeking in at the form buried under the blankets. It's wrong. I shouldn't be here. But the moonlight streams down and bathes my skin, pleasing the beast to no end. She wants to be here. She doesn't care about human rules of decency.

A family of deer passes through the next yard in search of food. I think she might decide to give chase, but food isn't what the beast wants. Her prey lies inside. I turn my gaze back to the window.

The bed is empty, covers thrown back revealing rumpled sheets. The beast growls within my chest, her irritation palpable. When a hand touches me softly on the arm, I spin around ready to attack with every ounce of her fury.

There he stands, right in front of me, clad in only a T-shirt and worn, faded flannel lounging pants. They look so soft, I want to reach out and touch them—to touch him. But I hold back, waiting for the inevitable "What are you doing here?"

But the words never come from his lips. He tips his head down, just enough so long strands of his glorious hair fall over his golden eyes. The animalistic eyes that call to the beast. All of him calls to me though. Trembling, I reach a hand up to push his hair back, but he touches me first, tipping my chin up, his lips inching toward mine....

And a shrill ringing escapes his mouth.

"Huh? What?" I shot straight up, slamming my head

against the underside of Cass's bunk.

She swung down to the floor and hit a button; the ringing stopped. "It's called an alarm clock." Turning around with a smile, she added, "Judging by the sound of growls coming from your bed though, it didn't fit whatever dream you were enjoying."

I wasn't sure what bothered me more: that I growled in my sleep or that she could tell what kind of dream I'd had from the sound. Giving her the finger, I flopped back on the bed and rubbed my head. "Is it Monday again? It sure feels like a Monday."

"Nope. Tuesday. Monday was the day that changed our after school plans for the foreseeable future." Cass threw open the closet doors then craned her neck to look at me. "And that means it's the perfect time for the new and improved Elle Jameson to go to school."

"The what?" It took a moment of watching her rifle through the closet before her words registered. "Why do we need a new and improved me?"

Cass tossed some clothes on the chair next to the desk. "Because the simple fact you didn't believe me when I said you were pretty the other night means you are in desperate need of a self-esteem boost."

Dragging myself from the bed, I wandered over and glanced at the outfit she'd so casually assembled. I picked up the top by the thin straps holding it together. "I fail to see how dressing like a slut is supposed to help my self-image."

She bundled up the rest of the clothes and thrust them into my arms. "It's only going to look slutty if you want it to. Trust me on this. Besides, maybe you need a little more sluttiness in your life." She held a hand up to stop the retort she knew was coming. "I was kidding. Just give it a chance. If you absolutely hate it, you can always change."

One look in her eyes, and I knew she wasn't going to cave this time. With a frustrated groan, I took the clothes with me to the bathroom. There had to be a way to get out of this without upsetting Cass, but even though I took an extra-long shower, nothing came to me. I wondered why I cared about her feelings considering the whole Jaxson thing, but she was my sister and just trying to help.

After combing through my hair, I gave up and sorted through the clothes. Thank God—my jeans. At least one thing would fit like it should. Since I was several inches taller, she hadn't had much in the way of options. Unless she'd tried to force me into a skirt, but she had more brains than that. I tugged on the denim and turned to the rest of the pile.

"When did I buy this?" I held up a pale golden yellow bra. It matched the panties I'd pulled on without a thought. Did Cass buy me underwear? When would she have done that? And why? After I shook off the rather creepy idea, I put on the bra.

The last item was another spaghetti-strap top, this time in an olive green. At least it wasn't pink. I pulled it over my head. Yep, it fit me just like I'd thought it would—like a second skin. The green suited me though, making my skin look even tanner than it actually was, and the bra straps peeking out gave a nice splash of color.

Part of me wished I hated everything about it, so I wouldn't feel bad when I handed the clothes back to Cass. But I didn't. I loved the colors, and I had to admit I liked the way the top accentuated my curves. I shook my head and color rose in my cheeks. What was I thinking? I couldn't wear this.

The run through the hall back to our room had never felt so long. "Cass, I'm sorry, but I can't go to school like this." My heart pounded, and I dashed toward the closet, frantic to find something that wouldn't scream "look at me."

Cass glanced my way and chuckled. "Of course not. Like that you kind of violate the dress code."

I turned around and opened my mouth to ask her why she'd had me put it on in the first place when something brown and fuzzy hit me in the face.

"Put that on and you're all set."

Once I yanked the brown mass off my head, I found a short zip-front cardigan in my hands. Slipping my arms into the sleeves, I felt instantly more comfortable. Funny how covering skin did that for me. I looked in the mirror and couldn't help but stare. I didn't look slutty anymore but....

"This isn't me."

Cass snuck up behind me and glanced in the mirror, her smile reflecting back at both of us. "Sure it is. It's just the you you try so hard to hide from the world. And like I said, you're gorgeous. Toss on some liner and gloss, and there isn't a head at school that won't turn when you walk in."

I couldn't do this. I wanted the security of my sweats back. Cass turned heads, not me. This wasn't my role in life. My hands shook and I started to strip off the cardigan.

Her fingers reached up and covered mine, holding them tight and unmoving. "Give it a chance. One day, Elle, that's all I'm suggesting. Stop hiding for one day." She let go of me and left for her turn in the bathroom.

I stared at my reflection, perplexed. Why would the girl who was bound to hook up with the one guy I was interested in want me to get noticed? More important, had I really been using clothes to hide? To avoid standing out? Was that what I wanted out of life? Was it what my parents would have wanted for me? I bit my lip, pondering the outfit. My teeth raked against my lip as it slid free. Had I been trying to break the wrong habit all along? I worried all this time about something as silly as chewing on my lip when I was nervous, when all this time, I was trying to hide myself away. Cass said one day; if that was enough to stop the questions and worries stampeding around my brain, it would be worth it.

"I can do this for one day."

Chapter Sixteen

Tuesday, October 25 - afternoon

"I can't give up cross country!" I jumped out of the plastic seat. The entire conversation with my counselor, Ms. Williams, was making me crazy. I got that I needed tutoring, but this was too much.

She leaned back in her fake leather chair and eyed me like she'd had to deal with too many wayward students already today. "Elle, when we set up the tutoring system, it was done for the convenience of the people offering their services. For the vast majority of them, their available time is directly after school." I started to interrupt, but she set her lips in a thin line and shook her head. "Look, you got yourself into this mess. Consider yourself lucky Mr. Lialios was able to find another student to tutor you on such short notice. Those who volunteered at the beginning of the year are booked with kids who asked for help from the get-go."

"But you don't understand...."

She stood up and held the door open. "I understand if you are really lucky, you might be able to make other arrangements with your tutor, but for now, consider your time after school taken."

I picked up my books and walked out, clamping my lips shut so I wouldn't argue anymore. There was no way I could make Mrs. Williams understand that I had to run in order to keep the beast at bay. If I couldn't run, I couldn't force her to sleep during the day. And awake, the beast would want out. There were no guarantees I'd be able to stop her. Walking toward band, I realized I didn't have a choice. If whoever offered to tutor me wasn't willing to do our sessions later, I was off the team, and I'd have to find another time to run. My late nights looked like they just got later.

And here I thought tutoring was supposed to help my grades.

❧

A late fall heat wave decided to roll through town today, and I found myself having to ditch the sweater during marching band. More glances than usual had come my way throughout the morning, but during rehearsal I felt like I was on a display rack and marked down for quick sale. I debated putting the cardigan back on, but I was already sweating.

Any hope I had that Lisa might avoid me from now on disappeared. She shot me more glares during that single class period than I'd ever noticed before. And I narrowly avoided being impaled by her flagpole when she "slipped."

Fifteen minutes before class ended, an aide came out to the field and handed Mr. Gartner a note. He yelled for the class to break into sections for the rest of the period. I picked up my sweater and flags to head to our practice area when the chestnut-haired man with the eternally smiling face waved me over.

"Yes, Mr. Gartner?"

"Mr. Lialios asked to see you if I could spare you for a bit. You're doing well enough with your routines that I don't think missing these last few minutes today will hurt you too much." He winked and displayed the grin that made more than one female band member swoon. Waving me off the field, he added, "Just put your equipment over here, we'll take care of it."

That meant the rest of the squad would take care of it. I laid my flags on the ground and gave Edie an apologetic wave as I walked past. She shrugged and turned to the other girls. I jogged toward the main building but turned when the little hairs at the nape of my neck stood up. This time there was someone watching me through eyes narrowed to slits. Lisa. I slitted my own eyes back at her then blew a one-fingered kiss her way before slipping on my sweater and heading inside.

Mr. Lialios glanced up from his desk when I rapped on the doorframe. "Yes, Elle, come in, come in." I stepped up to his desk, my hands twining and twisting. If he noticed my nerves, he didn't say anything. Instead he just handed me a slip of paper.

First the aide, now him. *What is this? Some secret society of paper pushers?*

"As I'm sure you heard, finding you a tutor was a bit of a challenge. Because of the nature of our class, your best bet was another student." He nodded at the note in my hand. "I'm not sure I can get you anyone else, and I definitely can't find someone who knows their stuff better. Don't screw it up."

Great. The secret society sounded like a lot more fun. "Thanks, Mr. Lialios. This is really important, I won't let you down."

He nodded. "Glad to hear it. Go see Mr. Barker and he'll fetch your tutor so the two of you can make arrangements on where to meet." He gave a casual wave toward the door.

One look at the clock, and I realized I didn't have time to be casual. The bell would ring in just a few minutes. I jogged to the gym and handed the note to Mr. Barker.

He gave it a quick look then nodded and pointed toward the hallway. "Go ahead and wait by the door to the boys' locker room. I'll get him."

I'd kicked myself for not asking Mr. Lialios who my tutor was, and stupid me hadn't bothered reading the note that obviously had his name on it. All I'd worried about was having to quit cross-country. Did it matter? I mean, as long as the guy could help, who really cared who it was? Well, as long as it wasn't Lisa, but I'd left her at band practice and last I knew she was still female, so it wasn't a worry. I bounced on my toes near the door, waiting. I guess I'd find out soon enough.

Soon is relative though, and apparently speed didn't concern Mr. Tutor-Guy, because I paced in the hallway for what felt like forever before I heard movement near the locker room door. I stepped into the alcove just as it swung open.

A gruff laugh sounded as my eyes went wide. "Yet another way to make your job easier, huh? Though really, if you wanted to hang out more, you could have just asked."

I would've loved to have a snappy comeback at the ready, but even the "not him" that had first sprung to mind flew out of my head when I looked at Jaxson. His hair slicked back, still wet and glistening from the shower. Jeans hung from his narrow hips and his muscles bulged from working out. Muscles free from the confines of a shirt. Shirts that could never in a million years do his chest justice. I swallowed hard, trying to moisten a mouth that had gone dry in the few seconds since the locker room door had opened. The beast stirred within, woken by my rapid pulse and fluttering stomach, not to mention the delicious scent of Jaxson.

He cleared his throat and filled the silence that stretched between us. "So, it's Ellery, huh? Interesting name."

The automatic reply squeaked out from between my lips. "No, it's Elle." I tore my gaze away from his muscles, which irritated the beast to no end. Of course, the fact that she'd wanted to rub up against him had played a part in the decision.

Jax arched his eyebrow and gave me a lopsided grin that made my knees turn to jello. He leaned against the doorframe, crossing his arms over his chest. "You're…a lot quieter than the last two times we spoke. Daylight not your friend?"

I forced myself not to look at the way his muscles pulled tight across his shoulders. It was my only hope to get through this conversation, and no matter how uncomfortable it made me, Mr. Lialios said Jax was my best option for a tutor. "Um, I am a night person, but I guess I just really wasn't expecting you to be the one that opened the door."

He shrugged, drawing my gaze back to his shoulders. "I could say the same thing. But the bell's about to ring and I'm not exactly presentable for chemistry. What do you say we meet in the courtyard after school?"

"Uh huh, sure, that'll be fine." My voice had progressed from a squeak to a whisper. Very impressive, I'm sure.

"All right, Elle, see you then." After giving me one last

heart-stopping grin, he stepped back into the locker room and let the door swing shut, forming a very effective barrier between us.

I sagged against the wall, able to breathe again. Though the beast settled in to sleep once more, I didn't have the luxury of relaxing. Jax had stood there, staring at me until the metal door blocked me from his sight. Cass and I had been watching him, but I had a feeling it hadn't been a one-way street. A chill ran down my spine as I stepped out of the alcove and into the openness of the hallway.

⁂

The rest of the day passed in a blur. Nerves tinged with a hint of excitement propelled me through English and biology. When the last bell sounded, I went in search of Cass, finding her opening her locker.

"Hey, Elle." She didn't bother looking up "Did you hear about the tutor thing? It sucks. I'm really hoping mine will work with me as far as cheerleading goes. I ended up with someone from Western; maybe it'll work out better with a college schedule to meet later anyway. Speaking of meeting, I'm supposed to be in the library—like now. So what about you? Think your tutor might let you stay in cross-country?" She talked a mile a minute, completely lost in Cass-land.

"I don't know, Cass." Closing my eyes, I leaned against the row of lockers.

Cass's head was stuck in her locker while she grabbed books and stuffed them into her backpack. "I'm sure they will. Did you get someone from the college, too?"

"It's Jax."

She yanked her head from the depths of the metal, static electricity forming her hair into a halo of nearly silver strands. "Where?"

I shook my head and managed a small snort as I reached to smooth down her hair. "Probably on his way to the courtyard. He's my tutor, Cass." I chewed on my lower lip, waiting for her to offer some brilliant, logical plan on how I should play things. Considering where my instincts, both human and animal, kept taking me, deferring to her seemed smart.

117

"Huh."

Seriously? Huh. That's all I get? "Cass, I could really use something a tiny bit more, you know, helpful..." My hands itched to throttle her neck, but with a large chunk of the student body still hanging out in the halls, I resisted, clenching them into fists instead.

She stuffed one last textbook into her bag then slammed the locker. "Well"—she hefted the bag and headed down the rapidly emptying hallway—"it isn't necessarily a bad thing. It'll give you the chance to get a feel for him. See if you get an evil vibe or something."

I rolled my eyes and mumbled just loud enough for her to hear, "Cass, I sleep with a vampire in the bunk over my head every night. I'm thinking my evil radar might be a teensy bit faulty."

Cass started choking with laughter, attracting the attention of several people who stopped walking just to see if they could get in on the joke. She waved them on. "In that case, maybe you can cozy up and get a better sniff, see if he's our guy." I gawked at her and she snorted. "What? He didn't seem to mind getting close to you at the dance. Use it."

We stopped at my locker and I shook my head while twirling the combination and snapping it open. "Funny, but I think it's far more likely he's using me." I jammed notebooks and texts into my backpack.

"What do you mean?"

One glance at her face told me she really didn't get it. How could she be so oblivious about these things? "Never mind. If the opportunity presents itself, I'll try." I grabbed my backpack and kicked the locker shut with a clang. "Good luck with Joe or Jill College."

Cass shrugged. "I don't need luck, I just need to stop slacking off and do my work. You on the other hand, well, I wish you all the best with Jax." She reached out and gave my hand a squeeze before turning toward the library.

What the hell is that supposed to mean? I didn't want to chase after her to ask since I might not like her answer. Instead, I sighed and walked toward the courtyard and the devil I knew.

Chapter Seventeen

Tuesday, October 25 - after school

"By the way, you look nice today." Jax pushed a Colonial map toward me.

I blinked about twenty times so fast that anyone who didn't know me would think I was batting my eyelashes at him. I forced myself to stop. "Um, thanks."

He shrugged, and I couldn't help but picture what his shoulders looked like without the cotton stretched across them. The instant I caught myself daydreaming, I gave my head a fierce shake and turned to the paper in front of me. Jax propped his arm on the back of my chair and leaned closer, the fingers of his other hand resting on the map at a town name I seemed unable to focus on.

"To be honest, I almost didn't recognize you. Every time I've seen you around school, you're dressed in sweaters a couple sizes too big for you. This look works though."

He sat close enough that the aroma of rosemary and cinnamon overwhelmed me. The beast rolled around inside my body like a feline high on catnip. It took a minute, but then the teenage girl in me reacted to his words and pulled the cardigan tighter. "What do you mean, seen me around. We just met on Friday."

Jax leaned back and smirked at me. "Yes, and every

moment prior to meeting you by my locker, I kept my eyes closed and didn't notice anyone or anything that happened at school." He chuckled and shook his head, causing his hair to fall over his eyes again when he turned back to the map. "Just because I didn't know your name until today doesn't mean I didn't know who you were."

"What about Cass? Have you seen her around, too?" I clenched my jaw and tried my best to keep my eyes glued to the map. Why had I asked that? Did I want him to talk about her? And why the hell did he have to smell so good?

"Huh?" I could feel him looking at me for a minute before he continued, "Oh, your sister. Right." I risked a glance as he shrugged, and I spun back to the map. "I'll admit it's kind of hard to miss a tiny platinum ball of bouncy cheerleader. To be honest, it makes a lot more sense seeing the two of you hang out knowing that you're sisters."

I squeezed my eyes shut. He'd admitted it. He was watching us both. My heart started to race. Cass and I hadn't discussed how to handle this. Did I confront him? Wait. This could all be part of his thing for Cass. He would look for her and see me with her. Wonder why the popular, beautiful cheerleader was hanging out with me. *Don't confront him. Talk to Cass first.* How the hell do I bring this up to her?

His finger tapped my back, and my eyes flew open. He was staring at me with an amused smile on his face. Blood rushed to my cheeks, probably staining them a shade of red I didn't even want to think about.

Jax tapped the map. "Let's get back to the American Revolution, shall we?"

I nodded, not trusting myself to talk without saying something stupid. We spent the rest of the hour reviewing the latest chapter we'd covered in class. Or I should say he did. I kept trying to take a nice deep breath of his scent without getting the beast too excited or doing anything to embarrass myself again.

I stifled a yawn, and he turned to me. "What? Am I boring you already?"

"No, it's not that. I mean, history isn't really my thing, but it's not you. You're great..." I held my breath then attempted to rally and make it sound like I hadn't just said what I'd just said. "I probably need more sleep, that's all. I mean, history might bore the pants off me, but I've never failed a test before."

Jaxson's laugh made me shiver. "Bores the pants off you, huh? That makes my job a little more challenging, but I'll see what I can do to make history more relevant to you and your life. Actually, it's kind of strange that you'd even need a tutor if it was really just one failed test."

He stood and stretched, his T-shirt riding up and baring a few inches of his six-pack. I tore my eyes away from the sight and started shoving books into my bag. I couldn't do this every day. He'd make me crazy.

Decision time. Give him personal information or not? Without Cass here to weigh the pros and cons, I had to go with my gut. "I've never done great in history, so one really awful test grade is a big deal. Plus, I'm a foster kid, so my grades matter to other people. You know, doing bad in school is some sign that I'm unhappy, or experimenting with drugs, or..."

"Or staying up so late that you're exhausted at school?"

I shot him a glance that must have had suspicion written all over it.

He held up his hands in mock surrender. "Hey, you were the one who mentioned that you needed more sleep. But, that does explain things, and it gives me enough background that I might have some ideas on how to make history mean more to you."

Now that was an opening I could drive a semi through. "Since we're talking about things that are important to me..." I bit my lip, and he arched his eyebrow—I really wished he'd stop doing that since it sent the beast into a flurry inside me. "I'm on the cross-country team, and doing this right after school means that I'll have to quit. Is there any way I can talk you into meeting later?"

He stared at me in silence for what seemed like an eternity. Too many thoughts rolled around in my brain to even hazard a guess at what he was thinking. Finally he asked, "Do you think the running thing helps you sleep?"

I jerked back in my seat at the odd question, but considering I'd have to run at night if I quit the team, I gave the best answer I could. "Yeah, if I didn't run, I'd probably be up later." Evasive maybe, but not an outright lie.

Nodding, he folded up the map and handed it to me. "Okay then, we'll make it work. The bookstore isn't far from here. Why don't you meet me in the coffee shop there after practice from now on?"

That was easier than expected. It made me wonder what else he might say yes to if I asked. *Don't be stupid, Elle. It'll crush you if he says no. Just let it go.* I stuffed the map in a pocket. "Okay, that'd be great. When should I tell Jen...I mean, my foster mom to pick me up?" Jen wouldn't like coming at different times to pick up me and Cass, but she'd do it if I asked. At least I hoped she would.

Jax grabbed his beat-up biker jacket and swung his arms into the sleeves. "You don't have to do that. I can give you a ride home. That way if we ever run late, she isn't sitting in the parking lot waiting on you." *One problem solved, I suppose.* He picked up my backpack and handed it to me as I stood. "It'll also give me the chance to maybe buy you a coffee, or something, sometime."

᪣

Cass inhaled her water and started choking, her hand over her mouth to keep from spewing everywhere. "He asked you out? And I thought I had news."

I couldn't tell from the tone of her voice if the question was surprise over him asking or surprise that he asked me and not her. With a shake of my head, I gritted my teeth and stuffed my lab report into my bio folder. "He didn't ask me out. He said he'd buy coffee." I rifled through the backpack and pulled out my algebra book.

"Or 'something', you said."

I should have stopped the conversation after I'd told her my covert sniffing only let me know my human nose wasn't sensitive enough. She'd latched on to the coffee thing and wouldn't let go. "Pretty sure it was just in case I didn't drink coffee. Which I don't."

Cass rolled her eyes and tossed her homework on my bed. "Why are you so sure he didn't ask you out?"

She really didn't get it. Had I been upset over nothing? I shook my head. No. Regardless of how Cass felt, Jax liked her. "I'm pretty sure he has a thing for someone else."

With a huff, she sat on the bed next to her papers, her brow creasing. "Oh." She picked up her homework without changing her expression, rifled through the pages, and then tossed them back on the bed. "Hey, at least he's letting you stay on cross-country though. That must be a load off your mind."

Her focus on my time with Jax made me squirm, and I definitely didn't want to bring up his reason for saying okay. My only way out was to shift the conversation in another direction. "Yeah, I have some hope for staying sane through all this. What about you? The cheerleaders need to look for a new pyramid princess?"

A mile-wide grin split her face. "I thought you'd never ask."

Oops.

Perching on the edge of my bed, she held her hands in her lap, from all appearances, doing her damnedest not to bounce up and down. "Corbin said staying on the team was important. In his opinion, extra-curricular activities shouldn't be discarded like they're nothing."

"Corbin? So it was Joe College rather than Jill, huh?"

"Oh my God, Elle, he is to die for!" Cass squealed, her eyes sparkling. "Do you remember that guy Bailey pointed out at the assembly in the alumni section? That's him! He's a double major in mathematics and education with plans on being a college professor. He's hot—and brilliant!"

Any lingering fear she might pursue Jax flew out the window, and a wad of tension eased from my body. Even though it had its own issues, this situation was preferable to what I thought we'd have to deal with. Plus, I'd never seen her like this over a guy—any guy. She was practically floating. My Jaxson issues could wait. I set my paper inside the book and closed it, turning to her with a genuine smile. "Tell me all about him."

And she did. His short, sandy brown hair. His hazel green eyes that reminded her of a wild cat. His strong, chiseled features. "And he's tall, like over six feet tall." She fell backward on the bed, her face a mask of bliss.

I laughed because I wanted so badly to share her happiness. Well, that and the image of tiny Cass with a guy towering over her by more than a foot tickled my funny bone. "So, boy-next-door gorgeous and a genius. Anything he isn't?"

Cass propped herself up on the bed and gave an evil grin. "I'll let you know."

Call me naïve, but at first I really thought she just meant it in a general way. Then reality hit me, and my mouth gaped open as I stared at her. I grabbed a stuffed animal from the top of the desk—a deer she'd given me for my birthday last year—and chucked it at her. "You wouldn't!"

She snatched it out of the air. "No, I'm not stupid. But as of right now, if he has a fault, I haven't found it. He is the perfect non-boyfriend-boyfriend."

"Dinner!" Jen yelled up the stairs.

I headed to the door with Cass. "So where are you meeting for your tutoring sessions since Corbin is so in favor of you kicking your leg in the air wearing a short skirt?"

Cass grabbed my arm and gasped. "Do you think he might come to a game if I asked? That would be so cool."

I shook my head and brushed her fingers from my arm. "Down girl. If you want him there, ask. Of course, Trey might not like it much."

"I think I will." Her eyes went dreamy for a second then she woke up and heard what I'd said. "Trey? Why would he care?"

It didn't matter how smart she was; sometimes Cass was just an idiot. "Trey's been chasing you for months. You need to take care of it before you go chasing Joe College."

"Hmmmm. Really?"

I nodded.

"I suppose if this thing with Corbin doesn't work out, Trey could fill my dating void."

This time, I tugged her to a stop. "Cass, you can't do that to him. Trey's a nice guy."

She shrugged, missing my point entirely. "That makes him the perfect person to deflect the idiotic questions of why I'm a cheerleader and single. Unless, of course, people think I'm involved with Corbin." She grinned. "Thanks for letting me know."

My body's only response was to blink at her with my mouth hanging open...again. Maybe I was part were-fish, too.

She flounced down a couple steps then turned back to me. "Oh, and for now, we're still meeting at school. Corbin said it would be inappropriate for him to take me somewhere else since he's older. Isn't that the sweetest thing?"

Cass left me there, staring at the place she'd been standing. I shook my head to clear it. She was completely head over heels, or at least as much as possible for her. "Sure it's sweet," I shouted after her. "It's also going to put one hell of a crimp in the whole 'boyfriend' thing."

Chapter Eighteen

Tuesday, October 25 – evening

I really couldn't wait for the day that dinner didn't ruin my night. Our conversation started out fine, with Cass and me telling all about our adventures in tutoring. We eliminated the less family-friendly details, of course. Then Jen talked about the big new client she landed for her freelancing business. It was all going so well. Until Eric announced he had a late night ahead of him working on some presentation, or review, or something, for work the next day. I cast a glance at Cass and saw her looking as worried as I felt.

As soon as we'd made it upstairs and shut the bedroom door, I leaned against the oak panels. "Great. What do we do now?"

"We stay in. It's that simple." Cass slid into the chair with her English book in hand, ready to dive into Shakespeare. "We can't do anything tonight, not with Eric awake."

Easy for her to say. She didn't have a hairy beast pacing within the cage of her body. "Earth to Cass. I missed practice today. I still need to run." I walked the length of the room, mirroring the beast's movements, knowing it would do no good, but desperate to do something anyway.

Her eyes went wide and then her brows drew tightly together as she turned to me. "Oh crap, I didn't think about that. Will you be okay to skip? It's just one night."

"Don't do that to your face—worry causes wrinkles, even for the preternaturally young and beautiful." She waved off my attempt at banter, and all I could do was shake my head. "To be honest, I really don't know. I might be fine, but I've run every day since I figured out that it kept the beast subdued. Maybe I can get up early and go for a run in the morning before I have to get ready for school." I threw myself across my bed. Even if pacing had worked, which it didn't, I couldn't spend all night walking our room.

Cass stood up and brought my backpack to the side of the bed. She perched on the edge of the mattress and brushed my hair back. "We'll figure something out. Maybe Eric won't be as late as he thought, and we'll manage to sneak you out. If not, we'll set the alarm for earlier. It'll be okay." She reached down, yanked a book from my backpack, and handed it to me. "In the meantime, we should probably just take the opportunity to get some work done."

"Yeah, you're probably right." I turned the book over in my hands. History. Of course. Opening the pages, I couldn't help but wonder if Jax would be spending the night in, too.

Soon enough, it became crystal clear fate didn't like me much. When I smelled Eric making coffee at eleven, I knew my chances of sneaking out for a night run had decreased from slim to none. So, to the sound of rain battering our window, I climbed into bed for some much needed sleep. Then, sometime in the middle of the night, we lost power, and neither Cass nor I had checked the alarm clock's back-up battery in recent memory. I suppose I should have considered it lucky that shortly after the jangling bells would normally have woken us, Eric rapped on the door and reminded us to get up. At least the power was on now and I could still get breakfast.

I scrambled into the bathroom and rushed through my shower. Sometime in the midst of rinsing my hair, I heard the door open then close seconds later. When I stepped from the steamy enclosure, I saw why. Next to the baggy sweatshirt I'd thrown on the counter laid the clothes Cass had dropped off. I stared at the two shirts as I slid into my jeans. She hadn't pushed, hadn't said a word. Hell, she'd even left the other option in plain sight, but I got the message loud and clear. Which Elle did I want to be?

Stepping into the bedroom, I had a hard time missing Cassidy's grin. "Willing to give it one more day, I see?"

"Yeah. Only because it'll probably be too hot for the sweatshirt though. "

She strode out of the room and shouted, "We'll take what we can get."

What's this "we" nonsense?

The reflection in the bedroom mirror had my head and wore my jeans, but I still didn't recognize her. The shirt wasn't as questionable for me as yesterday's had been. This time Cass had delivered a burgundy Henley with velvet trim on the neck and sleeves. It still fit snugger than I was used to and left me feeling a little naked. But, taking a good, hard look at myself, I realized I also felt strong. Cass was right. I had been hiding. As nervous as I felt in the clothes, I stood taller, held my head higher.

Crap, I like the new and improved me, too.

The "we" comment made sense when I settled in at the breakfast table. Jen wore a Cheshire grin that matched Cass's perfectly. At least I didn't have to worry about Cass buying me underwear; Jen had stepped in as mom and done the shopping. It also explained why the clothes fit so well. I'd thought they'd come from Cass's closet, but they'd been bought for me. I loved Jen a little more for the clandestine effort.

"Okay, you two, stop looking so damned proud of yourselves. I'm willing to give this a chance, but do me a favor?" I stared pointedly at Jen, who gave a shrug, promising nothing. "Next time you go shopping, at least take me with you."

All three of us started chuckling, and Jen could barely get out the word, "Deal." When Eric walked in, rubbing at his sleepy eyes, and asked what was so funny, we just laughed harder. I don't know what made it so hilarious, but it felt good to act like a normal family. For one moment, I was certain I'd made the right decision to not risk sneaking out the night before with Eric awake. I loved my new family too much to risk losing them.

I had second thoughts when we stepped onto the bus though. "Good morning, Ms. Crawford."

The bus driver turned to me with eyes that didn't hold even a hint of their normal twinkle, and I froze in my tracks. "Take your seat please," she said in a lifeless monotone.

I turned away and moved down the aisle, passing those in the front who wanted off the bus as quickly as possible. People waved greetings—I don't even know who—and I nodded in response, afraid to look at their faces. Afraid I'd see more of those blank stares. I yanked Cass into a middle seat, away from everyone else so we had some small bit of privacy.

"How is the altar-builder doing this?"

"Still sticking with that, Elle? You haven't picked a suspect yet? Seriously?"

A growl rumbled up through my chest as I glared at her. I felt the beast stirring again, clawing to get out. Today was the wrong day for Cass to be a bitch. Squeezing my eyes shut tight, I tried to force the beast down. "Actually, I still think Lisa's doing it, but I won't pretend I'm sure. Really, I don't think it matters much right now. What I want to know is how *whoever*"
—Cass rolled her eyes at me—"it is has managed to get to such a range of people. It doesn't make sense. Teachers, sure. Students, okay. Even Ms. Crawford I could get. But add on the bank teller and the librarian at Western? Those I just don't get. And I'm sure there are people we don't even know about."

Cass raised one shoulder in a half-hearted shrug and whispered, "How do bad guys always manage things? They just do. Really the how doesn't make a difference. We need the who so we can stop them. And actually, it isn't so out-there that either Jax or Lisa had to go to the college library for something. Or the bank for that matter. Hell, one or both of those women might live in their neighborhood."

I slumped against the plastic cushion, punching the back of the seat in front of us. Ms. Crawford didn't even flinch, though several students from a few rows up glanced back. "I just don't like not knowing."

"Fine. So tonight we focus on the things we can figure out. You said you got a good whiff of our buddy Jaxson." She waited for me to nod. "Good, get reinforcement today. Hell, see if you can get something with his scent on it. Then you can hit the cemetery tonight and compare." Cass turned and stared out the window at cars whizzing past the lumbering bus. Her way of telling me the conversation was over.

It wasn't finished for me though. "Because of course, the altar and all the blood will still be there, right?" I plucked at a string on the cushion, wondering if the altar disappearing would make things better or worse.

Cass shook her head and actually managed a quiet chuckle. "Elle, come on. If we've learned one thing about the horrible people of the world, what is it?"

She might have been able to laugh about her past and the things that had happened to her at the hands of "horrible people," but I wasn't. This time I didn't need to try to keep my voice down. I could barely whisper. "They never give up."

"Exactly," she kept talking, unaware of my discomfort. "Besides, I've kept my ear to the ground. No other disturbances. So either *whoever* is still at Indian Fields or they're keeping really quiet."

By the time the bus pulled up to school, the beast was howling, and I still hadn't decided which option scared me more.

I'd hoped things would improve once I got into class, but no such luck. The beast was awake and nothing I did was settling her back down. The press of bodies in the hall overwhelmed my senses, and I collapsed at my desk in history, for once happy to be there. I could still smell and hear everyone around me, but it wasn't like the hall. I could see straight and breathe here.

Then my friend Kris walked in, and the beast perked up. I turned my head the other way and tried to take shallow breaths. Closing my eyes, I tuned out everything but Mr. Lialios's voice, lecturing about the Colonies' allies during the Revolutionary War. But the Spaniards, French, and Dutch didn't matter to the beast, and they disappeared in a haze of red as she fixated on the one thing she cared about.

She smelled blood. Somewhere on Kris. Without meaning to, I turned toward the scent, my nostrils flaring. The American Revolution became a background echo, and the classroom blurred. Kris was the only thing that mattered to the beast.

Maybe if I let her sniff him out fully she'd let go, and I could get through the day. Or at least the class. So I closed my eyes and inhaled. Smelling deeper than the blood, searching for where it came from. The beast had too much control. I shouldn't be able to do that in human form. Then it was there. Unmistakable. The tang of steel beneath the blood.

My eyes flew open with one clear thought: *he has a weapon.*

Panic made my heart race. Why would he bring a weapon to school? I thought he was a nice guy. Nice guys don't carry weapons.

The beast didn't give me much time to worry about Kris though. She tried to grab hold of my anxiety and ride it to the surface. Frantic, I pushed against her with all my might.

My hand shot into the air. Mr. Lialios nodded to me, and I gasped out, "I'm really not feeling well. Can I have a pass to the nurse please?"

I must have looked pretty bad, because he waved me to the front and scribbled in my planner. Bag in hand, I dashed out. The heels of my boots hit the tiles of the hall with echoing clacks as I ran to the bathroom.

Leaning against the sink, I forced my breathing to remain shallow so I couldn't taste any scents on the air, trying like hell to get my heart rate back to normal. One glance in the mirror made it clear why my history teacher hadn't argued. My face had a contorted, pain-filled appearance. It wasn't pain though. It was *her.* I twisted the tap to cold and splashed icy water on my face.

"Go to sleep, you stupid bitch," I hissed. Tears threatened to fall, and I knew if I let that happen, I was screwed. She'd have her way and there'd be no more hiding. I choked on a sob. "Please."

Another healthy dose of water seemed to help. Either that

or she took pity on me because she quieted a bit and stopped pushing. I staggered to the office and claimed a migraine. "I just need to rest in the dark for a while." The nurse gave me a worried look and ushered me into the sickroom, promising to check on me in a half-hour.

Lying with a cold compress over my eyes, I worked on taking slow, calming breaths. The beast didn't like the antiseptic odors in the room and paced inside me, waiting. I had to lull her somehow, and I didn't think I could convince the medical professional in the other room that all I really needed was to go outside and run the migraine out of my system.

The nurse was kind—she gave me almost an hour. Apparently it was long enough that I looked better, because the emaciated health nut told me I could go back to class. Her dismissal gave me just enough time to walk back to algebra and suffer through the last fifteen minutes of class.

Too bad the beast woke as soon as I stood up. I made a detour into the bathroom and splashed more water on my face. Then I spent the remainder of the period trying to combine deep breathing with not smelling anything.

Of course, the beast didn't like that so much, and by the end of class, it was all I could do to keep myself from shifting as I raced through the halls.

Chapter Nineteen

The locker room was blissfully empty when I arrived. But even without the other girls crowded in, the stench still assaulted me. Sweat. Hair products. Perfume. I tore off my clothes and threw on the shorts and tank top I used for gym, leaving behind the locker room and its over-abundance of smells before anyone else even showed up.

I found Mr. Barker at the opposite end of the gymnasium, near a rack of basketballs. "Mr. B? I have a problem."

The big man turned to me and laughed. "What teenage girl doesn't have problems? What is your crisis of choice for the day, Elle? 'Female issues' won't get you out of basketball." He winked then picked up a ball and tossed it to me.

I caught it and shifted from foot to foot. The beast didn't find his attempt at humor the least bit entertaining. My control over her was slipping. This had to work. "I kind of *do* want out of basketball"—his face turned stern and he opened his mouth, but I plowed ahead—"but not out of class. I missed cross-country practice yesterday because of tutoring and I really need to run." His mouth snapped shut and he eyed me, probably looking for a lie. A spasm hit me as my insides tried to twist. The beast was winning. I decided to push a little harder. "I just can't focus and it's affecting all my other classes."

"Elle, as much as I like you, I can't just let you bow out of a lesson, you know that. If I do it for you, I'll have to leave the option open to everyone."

I was screwed. I'd have been better off just skipping class altogether. No. Because cutting class would get tacked on to the grade thing and mess with life at home. I was right; the fates were out to get me.

Then Mr. Barker leaned in close and whispered, "But, you're a smart girl who knows the rules and penalties in here. I'm sure you can figure something out." He squeezed my shoulder and moved across the gym to call people out of the locker rooms for class.

I searched my brain for all the gym rules while we stretched and ran two circuits around the gym for a warm-up. The only things that popped into my head would get me in a lot more trouble than I wanted. At least the short run calmed the beast a tiny bit. It wouldn't last though.

"Split into your assigned groups and we'll start with shooting drills," Mr. Barker bellowed.

My toes were barely on the free throw line when Mr. B lobbed the ball into my hands. I dribbled it twice then started to shift into shooting position when I caught him looking at me. Mr. Barker jerked his chin toward the net then moved on to the next group.

I glanced from the ball to the net, and my lips curved into a smile. The beast must have felt the change in my emotions because she growled and tried to push her way out again. This time, I used her energy. I rushed the net, leaped and dunked the ball, hanging onto the rim for a few more seconds than probably necessary. But hey, I wanted to make sure I gave Mr. B plenty of time to see me.

"Elle Jameson!" He yelled, doing his best to keep his lips from twitching into a smile, and pointed to the line along the outside of the gym. "Run it out!"

The sound of his voice was music and drowned out the angry howl of the beast. I pretended to sulk as I walked over to the line, thanking my lucky stars most of the teachers liked me well enough that I got away with things every once in a while. I spent the remainder of class running like my life depended on it. Considering all the sticky outcomes I could imagine if I shifted into wolf-form during class, death might not have been too far off the mark. When Mr. B blew the whistle signaling the end of class, the beast had bedded down for a nap and I dripped with sweat.

"Feel better?" he asked when I walked by on my way to the locker room. I nodded breathless thanks. "Nice dunk, by the way, you might want to consider the basketball team this winter."

I started to laugh, but combined with how hard I was breathing, it turned into a choking fit. Mr. Barker clapped me on the back, and I managed to inhale again. "Thanks." I smiled. "For everything."

He let out one of his great belly laughs. "Any time, Elle."

"Hey." Jax smiled when I entered the bookstore and waved me over to a sitting area adjacent to the coffee shop. He already had books and maps spread out on the low table in front of a couch.

"Hey yourself." I tossed my jacket and backpack at the end of the couch and sank into its micro-suede softness. Jax sat down next to me, and I realized just how small the couch was—it barely qualified as a loveseat.

Jax glanced at me then at the coffee cup in his hand. "You want something? I could go grab it while you get your stuff out."

Personal space for ten seconds or get to work so we could finish? His shoulder brushed against mine and a tingle ran down my spine. No question. I needed to compose myself for this. "Uh"—I ripped my tongue from where it had stuck to the roof of my mouth—"actually a bottle of water would be fabulous." He didn't need to know about the one in my backpack, right?

He flashed a lopsided grin. "One bottle of water coming up."

I took some deep breaths, reminding myself that he could

very well be the altar-builder and that I had to concentrate on doing my job. Then an icy trickle ran down the back of my shirt as he pressed the bottle to my neck. My eyes rolled back; it felt so good. *Focus, Elle.* I reached my hand around and grabbed the bottle. "Thanks." I twisted the cap off and took a long swig.

Settling in next to me, he leaned forward and grabbed his book. "No problem, I saw you running earlier and figured you might need some cooling off."

Water sputtered out of my mouth, and I tried my best to keep from spitting on him. Raising a hand to my lips, I said, "You watched me run?" *What kind of person does that?*

He brushed his hair back and shrugged. "I was on my way inside when I saw all these crazy track people go flying by. It's kind of like a train wreck, you know? You notice it, and you can't help but stop and stare." He gave a little laugh.

The sound tickled the fancy of the beast, who twitched in her sleep like she was chasing something tasty. Which, in turn, made me squirm a little. I couldn't even tell if I was attracted to him anymore or if it was just her rubbing off on me.

"Anyway," he continued, "while I stood there like a slack-jawed idiot, you cruised by, passing people like a madwoman. It was kind of scary to tell you the truth." The lopsided grin made a repeat appearance.

"Oh. Okay." What he said made sense, but I couldn't shake off the feeling he was *trying* to put me at ease. To make me comfortable. So I'd let my guard down. Immediately I shored up every mental wall I could. I didn't care how much I liked his smile or his smell, I wasn't going to let him get to me so easily.

He cleared his throat. "Let's get to work then. Since I heard you skipped out on class early today, it's probably a good idea if you get caught up on notes." He shoved his notebook toward me and leaned back, sipping his coffee.

"Yeah, that would be very helpful."

His jagged scrawl stared up at me from the pages as I started copying, and I could feel his eyes glued to me from the other side of the couch. I could also feel his leg touching mine far more than the confines of the loveseat necessitated.

The walls started crumbling, and I had to do double duty taking notes and trying to keep my guard up. *One of these days I will figure out how to concentrate on history. Really. I will. Just thinking it isn't going to be today.*

We were packing up our things to leave an hour later, when Jax leaned close and whispered, "You smell really nice today, by the way."

"So do you." *Oh my God. Did I really just say that?* Thank goodness I'd left my hair down after practice. It covered my cheeks as blood rushed to stain them scarlet. I bent over my backpack a few seconds longer, hoping the color would dissipate. At least a little.

When I looked up he was smirking at me. "I don't wear cologne, but thanks all the same."

I gulped. "It must just be you then." How many stupid things would I say before we left? Why couldn't I just learn to bite my tongue around him? "I don't wear perfume either." That had to be safe.

His low chuckle sent a tremor through me, from my flushed cheeks to lower regions best left unconsidered. He leaned in close again, his lips brushing the curtain of my hair. "Maybe that's it. Maybe I just like the natural scent of you."

My cheeks got hotter, and I found it hard to breathe with him so close. Too much of me wanted to turn my head and press my lips against his. Which was completely insane. Instead, I searched for something to say. A way to shift the moment back to normalcy. Then the truth hit me.

"Um thanks, but I just realized. It isn't really me you're smelling. Susie Carmichael sprayed perfume all over herself after practice. I had to walk through it to get out of the locker room." I stood and shouldered my backpack, a plan formulating. "If you want, I can ask her what kind it is so you can pick up a bottle for your girlfriend."

Jax reached over and brushed back some hair that had fallen into my face. He tucked the strands behind my ear, his fingers lingering. "No girlfriend to buy it for, but whatever it is, it smells good on you."

I froze, staring at him. My mouth too dry to form words.

Every second he spent touching me just made me more afraid to move. Afraid I'd break whatever delicate spell had created the moment. I wanted to stay this way forever, but I knew it couldn't last.

All too soon, a cell phone rang nearby, crushing the silence holding us in place. I swallowed hard, storing the moment to pull out and examine again later. Jax dropped his hand and gave me a smile that didn't reach his eyes. "Come on, Elle the super sniffer, let's get you home." With that, he headed toward the door, and I took a deep breath and followed.

Super sniffer? If you only knew the half of it.

We stepped outside into a warm breeze, but I could feel a taste of the cold front headed our way. Instinctively, I pulled my thin jacket closer. "So, where's your car?"

"At home." He didn't look at me when he said it. He just strode into the parking lot, oblivious to the way his actions contradicted his words. I stayed on the sidewalk and waited for him to turn back toward me. "What?" he asked at last.

"I thought you said you'd drive me home."

The lopsided grin I was coming to both love and dread made another appearance. "Trust me. Just a little bit, okay?" He waved me into the parking lot.

I so wasn't sure I *should* trust him, but I really wanted to. I wanted to believe there was nothing more evil about him than his bizarre love of history. So I followed him. Baby steps and all that. "Where are we going, Jaxson?"

He stopped and turned around so abruptly that I almost ran into him. Reaching out, he grabbed my arms to keep me from falling. "Right here."

My eyes were glued to his face, and I found myself breathing harder. He hadn't let go of my biceps yet. Maybe he planned to throw me in a car and tie me up until he could take me to the altar. Maybe I'd been wrong about him liking Cass all along and he was about to lean over and kiss me. Maybe…

Jax jerked his head to the right, and I glanced that way. Then I stared.

Is this some kind of joke?

He'd indicated a parking space containing a black and

chrome motorcycle. I didn't know enough about motorcycles to know anything other than it was big and beautiful. With my mouth still hanging open a little bit, I stepped over and ran my fingers along the slightly worn leather seat and took in the name emblazoned on the side of the tank: Indian. The bike wasn't new, that much was obvious, but it was well cared for. It fit him. A bit rough around the edges, but absolutely stunning.

"Do you like it?" His voice came from right over my shoulder, and my heart started to race as I nodded. He reached past me, unhooked a bungee cord from the seat and offered me one of the two helmets he'd had strapped down. While he stuffed his backpack in a saddlebag, he asked, "In that case, can I still give you that ride home?"

As he spoke, his breath tickled against the side of my neck, making it hard for me to think. *Trust, Elle. Remember, it's all about trust. You're going to have to give a little to get the answers you want.* It felt like the world stood still, holding its breath while I made my decision. A smile played at the corners of my lips as I nodded again and slipped the helmet over my head.

He put on his own helmet and climbed on, giving me a moment to mount behind him. He flipped his visor open. "Just make sure you hold on and move with me, okay?"

The beast rolled over inside me and arched her back, thrilling at his closeness. "No problem." I wrapped one arm around his waist then leaned against him, taking a lingering inhale of his scent before I snapped the faceplate shut and wormed the other hand into position.

Who says work has to be boring?

Chapter Twenty

"I don't know, Elle. I'm just not very comfortable with you riding on that boy's motorcycle."

The spoonful of stew stopped halfway between the bowl and my mouth, and I blinked at the den-mother tone in Jen's voice. She'd never seemed like a worry-wart before. "Um, we both wore helmets, and he drove very carefully." I looked to Cass for some support, but she was doing her best not to laugh.

"What kind of motorcycle is it?" Eric asked.

Great. More questions. And why would that even matter? "An Indian? I think that was the name."

Eric nodded, his eyes twinkling. "Nice. A true American original. I approve."

I breathed a sigh of relief; Eric backing me up pulled a lot more weight than anything Cass could have said.

"Eric!" Jen turned her irritation on him.

He just chuckled. "Come on, Jennifer, cut the girl some slack. If she has a cool tutor, maybe it'll be enough to encourage her to get that grade up to an A and keep it there." He popped a piece of bread in his mouth and winked at me.

I forced my face into its most innocent expression. "I suppose if you like the idea of coming twice to pick up Cass and me, then I'll tell Jaxson I don't need a ride anymore."

Jen slapped her butter-coated knife on her bread in short, fast strokes. I had her trapped between a rock and a hard place, and she knew it. "Fine. But if I ever see you on it without a helmet..."

I held up a hand to ward her off. "I promise. Never without a helmet."

She narrowed her eyes at me, still not happy, but she let the matter drop. Eric and Cass picked up the slack in the conversation, but it was obvious it'd take some time for Jen to like Jaxson. I just hoped he would be around long enough for me to worry about it.

As soon as we were back in our room, Cass burst out laughing. "He rides a motorcycle? How bad boy cliché can you get?" She straddled the chair and raised her eyebrow in an eerie impression of Jaxson. "Hey, Elle, want a ride on my motorized manhood?"

I grabbed the pillow off my bed and threw it at her. "First off, we don't know if he is the bad guy. Secondly, clichés aren't all bad; Hollywood has made millions on the backs of clichés. More than once." I picked up my biology notes and flipped through them to make sure I'd reviewed everything for my test the next day.

"I said bad boy, not bad guy. But that doesn't matter. We don't know he isn't our guy either." She tilted her head to the side and looked at me with an odd expression on her face. I made a point of burying myself in my notes. Apparently it was a bad move. "That's why we planned to go back to the cemetery so you could sniff things out again, right?"

I didn't answer.

The chair scraped against the floor as she stood. Seconds later, she ripped the papers from my hands. "Right?"

I grabbed the papers back, but a note of desperation crept into my voice over the air of irritation I wanted to project. "I'm not sure we need to. I don't think it's him." I stuffed the pages of notes back into my folder and walked over to put it into my backpack.

"You mean now that you've gotten a better whiff of him, he smells wrong?"

I examined a scratch in the desktop.

"That *is* what you mean, right?" I could feel her eyes on me as she stood there, tapping her foot and waiting for me to respond. "Or is this about Kris? Because I agree that we need to look into the weapon thing."

"Yes." At least she'd glommed onto the Kris thing, too. I hated the idea I might be frivolously going after one of my best friends. I wanted to leave it there, but I couldn't lie to her, not when it mattered this much. "No. I don't know, Cass. I just don't think it's him." I threw my head back, squeezed my eyes shut for a second, and then stared at the ceiling.

"Oh crap, Elle. You really are into him, aren't you?"

Again, a lie would have been so convenient. Say no and make up some reason about needing him as a tutor because I didn't want to lose our family. But in the end, I had no choice. Even with my head at its odd angle, I nodded. Then, since I'd started, I figured I should throw everything on the table. "It doesn't matter though. He likes you."

"What? That's ridi...you know what? Who cares? I don't like him. He's not my type, you know that." She waited until I brought my head back up and nodded. "But we can't just pretend he isn't a suspect—and a strong suspect—just because you have feelings for him. If anything, it means we need to be even more careful. We don't know what kind of power the person doing this has. For all we know, Jax is *making* you like and trust him."

His request to do just that echoed in my head and my heart lurched. Could the things I felt around him be something he pushed into my head? Could he make even the beast fawn over him?

Cass took my hand and squeezed. I hadn't even noticed she'd moved—too caught up in my own thoughts. "Look, Elle, I don't want you to end up with zombie eyes. So we're still going to the cemetery, okay?"

The beast howled inside me, woken by my conflicting emotions. I put all of us at risk if I was getting close to the enemy, if I was letting him invade my dreams and my heart. "Yeah, as soon as Jen and Eric are asleep we'll go and get it over with. I need to know, one way or the other."

c‍ꙅ

Icy wind whipped through the trees and made most of the remaining leaves fall in crunchy avalanches. The entire scene would have fit Halloween week better with a slightly gentler wind. One that made the trees groan. In this mess, they flailed about like they could fall and impale us with their bare branches at any moment. Then again, maybe that was scarier after all.

Across from Indian Fields, I stopped. "You okay, Cass? The blood…"

She waved me off. "This wicked wind is good for one thing: it's blowing the smell in another direction. I'm not feeling anything at all, but if you want, I'll still stay over here just in case it shifts or something."

I examined her face in the dim light from the street, and she gave an obliging smile. She was telling the truth. Blue eyes and not even a hint of fang. Plus, her voice sounded normal, not haunted in the least, but I didn't see any point in risking things. "Probably a good idea. Not much you can do to help me with a comparison sniff."

Hiding behind a tree and a clump of bushes, I stripped. The beast snarled inside me, wanting out. I'd kept her chained for too long. The change came hard and fast, making not only my muscles ache, but my head, too. The duffel bag weighed on my jaw as I padded over to Cass, causing shooting pains to flare behind my eyes.

She reached down for the bag, freeing me from the added agony. "If something goes wrong, I'm coming over. Blood or no blood."

I snorted, knowing the headache wasn't just from the shift. It had started earlier; it just hadn't been this intense. Both Cass and the beast sensed something. Probably the same thing I'd felt. Something was in the air tonight. Good or bad, I couldn't tell, but it was there. Crouched. Watching. Waiting. Squaring my shoulders, I decided to face it head on.

Brave choice since I couldn't avoid it without giving up.

I trotted over to the cemetery and made sure to keep to the

shadows as much as possible without making it look like I was trying to keep to the shadows. Maybe it was silly since I looked like the beast, but I didn't want to draw any undo attention, especially if the altar-builder was at work. Indian Fields appeared empty, but with the wind, my canine senses had been useless across Milham Road. Once inside the cemetery, I stalked around the perimeter, searching for anyone hiding in wait behind the shelter of the aged and broken headstones.

No one.

One challenge down, and I wasn't running for my life yet.

I leaped over the fence at the back and wended my way around until I was downwind of the altar. Then I eased forward until all my senses could verify that it was unattended.

Two down.

Old blood still covered the ground and cloth, visible only as shades of gray. But once again, there was more. Most of it had dried, but my nose could tell some of it was pretty fresh— within the last day or two.

Time to get this over with.

I inhaled, snuffling at the ground. My lip curled into a snarl. Rosemary and cinnamon. Could this be Jax? Those parts were the same, but I smelled other things, too, stronger in the blood than any of it had been as just a scent trail. I growled my frustration. I just couldn't tell for sure. Yearning to rip something up, I spun from the altar and its tempting cloth, and headed back toward the road.

A sudden ruckus near the cemetery entrance drew me that way. I bounded over with my teeth bared.

Against the stone wall, I found Cass in a similar state. The only difference was her fangs glistened in the streetlights inches from Jaxson's neck. A low growl rumbled through my chest and throat. Both their heads turned my way.

"Looks like your instincts failed you on this one," Cass announced, her speech slurred from trying to talk around her teeth. "There's only one reason he'd be here."

"I don't know what you're talking about, I…" Jax began. Then Cass pressed her arm against his throat, pinning him against the wall and cutting off his words.

Cass was strong for a girl her size, but not like me. Jaxson wasn't even trying to get away. I squinted in what was probably a very non-wolf-like manner as I stared her down.

"Fine." She flashed her fangs. "I'll just hold on to him for now." She grabbed the bag of clothes from near her feet and swung it over the fence.

Giving them one last warning growl, I ducked behind the wall and begged the beast to let me shift back without any problems. As soon as I was human again, I snatched my long coat from the bag, threw it on, and, holding it closed, walked around the barrier. "What the hell are you doing?"

Cass turned my way, saliva dripping from her fangs. "Saving your furry butt. He followed us here. He came out of the woods, heading right for the cemetery. Call me crazy, but I don't buy the damn coincidence."

I cocked my head to the side, glaring at her. "Neither do I. But jumping him and saying 'look at my pretty fangs' might not have been the smartest way to handle things."

Her eyes widened and she let off Jax's neck a bit as she realized what she'd done.

I rounded on him. "She's right though. What the hell are you doing here?"

"Truth?" His voice trembled the slightest bit. I nodded. "Following the two of you."

Cass shoved him against the wall.

He rushed on. "Hey, I'm sorry. The whole 'we'll be watching you' thing kind of put me on high alert. Especially after I somehow ended up as Elle's tutor, I figured a smart person would make a point of watching the watchers."

I jerked my head toward Cass, who hadn't let him go yet. "Rethinking that logic now, aren't you?"

He swallowed, his Adam's apple bobbing. "A bit. But crap, what are you two doing out here that's so secret you attack a guy just for getting close anyway?" His eyes darted from me to Cass and back again.

Not "what are you," but "what are you doing"? Like he wasn't surprised at Cass's, um, new appearance. Or mine for that matter. I glared at him and Cass pushed harder against his throat. I wasn't imagining things, she'd noticed, too. "We were checking up on you actually."

Jax didn't flinch, but he did arch his eyebrow. "Okay, I'll bite." I rolled my eyes at his attempt at humor. None of this was funny. "How are you checking up on me here? I followed *you*. And why are you checking on me at all for that matter?"

Cass clenched her jaw. I wasn't sure if it was just anger or if she had to do it to keep from attacking him. She barely moved her lips when she spoke. "Our dear friend Elle needed to see if it was your scent we found all over this place."

"Why the hell would it smell like me here?" He tore his gaze from her and looked at me, his eyes pleading. When I didn't respond quickly enough, he asked, "Does it? And what does that mean?"

I shook my head and bit at the inside of my cheek. He didn't look guilty, but considering what I knew about Cassidy, I wasn't about to be deceived by appearances. "There's stuff happening in this town, Jax, and you are either a part of it, or you need to stay far away from it. There really isn't much wiggle room in between. As for your scent?" I shrugged, more for Cass's benefit than his. "I need a direct comparison of your blood to be sure of anything."

He spoke quickly, trying to hide the slight tremor in his voice, like somehow he expected all this to be fine and dandy once he played stupid. "Then do it. Compare. Whatever you need."

I narrowed my eyes, trying to read him. Legit offer or divide and conquer? Did he know Cass couldn't go in there? Giving a nod, I made my decision. "In that case, Cass, let him go."

She eyed me warily and didn't argue, but simply waited for me to explain myself.

"Look, if he's offering, I'm going to need his blood, and things could go ugly if you're too close."

"You need to shift for this, right?" she asked.

"Yes." Color flushed my cheeks. Jaxson knew what I was. How was I going to deal with that?

"Then I'll let him go after you're done." She turned her swirling blue-black eyes to him. "I will only give you this warning once. You try to run? I *will* catch you. You hurt her? I *will* kill you."

I snorted as I ducked back behind the bricks. She probably stood there holding him against the wall in true brooding-vampire style for the entire time it took me to shift again. Changing this many times would leave me sore tomorrow. The human body just isn't designed for that much wear and tear. It'd be worth it though; I needed an answer.

Padding around the wall, I watched Cass release her hold on Jax with excruciating slowness. He straightened his jacket, trying to regain a tiny bit of composure. It didn't work; his sweat still reeked of fear. I couldn't help but be impressed though; he walked along the fence line with me like he was just out for a late night stroll with his dog. As soon as we stepped away from the roadside, I stopped and stared at him. When he didn't do anything, I sank back on my haunches and snorted.

"Oh, right. The blood. I guess I just figured you planned on biting me."

I blinked. Was he an idiot or was it just the fear talking? He stepped to the wire fence, searching around until he found a sharp edge. Without a sound, he yanked his hand along it, slicing it open. A hiss of pain escaped from between gritted teeth. I took his pant leg between my teeth and gave a tug.

"I hope you appreciate this, Elle." He clenched his bleeding hand into a fist and followed me.

I better appreciate it? Oh, Jax, I saved you from being Cass's midnight snack. Let's not pretend you're doing me a favor.

We approached the altar, and he froze. He stood staring, slack-jawed, at the display in front of us. I wanted to believe his shock was genuine, but it could've been an act. I needed to be sure once and for all.

I walked right up to the altar and inhaled deeply, almost tasting the scents left behind by its builder. Then I strode back to Jaxson and snuffled at his hand, rubbing my nose in the dark gray fluid that leaked from the cut. Before I could stop her, the beast let out a howl of joy.

I didn't wait for Cass to react to the sound; I turned tail and rushed back to the fence, ducking behind and forcing the shift as quickly as I could. Not even bothering with the coat this time, I peeked my head out from the shadows. Jax must have chased me, because Cass had him pinned to the damn wall again.

"No, Cass!" She turned to me. "Back off. It's not him." As soon as the words left my mouth, she let him go. I went back for my clothes, repeating in a whisper just for me, "It's not him."

Cass's voice reached me as I tugged on my jeans. "Great. So Jax here isn't our guy, but because of my screw up, he knows what we are. What do we do now?"

I got down on my hands and knees. "Right now I search for my damn bra. It must have gone flying when I dumped the bag to get my coat."

Jaxson's voice filtered around the corner, "Are you decent?"

At least Cass was letting him breathe. I glanced down, confirming everything, including the coat, was in place. I held it closed. "Yeah, I guess."

"Would a light help?"

"You brought a flashlight to follow us? Very sneaky of you."

Stepping around the corner of the fence, he said, "Not exactly." Jax held out his hand, palm up, like he wanted me to take hold of it. I reached forward just as fire sprang from his skin, lighting up the night, and the smirk on his face, as I gasped and jumped back. "Found it." He picked up my bra with his other hand, the one now wrapped in a makeshift bandage, and held it out toward me. "Nice shade of blue, by the way. I bet it really brings out your eyes."

Chapter Twenty-One

Wednesday, October 27 - after midnight

I snatched the bra from his hand, nearly missing it because my eyes were glued to the fiery display in his outstretched palm.

As soon I had my bra back, he squeezed his hand into a fist, extinguishing the flame. "I'll give you some privacy for a minute. Then I think maybe the three of us should have a little chat."

He didn't wait for me to respond, but simply walked around the wall, dragging Cass along with him. I threw on the bra and shirt and was still tugging the coat back on when I rounded the corner to find Jax and Cass deep in conversation. They stopped talking once I appeared.

The flush coloring Cass's cheeks told me as much, if not more than, hearing what they'd said would have. Maybe she hadn't found Jax attractive before, but the appeal of a guy she didn't have to hide from looked like it was too much for her to resist. Sighing, I realized my tiny window of opportunity with him had just closed. "Come on, you two, we should probably get off the street for this."

"Yeah, because all the rest of what happened here tonight was suitable for public viewing." Jax rattled something in his hand. My muscles tensed until he held up a set of keys. "This way, ladies." He led us to the corner, across Portage Road, and onto a tiny dead-end street. He strode up to the one and only car parked there and yanked on the passenger door until it opened with a groan.

The moonlight had to be playing tricks with my eyesight. I mean, the guy had a motorcycle Eric drooled over. This oddly mottled hunk of steel elicited a different biological response. I tilted my head, trying to get a better look.

Cass took the more direct approach. "Jaxson, can we get some of that light again?"

He shrugged, and his palm blazed, illuminating the pile of metal behind him. The paint on the side panels was blue, the hood deep red, the rest of the body black. At least the trunk had the fashion sense to match the hood. I was sure a closer examination would reveal patches of rust all over it.

Cass summarized what we were both thinking. "What a hunk of junk."

"Yeah," Jaxson responded, his lips twitching to the side, "and right now she goes from zero to sixty in about fifteen seconds. But someday she'll be gorgeous and fast." He caressed the car. When he saw us looking, he closed his other hand and the street went dark. "Do you want a ride or not?"

"Do you promise once we get inside it won't fall apart and crush us all?"

I whacked Cassidy on the arm with the back of my hand. "Yes, Jax, we could use a ride home." Leaving Cass standing there rubbing her arm, I walked over and started to climb in.

Jax put out a hand to stop me. "Naysayers take the back." He waved Cass over and held the seat forward until she shimmied inside. After slapping the seat into place, he waited for me to take shotgun before slamming the door with bone-jarring force.

The seat squeaked as Jax climbed behind the wheel and nothing fell off when he slammed his door just as hard. If the death-trap could survive that kind of abuse, I figured Cass's worries were unfounded.

"All right, I get that you said you were watching us, too, but what the hell made you come out here? No offense, even though your scent doesn't match, it's still pretty screwed up to have you at the scene of the crime."

"It's like I said, I started watching you right back after you 'found' me at my locker. Even when you were heading to the stadium, I figured there was something different about you when you turned around and stared right at me like you knew I was there even though I was sure the shadows were dark enough you couldn't see me." His hands twisted back and forth on the steering wheel nervously.

At least now I knew who'd caught me that night. "Okay, so that explains Friday, and obviously you went to the dance Saturday for similar reasons." He opened his mouth and started to say something, but snapped it shut instead and nodded. "Still doesn't explain tonight."

Jax clenched his jaw and shrugged. "Yesterday you mentioned late nights." Cass made a noise from the backseat and I knew I'd be in trouble when we got home. "And it got me to thinking maybe there was more of the picture than I got to see at school. So I staked out your house last night." I tensed as Cass kicked the back of my seat and something inside of it popped. "I figured I'd give it another go tonight, and we ended up here."

"We were that easy to track?"

"Between her hair and your blue coat? Yeah, kind of."

Cass kicked me again. "I told you to start wearing more black."

"Shut up, Cassidy." I turned back to Jax, eyeing him. "And your lack of surprise over what you saw us do?" He had easy answers for everything else, but as much as I wanted to believe everything, I just didn't trust people that much.

He snorted. "Well I kind of noticed you sniffing me on the ride home today, and I watched while she stopped at your neighbor's house. I'm guessing she wasn't giving that dog a lingering embrace for no reason. While I trailed you, I worked through the most obvious possibilities. So, no, neither of you came as a huge shock."

Cass leaned forward, her chin resting between our seats. "And running into two other supernatural teens didn't hit your radar as odd?"

"You know, all things considered, I would have figured it was odder if I was the only one out there." He shrugged and slid the key into the ignition.

"I felt that way a year and a half ago." I reached behind my shoulder, and when I didn't feel anything, I twisted around to search for the seatbelt.

"Oh, yeah, about that—they're on order." He turned the key and the engine grumbled to life.

I hoped if we had to ride in his car more than this once a new engine was on order, too.

He pulled out of the street and turned toward our neighborhood. Leaning over, he spoke just loud enough to be heard over his car. "And you wondered why I drive the motorcycle? Now you know."

"Hello? I can still hear you," Cass grumbled. "Besides, whispered conversations are just rude."

A snicker escaped my lips before I could stop it. He was whispering—sure. I made a point to yell over the engine noise, just to appease her. "Okay, Jax, so what gives? Super cool bike and…this?" I waved my hand toward the dash.

"I bought the Indian for a steal when I turned sixteen. Mom kicked in half and it's paid for now. This," he ran a hand gently across the dashboard, "used to belong to my mom's cousin, Jim."

"And what? Your evil second-cousin Jim decided to curse Pyro-boy with the messed up car?"

He ignored the jab from Cass. "Jim's wife was done with his mid-life crisis 'project' about a month after it took over the garage. Rather than try to sell it, he ended up giving it to me." Jax stared into the rearview like he wanted Cass to know the next part was directed at her. "It's a 1968 Chevelle—and a classic."

"So is *War and Peace*. And the book is probably worth more."

"Cass, give it a rest." I turned to Jaxson and squirmed in my seat as a spring poked me in the back. "We can delve into the merits of your car some other time. What I want to know is what the hell are you?"

His lips twisted into a half-hearted smile. "Wish I knew, Elle. I really wish I knew."

My brows knit together, and I pursed my lips. When he'd shown us his ability, I assumed we were past secrets. "Come on, Jax, that's hardly fair. You know what we are. Fess up."

I watched him, but the dim glow of passing streetlights didn't help me read his face at all. "I'm serious. I only discovered the ability a couple years ago. Last spring, I accidentally burned down our house. It was part of why we moved here. Since then, I've spent most of my time trying to control the power. Giving it a name took a backseat to that."

"Fine. Then until further notice, you are officially dubbed Pyro-boy," Cass announced. I tried to ignore her, pretend she didn't exist, but then she had to go and say something logical. "Since we can officially cross Jax off the suspect list, what do you want to do now?"

Tearing away from studying his face, I turned to Cass, knowing by the look in her eyes she didn't really trust him yet. "Now we figure out how he can help us."

Though Jax didn't raise any general objections to helping, in the end we decided morning was coming upon us too quickly to start discussing it tonight. Which suited Cass just fine. Besides, none of us could really afford any more missed sleep. So he dropped us at the end of the block, hopefully preventing the sound of the Chevelle from waking all our neighbors.

We hadn't even reached the house when Cass gave voice to what I'd suspected in the car. "I still don't trust him."

"Of course you don't."

"What? You *do* trust him?" She swung up into the tree outside our window with unnatural grace.

I scrambled up after her, my voice coming from between clenched teeth. "I know he isn't the altar-builder, and I want to trust him. You know that, so it's your job to be the logical one who stands back and makes sure we can." I hooked the last branch with my leg, and Cass grabbed my hand to pull me up. "For now though, let's just get to bed."

❦

The hands on the school clocks moved at the pace of comatose snails all Thursday. Only the promise of the night to come kept me on task. We'd arranged it so Cass would meet Jaxson and me at the bookstore. Jen was ecstatic when we mentioned the plans to her over breakfast. She'd said it was because she had a lot of research to do for her new client, but I was pretty sure part of it had to do with the fact that Jax couldn't drive us both home on his motorcycle. I found it funny how much she worried about the things Jax and I could get up to on a motorcycle but totally ignored the trouble two or more of us crazy kids could manage in a car.

And in fact, the things Jax and I could get up to in his car stayed with me all through practice. I made a point of taking as cold a shower as I could stand afterwards. People who say that works are full of shit.

By the time I sat down on the loveseat in the bookstore, I was as far gone as ever. Jax radiated a heat that I doubted had anything to do with his ability. Of course, with the fingerprints he'd burned onto my back at the dance, I couldn't be sure.

I tried to talk to him about his power, but he stayed intently focused on the American Revolution. Much to my frustration to say the very least. At least he'd kept his promise to make history relevant to my life. Comparing the American settlers to orphans made their plight a lot less distant.

"Essentially, their family didn't want the responsibility of them anymore. They just wanted all the good things, like respect, that come with being a good parent. Not to mention the tax write-off." He jerked his head toward a couple pregnant women, one of whom had mentioned she'd planned her baby so it would be born prior to the end of the year.

I stifled a laugh.

"That last bit was the part that really got under the skin of the Colonials," Jax continued. "They felt used. They had no real rights. In fact, their wishes weren't even represented within the British government, but they were still expected to pay, just like any other citizen of the crown."

This made so much more sense than anything I'd heard in

class. "So the settlers felt like…" I struggled for the right words "…abused children?"

Jax leaned back against the couch and bopped his head back and forth. "Not exactly. Neglected is probably more appropriate. Except for when they proved useful, the Colonists were ignored. The problems of the Colonies were not the problems of the crown."

We continued on like that, him teaching, me soaking it up for I don't know how long. I also don't know how long Cass stood there before she cleared her throat. My head shot up and she laughed. "Hey, don't let us interrupt. I'm sure it's entrancing stuff."

"Oh. Hi, Cassidy," Jax said, shifting away from me.

I didn't say anything; I was too busy taking in the other half of her "us." That and trying to ignore the stabbing hurt caused by Jaxson's sudden distance when he saw her. But I really tried to let that go. "Hi. Who's your friend?"

The prepster standing next to Cass in his pleated dress pants and starched collar gave a dazzling smile and reached out his hand. "You must be Elle. I'm Corbin. Corbin Daughtry."

I resisted the urge to make a James Bond joke as I stood and shook his hand. Of course, if Bond had that weak of a grip, I couldn't understand why the bad guys were always afraid of him. Corbin was cute enough in that buttoned-up, brainiac kind of way, but I just couldn't see him having a lasting relationship with either shiny, happy Cass or her evil twin who came out at night. If I was wrong, I sure hoped he toned down the cologne, or we'd never be able to hang out. "Nice to have the chance to put a face to the name. Cass has told me a lot about you."

If looks could kill…but as it was, Cass would get me for the comment some other time. I glanced toward Jax, who was more withdrawn than I'd ever seen him. I tried to see things from his perspective. Cass standing there with another guy, glancing up at him with adoring eyes. Yeah. Had to suck for Jax. Funny how I didn't feel very bad for him.

Corbin must have noticed the tension because he shifted

the conversation away from him and toward Jaxson. "I heard part of your lesson with Elle here. Brilliant spin on things. You must be the most sought after tutor at Portage Northern."

The way his lips twitched, I could have sworn Jax tried not to laugh. "Hardly, but thanks." He held out his hand. "Jaxson."

I don't know if it was Jax's superior grip or if Pyro-boy put a little extra heat into the handshake, but Corbin's face paled a bit as they shook hands. "Nice to meet you, but now that I've delivered Cassidy safely into your hands, I should be going." Corbin nodded at the two of us then turned and gave Cass a tiny bow that made her blush crimson.

Through eyes narrowed to slits, Jax watched Corbin leave. "I don't like him."

"Big surprise there." I snorted and started gathering my papers and books.

"What's that supposed to mean?" He loaded his own backpack and slung it over a shoulder.

I zipped my bag shut with a resigned sigh. "Nothing. Never mind. Let's just go." I led the way to the door.

Jax muttered, "There's just something about him that seems fake. He's too…perfect."

"Nothing wrong with a little perfection." Cass brushed by Jax and linked her arm in mine as we walked into the parking lot.

Needless to say, the drive to our house passed in silence. Well, other than the ear-splitting rumbling of the Chevelle.

If Jax coming into the house surprised Eric, he didn't let it show. He offered to take his paper into the family room and give us the kitchen. When Cass said we'd work upstairs, Eric didn't even flinch; he just waved us up.

Cass closed the door behind her and got right to business, spinning things just like we'd planned in advance. "Okay, Jax is obviously off the suspect list. So who does that leave?"

"Yeah, thanks for that," Jax muttered, moving around the room like he didn't know what to do now that he was here.

"Just make yourself comfortable, Jax. Chair. Floor. Bed." Color rushed to my cheeks as I said the last one. I turned to Cass so he wouldn't see. "By my count that leaves Lisa and

Kris."

Jaxson had taken my offer and sat on the edge of my bunk, waving his hand in the air. "Forgive the new guy, but who the hell are Lisa and Kris, and what exactly do we suspect them of? I mean, I saw the mess last night, but you haven't exactly filled me in."

We'd anticipated that, too, and explained everything—if he was in it with the altar-builder, he already knew, and if he wasn't, it was necessary information. "So"—I leaned against the wall next to the bed—"Lisa McLeod is the only person other than you who smells remotely like the scent at the altar, and she's an all-around bully. Kris Benson is a really good friend of mine, but he had a bloody knife in school yesterday. Which, while not a direct connection to the altar, still makes him a suspect, even though I never thought to sniff him out." Considering how uncontrollable the beast had been that day, I doubted it would've worked anyway.

"Kris Benson? He's in our grade, right?" Jaxson asked, leaning back on the bed to look at me.

I nodded. "Yeah. Tall, blond spiky hair, blue eyes. He's in my history class." Oh yeah, like that explained everything.

"That's where she smelled the blood," Cass added from her perch on the only chair in the room.

"If it's the guy I'm thinking of, he's in gym with me. The office yanked him from class yesterday. I heard he got expelled." He picked up the stuffed deer that had somehow ended up on my pillow and cocked an eyebrow at me.

I snatched the thing out of his hand. "He wasn't in history this morning, but I hadn't really noticed. I guess I don't have to feel guilty about not reporting the knife then."

"True, but if he's expelled, we don't have an easy way of keeping an eye on him. He can go anywhere. Do anything." Cass scraped the chair across the floor as she stood up. She came closer and leaned against one of the uprights of the bunk beds.

I gave a curt nod. "In that case, we stick with the one we *can* track easily first. Figure out what's up with Lisa."

"Okay, so what's the plan?" Jax asked. "The three of us

stake out her house all night and grab her when she leaves?"

Cass glanced at me, and I knew what she was thinking: he shouldn't be so into this so quickly. There should have been more questions, more worries. So she ran with what we'd agreed on before he entered the picture. "I don't know about you, but we can't really afford to pull an all-nighter." After all, our life here depended on our grades.

I nodded. "She's right, and I have other plans for Jax anyway." Cass shot me a look that screamed "I'll bet you do," but I pointedly ignored it and turned to him. "Something about you makes you smell like the altar-builder. I'd lay heavy odds it's connected to your ability."

His face went stony.

I had to crouch down by the bed in order to meet his eyes. "I hate to say this, but your worry about controlling your power needs to take a backseat to figuring out what you are."

Setting his jaw, he pushed off from the bed, stalking across the room. "I get it. That'll give us some clue as to what this altar-builder is."

Cass shrugged when I glanced her way. Biting my lower lip, I followed Jax and laid my hand on his arm. His muscles bunched under my fingers. "And hopefully how to beat whoever it is."

"Yeah. Like I said, I get it." His voice told me he might have understood, but he didn't like it. He sucked in a breath and let it out slowly before laying his hand on mine and squeezing. He turned back to me. "And what about you?"

"I'm thinking tonight is the night we stop trying to wait for people to do something and we lure Lisa out instead."

Cass laughed from across the room. "And how do you propose we do that? Your charming wit and sparkling personality don't seem to appeal to her."

"I'll think of something." I jerked my head toward the computer. "What do you think I keep you around for?"

A sharp rap sounded on the door.

"Come in," Cass and I chorused.

The door creaked open, and Eric stuck his head inside. "Hate to interrupt, but Jen called to say she's running late. I'm calling out for dinner. Jaxson, you interested in hanging around for some food?"

Between the dinner invite and the motorcycle, Jen and Eric had drawn the dating-police lines. Eric had drawn the role of good-cop.

Jax glanced at Cass and me.

Oh yeah, like this isn't new to us. I shrugged, leaving the choice up to him.

"Uh, sure, Mr. Smith. I'll have to call my mom and make sure she's okay with it."

"Perfect answer. Glad I came prepared for it." Eric lobbed the cordless handset into our room, and Jax snatched it out of the air. "And Jennifer questioned whether you were the right guy for our girl. I'll call you down when dinner's here."

The door swung closed as I wondered if I'd stopped breathing. Eric had just thrown it out there. My eyes felt too wide, my heartbeat too slow. *Please let me pass out. Cass can make some excuse for what Eric said.*

But air must have still flowed into my lungs because the world didn't go black. I saw every step Jax took back toward my bed with the phone pressed to his ear. I'm sure I heard his side of the conversation with his mom, but none of it registered. When he clicked off the phone and sank back onto my bed, his irritation had disappeared. The expression on his face was almost playful.

He's happy?

Jax tossed the phone on the bed. "So, I had a random thought. Do you guys have a name for this little group we're forming?"

Cass didn't say anything, and I stared back blankly. *A name? This has to be some kind of a joke.*

When neither of us was forthcoming, he continued, "You know. A way we can refer to it without screaming to everyone what we're doing? Maybe something that sounds like a TV show, or a band, or something."

Cass piped up. "Actually I was thinking something along the lines of Paranormal Response Unit, PRU for short."

My head swiveled in her direction. *She's thought about this?*

When? Why? I refused to take this idiocy silently. I was an equal partner in all this. At least an equal partner. And why were we playing chummy if we weren't supposed to totally trust him anyway? "PRU? It sounds like prude. I guess the two of you don't plan on getting dates any time soon."

While plucking at the threads of my denim bedspread, Jax made a face. "What if we go for Team instead of Unit? Paranormal Response Team?"

Cass nodded with enthusiasm.

The idea crossed my mind that maybe I had passed out after all and this was all some bizarre dream caused by lack of oxygen getting to my brain. A nice idea, too bad I didn't believe it. "PRT? Pretty? Come on. Why not just call ourselves Supernatural Teens' Undercover Paranormal Investigative Division? You know. STUPID."

Jaxson chuckled, abandoning his destruction of my blanket, but Cass just shook her head. "No. I like PRT; we'll go with that."

I'd been outvoted. Maybe Jax joining us wasn't such a great idea. When it was just me and Cass, this crap didn't happen. "What's next? Are we going to have a slogan, too?"

They ignored me. The decision was made.

For better or worse, the PRT was born. Too bad I was the only one who seemed to be experiencing after-pains.

Chapter Twenty-Two

Thursday, October 27 - early evening

Eric played dad pretty well, grilling Jax without being a jerk about it. They talked cars and motorcycles, and they even went out to look at the Chevelle. Eric came back in grinning like a little boy. He'd definitely stand in my corner if Jen ever had another tizzy about Jaxson.

While the guys talked and we did dishes, Cass took the opportunity to regale me, yet again, with tales of her tutor.

"Corbin is hot."

"Corbin is brilliant."

"Corbin is so funny."

"Corbin makes me feel all warm and fuzzy just by being around."

Corbin is so sweet he managed to give me indigestion without setting foot near our kitchen.

I was busy trying not to puke on the saccharine Cass poured all over when Jaxson came into the kitchen. "I'm sorry to eat and run, but I've still got that research project to work on tonight." He winked at us.

"Oh, yeah, let us know how that goes." I twisted my hands in a towel nervously. Would Eric ask about the "project"?

"Definitely." He called in to Eric, "Thanks again for dinner, Mr. Smith." Then he walked over, and after giving Cass a nod and a wink, he reached up and tucked a piece of hair that had come free of my ponytail behind my ear. "And I'll see you ladies tomorrow at school."

He showed himself out. Which was probably a good thing, because I don't think I could have moved, and Cass was too busy trying not to laugh me. I could only imagine the expression on my face, and her reaction left me wondering if she actually liked him or not, especially with all the Corbin talk.

Cass and I had been back at our homework for a while when I heard Eric pacing downstairs. I glanced at the time. Ten o'clock. Jen had said she'd be a bit late, but from the repetitive pattern of his strides, Eric expected her home before now.

I tried to focus on my lab report for biology, but kept glancing at the clock, watching it grow later and later. By the time I closed my notebook on the finished report, worry had settled firmly in my gut, and I found myself wishing I could pace with Eric. Jen should have been home by now, or at least called.

At ten forty-eight, the garage door rumbled open, and the incessant movement downstairs stopped at last. I breathed a sigh of relief and relaxed against my pillow, determined to finally settle into the last few chapters of my assignment for Mod Lit.

"Jesus Christ, Jennifer! What the hell happened?" The shrill tone in Eric's voice plunged my heart into ice water.

I found myself down the stairs before I even realized I'd moved. I couldn't speak. Couldn't breathe. All I could do was stand there and gape. Jen's face was ashen. Her hair disheveled. Her clothes torn and muddy. She sobbed in Eric's embrace and couldn't seem to stop shaking.

My mom. Someone hurt my mom.

Cass spoke from behind me. "I'll make her some tea." She touched my arm, and I flinched. "Elle, go get her a blanket and a wet washcloth."

She'd used her calm, logical voice; I could listen to her.

My limbs felt stiff and unresponsive as I went about the assigned task. I had to go back to the bathroom because I'd forgotten to wet the washcloth. I stared in the linen closet trying to remember why I was there until Cass yelled up asking for the blanket.

When I made it downstairs, Eric draped the blanket around Jen's shoulders and then picked her up and carried her to the couch. She looked so small in his arms. As soon as he put her down, he took the washcloth and started mopping her face.

A towel. She'll need a towel. She won't want her face all wet. I turned to go back upstairs and get one.

"Please don't go," Jen's voice cracked. "I need all of you here for a little bit." She stared at me with wide, frightened eyes. "Please."

Thoughts of the towel forgotten, I sank onto the couch next to her and swallowed the stony lump in my throat. Cass joined us, pulling up an ottoman so she could sit close. Jen didn't say anything for the longest time. She just lay against Eric's chest, trying to stop trembling long enough to sip at her tea.

She tipped her head up to look into Eric's face. "I'm so sorry. I don't know how it happened."

He shook his head and hugged her tightly. "It's all right, sweetheart. The only thing that matters is you're safe."

It was like she didn't hear him. Didn't feel Eric's strong arms holding her. Her eyes were haunted, like she couldn't stop seeing what had happened. Then she told us.

"He grabbed me. He was so strong. I didn't know how to fight him." Tears streamed down her cheeks from eyes that never blinked. "I don't even know what he was doing. It was so hard to breathe. So hard. I managed to scream, and someone must have heard. People came running. He shoved me away. He just let me go and dashed into the dark."

Her words didn't belong in this house. This haven with the warm oak trim and the earthy, comforting colors. With its books and family photos. This house was a place of love and happiness. A place of safety.

I choked the heartache down. Whoever did this to Jen had tried to break that. They'd tried to break her. To break our home. The tears welling up in my eyes didn't dry, but they didn't fall either. A fierce, protective fury joined with the hurt, and I felt my lip curling up into a snarl. The beast was so close to the surface, I could barely contain her. I promised her vengeance and forced my face into a more acceptable, blank expression.

Jen's chin quivered, sobs threatened, but the rest of her tremors had ceased. "It was stupid. I should have waited for help. But I was terrified he'd come back. I crawled toward the car until I could walk again. Then I got in and drove as far from campus as I could. I wanted to call, but I couldn't find my cell. I don't know where I lost it, but I couldn't stop anywhere to call you. Not like this."

She gestured at herself and started crying again. Eric smoothed her hair, rocking her back and forth like a child.

"I'm so sorry, Eric. I came home as quickly as I could."

He shook his head and held her tighter. "There's nothing to be sorry for. You're here. You're safe." He squeezed his own eyes shut, seeing things I didn't want to imagine. "I'm just glad you're home now."

"Me, too," whispered Cass, reaching over and gripping Jen's hand.

"Are you sure it was a guy?" I asked, my voice tense and cold. The beast had chased my sadness away, all that remained was the intense need to find her attacker and make sure this never happened again. Make sure the attacker paid for daring to lay a hand on my mom.

"Ellery! What kind of question is that at a time like this?" Eric's tone had gone from soft and soothing to furious in an instant.

He probably wanted to send me away, and I understood. The beast wasn't about to back down though. It didn't matter how hard I fought her. She was right. What I had to say would hurt, but it needed to be said, no matter how much I hated causing Jen more pain.

"The kind the police will ask." I stared him down. "The kind she needs to think about if the person is going to get caught."

I could almost hear Cass screaming at me to shut up. She had to know where my head was.

Trying to soften the blow, I added, "I'm sorry, Jen, but it's the truth. You have no idea how glad I am that you're home safe, but they're going to ask you to describe the guy." Maybe it wasn't much softer after all. I twined my fingers in hers.

She squeezed my hand and tried to smile, looking much more like her normal self for the effort. Like she'd gained strength from the truth in what I'd said. "You're right, Elle. But I can't describe him. I never saw his face. He had a hood on, and it was so dark." She pressed her eyes shut as another shudder wracked her body. "And no, I'm not one-hundred percent certain it was a man. I've never met anyone that strong before though, so can't imagine it was a woman."

She couldn't be sure though. My mind flashed immediately to Lisa. I forced myself to deal with *this* instant; Lisa could wait a couple hours. Then I'd let the beast have her. "All right, Jen. I…I'm sorry for pushing."

Jen released my fingers and pulled me into a one-armed embrace. "It's okay. *I'm* okay. I'm home. I'm safe, and I will do everything in my power not to let this happen to anyone else. I'm sure the police will have questions we can't think of that will help them find him."

She kissed the top of my head like I was a little kid.

Casting a glance over her shoulder at Eric, Jen said, "I could use another cup of tea, and I think the girls should have a warm drink to settle their nerves before bed. After all this, I bet they're going to need all the help sleeping that they can get. I know I will."

He leaned forward and helped her into a more upright position then kissed her cheek, his lips lingering for a few seconds. "I think we all will." Eric stood and moved toward the kitchen.

Cass jumped to her feet. "I'll come help."

Jen still held Cass's fingers though and didn't let go. Pulling her toward the couch instead. "Come sit by me, Cassidy. I need you girls close for a little longer."

"I was just going to help Eric with the drinks."

"Don't worry about Eric, he can handle it."

I flinched at the implication that Cass might not be

worrying enough about the right person.

Jen inclined her head toward the side of the sofa Eric had vacated. Cass settled into the seat, and Jen held us both close. "I'm really sorry for scaring the two of you. I wish Eric hadn't yelled when I got home."

I stiffened and my brows pulled together. "You mean you wouldn't have told us?"

"No. Yes." She shook her head. "I don't know. I just feel awful that you had to see me like this."

The tension still held me in its grip, not releasing a single one of my muscles. "I thought we were a family, Jen…" I couldn't finish.

She smiled, but it didn't come anywhere close to her eyes. It looked like the smile people put on at funerals when they are trying to look strong. It was a lie in a pretty package. "We are, but every once in a while that means I get to protect you from the ugliness in the world. Heaven knows you've both seen enough of it to last most people a lifetime." She held on to me and Cass as if she thought we might fly away. This part was Jen. It was real. This felt like home.

Finally, Eric strode back into the room with four steaming mugs on a tray. He handed Jen her tea. There was one other mug that smelled like green tea, but the last two were filled with hot chocolate, complete with whipped cream. He handed them to Cass and me.

My lips twitched. I'm sure Cass was having similar thoughts. We both would have preferred tea. Then I looked at my awkward little family and decided I could indulge Eric's need to look at us as young, innocent girls. I sipped at the cocoa, and Cass mirrored my moves. Soon enough, we'd drained our mugs, and Eric shuffled us toward the stairs.

"But the police—" I stifled a yawn.

"I'll call them right now. There's nothing you girls need to be down here for. I'll give Jennifer something to help her sleep once they're gone."

With my hand gripping the banister, I nodded. Tonight had exhausted me. We'd have to set an alarm and sneak out after the police left. In the meantime, I planned on squeezing in a nap. I shut the door and walked over to my bed, tripping on something I couldn't see on the floor.

Though I stumbled into bed, Cass just leaned against the rail. She looked as tired as I felt. "And now we're down to Kris."

Lying back against my pillow, I yanked my blanket up and shook my head, still not willing to believe someone I'd been friends with for over a year would attack Jen. "Maybe, but she wasn't sure it was a guy," I insisted, fighting the urge to close my eyes. "I say once the cops are gone we still use tonight to check out Lisa."

Cass sighed, gave a stretch and climbed into her bunk. "I don't know, Elle," she murmured. "Something just smells funny."

I groaned and crawled out of bed to click off the desk lamp. "Cass, you're a vampire. Unless it's blood, you're better off leaving the sniffing to the canine." At the last second, I remembered the alarm. By the time I snuggled back under the covers, Cass was already snoring. She hadn't even shot back a retort to my vampire comment.

For a few minutes, it was quiet downstairs. My eyes had drifted shut and I felt sleep pulling at me, seducing me. When the voices started, my eyes snapped back open.

It's just the police. They got here really quick. Maybe Jen's not the first to get away.

Then it hit me that the only voices I heard were Jen and Eric's. Maybe the police were recording their statements. I strained to listen in, but sleep still clouded the edge of my brain. Every time I caught a piece of the conversation, I seemed to lose it just as quickly.

Eric's voice. "Of course not. I'm not stupid enough to call..."

Then Jen's. "...we still don't even know if they understand..."

My eyes could barely stay open, and the voices faded in and out no matter how much I concentrated.

"...the group is fairly sure...can't exactly bring it up at dinner...we'll keep watching and listening..."

"…they're just teenagers…"

I stopped fighting the pull on my eyelids and let them drift shut, hoping it would help me to focus on the voices downstairs, but the next thing I heard was the piercing cry of the alarm clock.

It was morning.

ᑫᐤ

Cass and I were both too groggy to talk on the bus. We didn't trust ourselves to keep our voices down. Finally at lunch, we managed to find a few minutes away from everyone else.

"You think they drugged us?" Cass asked. "What possible reason would they have to do that? Are you sure we weren't just in shock and the emotional strain made our bodies shut down and rest?"

I rubbed the back of my hand against my chin. "Maybe, but it seems weird that we'd *both* fall asleep that quick. It's never happened before. And"—I'd strained all day to remember the snippets of conversation I'd heard while I fought sleeping—"I think they were talking about us."

Cass picked at the fruit on her tray as she slipped me the uneaten half of her burger under the table. "Well, you know, maybe they slipped us something to help us sleep. Didn't Eric say he was going to give Jen something?" I nodded. "Maybe he was just trying to be parental and keep us from sitting up all night thinking about what happened to her."

My shoulders lifted in a half-hearted shrug. "Maybe, but I know what I heard. Why would they have been talking about us? Jen was the one who got attacked." I bit into the burger, chewing thoughtfully and not tasting it at all. "It just doesn't make sense. Talk about the cops. Talk about the attack. But us? Other than a random 'I hope the girls aren't traumatized by this'? Plus I set the alarm to wake us at like three."

Cass stretched and rolled her eyes. "Like three? You don't even know what time you set it for. How can you even be sure you set it at all?"

I chomped into the burger again. I couldn't be sure. Maybe I'd dreamed the whole thing.

Standing up, Cass grabbed her tray. "Whatever happened, there isn't much we can do about last night now. So we just shift our activities. Since you are so insistent, we'll spend tonight testing your theory about Lisa. Even if it takes all night. This fight getting a bit more personal now."

"Yeah." I couldn't stop picturing Jen with zombie eyes. The beast needed something to attack, so I tore into the burger again. Then I stopped chewing. Out of the corner of my eye, I saw something going on across the cafeteria. People were laughing hysterically at a behemoth in a pink bow and painted-on makeup. I wanted to believe it was someone from the football team who had lost a bet, but I knew with a fair degree of certainty what I'd see when I turned.

The moment our eyes met—hers devoid of life, devoid even of hatred—I closed mine and slumped in my seat. "Never mind, Cass; you were right again. Scratch Lisa off the list."

Chapter Twenty-Three

Friday, October 28 - late afternoon

The only thing I could think about for the rest of the day was Kris. When I pictured him threatening Jen, attacking her, leaving her with blank eyes, I wanted to throw up. So much for being a friend; he was nothing but a liar. We had to get him. Tonight.

I made a point of hanging around the gossip mill, but none of the girls I asked knew anything. Some of them didn't know him at all. They felt sure enough to spout rumors, but I didn't have a clue if any of them held a sliver of truth. All I could do was hope that someone else had a little more luck.

I jogged over to the bookstore after practice trying to figure out the best way to stake out Kris's house when something on the back of the building grabbed my attention. There, mingling with the older graffiti, were the emblazoned the words "PRT - Saving the world before breakfast." I squeezed my eyes shut for a second, but when I opened them, the words hadn't disappeared.

I reached into my backpack and wrapped a fist around my nasty gym shorts. When I rubbed at the paint, the brick crumbled away like ash. The few inches of paint I'd cleared hadn't made a difference. They'd made a dent though. The letter P was etched right into the bricks.

"I don't freaking believe this."

Jax had burned the words into the wall. Apart from destroying the entire section of masonry, his "artwork" was there to stay. Instead of researching and helping us like he promised, he'd done this. Maybe Cass was right; maybe we couldn't trust him.

I couldn't even bring myself to look at him during our tutoring session. Instead, I kept my lips clamped in a tight line and fumed while he talked about history. I nodded and gave monosyllabic answers whenever absolutely necessary. I feared if I tried talking to him, I'd blow up.

As it was, he inched farther and farther away from me as the hour went on. At least I didn't have to delude myself into thinking he didn't get that I was pissed. He knew.

And lucky us, we'd made plans to meet up with Cass and Corbin when we were done here. The short drive over to the cafe felt like hours as the silence stretched between us.

When I let go of the door as I walked inside, I had a fleeting hope that it would slam on Jax's spray paint finger. Then it hit me that he'd just skip the paint and settle for burning things.

Corbin popped up from the table where he sat with Cass and reached his hand out to me with a smile. The motion made me stop dead and reevaluate my scowl. Though I'm sure I still looked confused, I managed to force my lips to curve more up than down as I took his hand.

"It's lovely to see you again so soon, Elle." He scooted out a chair for me, and I slid into it, biting my lip to keep from giggling at the gesture. He stepped back and gave a curt nod. "Jaxson." Oh, I was understanding Cassidy's attraction more and more.

"Good to see you, too, Corbin."

Jax sat next to me, pushing his chair as far from mine as he could without it looking bad. "Hey, Cass. Corbin."

Corbin's brows pulled together as he watched us for a minute. "Yes, well, I just ordered drinks for Cassidy and myself. Would either of you like anything?"

I reached for my wallet. "A chai tea latte sounds great. Let me just grab you some cash."

Jax pushed his chair back, scraping it against the floor tiles. "I'll get it."

"That's not necessary, Jaxson." Corbin waved Jax back toward his seat. "I'm more than willing to treat everyone."

The temperature rose noticeably at my back. "Thanks, but I've got it." An instant later, the heat was gone, making me shiver as a chill ran down my spine.

"Trouble in paradise?" Cass asked with a lilt in her tone, but a touch of darkness in her eyes.

"I noticed things seemed a little colder, too." Corbin looked truly concerned, like we were all besties or something.

"Nothing a good swift kick won't solve," I grumbled, feeling a little bad about the vague response.

Corbin laughed, and Cass gave a nod full of meaning. Jaxson returned with all our drinks a few minutes later. When he handed me mine, I noticed something sticking out of the sleeve around the cup. I slipped the piece of paper between my fingers as I set my cup on the table. With my hands where Cass and Corbin couldn't see, I unfolded and read it. *Whatever I did, I'm sorry. Consider this a peace offering?*

I crumpled the note in my fist and shoved it in a pocket, but when I shook my head at him, I felt the ghost of a smile on my face. Could I really stay mad? I looked at him and his twinkling amber eyes hiding behind the curtain of his hair. As it had been since we came into the close space of the café, his scent intoxicated me. It seemed heavier here than it ever had before, more intense. I gave my head a fierce shake. Of course I could stay mad. He'd screwed up.

We all made nice. Me still angry with Jax. Jax still not liking Corbin. It was weird. Cass was in a social mood though, so she got us talking. We got to know each other a little better. Actually, Corbin got better acquainted with us, since nothing came up that the rest of us didn't already know about each other.

"So, Corbin"—Jax leaned back in his chair, lacing his fingers behind his head—"we're all open books to you now. What about you? What's your story?"

Cass and I both turned to Corbin, me with curiosity, her

with adoration. I really hoped some small part of the way she looked at him was an act. Part of the bubbly cheerleader persona. Because this Cass was not someone I'd hang out with by choice.

After taking a long swig of his coffee, Corbin fiddled with the sleeve for a bit, peeling back the edges. "Like the girls, I'm an orphan. I was a little more fortunate though that my parents didn't pass away until just last year."

Cass gave a sympathetic "oh", and I reached across and squeezed his hand.

Jax pushed. "Really? That's awful." His voice didn't sound like he gave a rat's ass. I kicked him under the table, but he kept going. "How'd they die?"

My eyes went wide and I gripped the edge of the table. Cass gaped at him. She tried to say something, but her mouth just kept opening and closing like a fish.

I couldn't imagine what was going through Corbin's mind. Had anyone ever asked me about the death of my family like that, I don't know what I would have done. Probably attacked them.

Corbin handled it really well. Though, considering what he told us, I guess it didn't hit him in the same way it would've hit me. "There was a fire at Dad's company. He didn't make it out in time. Mom couldn't handle his death. She killed herself a few days later—swan-dived off a building." He clenched his jaw. "People think I'm cold because I'm not still torn up about it, but the reality is I was never close with my parents. They were distant and cruel. My entire life with them was one lie after another."

"That's...awful." I bit my lip, unsure what else to say. Cass had never known her parents, and mine had been ripped from me too soon, but at least they'd loved me.

Cass looked like she was about to cry. This time, I couldn't tell if it was an act or if he'd managed to touch one of those emotions she kept locked away inside.

He smiled wanly at her. "At least they left me their legacy. I get to go to college. I have a place to live. Enough money to buy pretty girls..." He glanced over at me and Jax. "Sorry, *a* pretty girl coffee every now and then without worrying."

Jaxson played with his coffee cup, twisting it in his hands. A quick glance over showed him staring at the table. Looked like he finally realized he'd stepped over the line. The death by fire thing might have had something to do with it.

Unfortunately, silence had descended. None of us was sure where to take the conversation.

Corbin's eyes widened a bit when he checked his watch; he drained his cup right after. "I hate to dump my sordid family history on you and run, but I have plans tonight so I need to take off."

Cass's face fell, and I figured if the bandage needed to be ripped off, it might as well happen now. "Hot date?"

He laughed as he swung his jacket on. "No. No girlfriend at the moment. It's just a small party I need to make an appearance at. It was great seeing the two of you again." He nodded to Jax and me then he raised Cass's hand and brushed his lips across her fingertips. "I assume we're still on for tomorrow's tutoring session?"

She managed to stop swooning long enough to nod.

"Then I'll see you tomorrow afternoon."

Corbin left, and I'll give Jax props, he didn't glower. He didn't exactly look happy either though. I suppose it could have been guilt over grilling Corbin like a steak, but it was just as likely he was upset over Cass's reaction.

Great. One more issue that I'll need to deal with or try to ignore. Again.

None of us fought the engine noise to talk on the way to the house. Maybe that's why Cass barely waited until the bedroom door had shut to dive into our investigation and the brick wall we'd hit. "So, I'm assuming Elle told you about Lisa."

Jax looked at me, and I made a show of stacking my books neatly on the corner of the desk and rearranging them when the silence stretched on. He finally broke it. "No, she didn't."

Cass glowered at me before filling him in. "Which means we're changing plans and going after Kris tonight."

"Good luck with that." Jax wandered over to sit on my bed, pausing when he saw it was unmade. "He's gone."

"What do you mean gone?" Cass asked, wandering over and pulling up my sheet and bedspread.

Screw that. Leave it. He can sit his ass on the floor. Of course, she didn't hear me; mind reading wasn't one of the vamp traits she'd inherited.

Jax still didn't sit down. Maybe he realized he wasn't welcome to. "I did some poking around. After Kris got booted for bringing his hunting knife to school, his dad threw a fit. Put in an official complaint, supposedly he even included a thank you for giving his kid time off for a long weekend of hunting."

"Hmm…" Cass grabbed her stuffed bunny and flopped onto my bed. "We'll still have to check it out and make sure they're really gone. But this doesn't sound good."

"Yeah. It means we have to start all over on a suspect list. I'm new at this, so help me out. How do we start?"

I could feel him looking at me, trying to bridge the chasm between us. *Screw that.* I spun around, glaring at him, at last giving my rage at him and at Kris an outlet. "Our best bet would to stake out the cemetery. But until we know what we're dealing with, that's a little too suicidal for my tastes. So we were relying on you to find something with your research last night." I stopped for a breath and glared at him, then plowed ahead. "Oh, wait, I forgot. You were too busy playing badass with spray paint to bother actually doing your job." My chest heaved, and my racing pulse woke the beast.

Jaxson didn't blink as he stared back at me. The beast bristled, and a low growl rumbled from my throat. Jax snorted and shook his head before turning to Cass. Apparently she found the entire thing funny. Between the two of them, the beast clawed at me, furious and wanting out.

"Is she safe to talk to when she's like this?" Jax had the nerve to ask.

Cass shrugged, still chuckling a little. "She is for me. I guess if you want to talk to her, you'll just have to take your chances."

Glancing at me, he rolled his eyes before turning back to Cass. "Not worth the fight right now. I might as well just talk to you."

Cass waved a hand, offering him a seat next to her.

On my bed.

I didn't know what to do, so I ended up standing there, blinking at them like an idiot. I wanted it to all be a horrible dream, but there they sat, so close they were almost touching. My sister and the guy I couldn't seem to stop myself from falling for. Sitting on my bed. Talking in near whispers.

One handy thing about the beast was that she managed to ignore the sound of blood rushing through my burning ears and heard every word they said. Including Jax telling Cass that he'd done the research last night. And that the graffiti was a brazen display he'd tossed up while waiting for me to finish practice. Because he was bored waiting for me to get done at practice. It might have been stupid, but not as irresponsible as blowing off his assignment. After my brain grasped that, the anger started to fade and I focused on catching up with the conversation.

"...from what I've been able to dig up, I figured out why my dad disappeared when I was young." Jax laughed. "I always wondered why my mom wouldn't talk about him. I guess I get it now. A lot of supernatural powers, like my pyrokinesis, are caused by demon blood."

"You're a demon?" I blurted out, trying to focus on our investigation and ignore the fact that they sat mere inches apart. He in all his darkness, and Cass all light and aglow on the backdrop of my indigo bedspread. *Yep. Totally focused on the task at hand. That's me.*

"Half-demon," he corrected, looking my way, but not meeting my eyes. "And I'm not positive, it was just the most logical theory I could find."

I wanted to walk over and wedge myself between them. She had Corbin, or at least close enough for Cass's happiness. He'd kissed her hand for crying out loud; she should have been ecstatic. But I couldn't do it. I pulled out the desk chair and sat there instead. "What exactly do you mean?"

"Elle"—Cass sniffed tartly, waving me off—"don't be dense. It means half his DNA comes from a demon."

My nails dug into my palms as I clenched my fists. Good

thing I kept them cut short or I'd have drawn blood, and I didn't think Cass had fed yet. I had to keep my anger in check. I might not have been exactly happy about their proximity or attitude, but the beast was still fuming. "I get *that*. But does it mean"—I winced, realizing there was no polite way to ask—"that you're like inherently evil?"

Jax recoiled like I'd struck him. "Um, I'd kind of like to think not. I've screwed up plenty in my life, including today obviously, but as far as I can recall, I haven't ever done anything *evil*." He paused, looking directly at me. "I mean, does being a werewolf make you inherently some kind of animal?"

That time I felt the emotional blow, like someone had punched a hole in my chest and was squeezing my heart. My voice came out as a whisper when I answered.

"Sometimes."

Chapter Twenty-Four

Friday, October 28 - evening

Cass reached out to stop me, her body already off the mattress, but I couldn't stay there with them. I jumped from the chair, knocking it backward in my haste to reach the door and get away.

The part that killed me the most was hearing Jax say, "Let her go."

No more delusions. No more pretending that maybe I'd been wrong. That maybe some part of him liked me. The part that brushed my hair off my forehead. Or pressed an icy water bottle to my neck. Or burned little reminders of him into my back when we danced.

I flew through the kitchen, thinking of nothing other than my desperate need for a distraction. Then Jennifer stopped me. "Where's your friend?"

The fist squeezing my heart tightened a little more. "Upstairs with Cass." I swallowed hard, forcing the words out. "They started talking, and I felt like I was intruding." It wasn't a lie, but there was so much more. I wished I could really confide in Jen. Hell, I wished the biggest problem in my life was boys. The truth was, even in this case, the male half of the species just complicated everything else.

Her forehead furrowed as an expression of bewilderment

crossed her face. "Cass? Really?" I shrugged. "I'm a little confused. I thought she had a huge crush on some guy named Corbin."

Grabbing an apple off the countertop, I gave a tight laugh, wanting nothing more than to strike back at them. And Cass was the easier target. "Corbin? You mean her twenty-year-old tutor? Yeah, she's crushing hard, but I guess she realized you might not approve of them dating."

Jennifer's jaw dropping was all the response I needed. I stalked into the family room, turning on the news and letting myself sink into the worries of the rest of the world for a few blissful minutes.

It didn't take much time before Jen decided they'd been alone upstairs for too long. I had a clear line of sight to watch as Jax and Cass said goodbye at the door. Had I been thinking, I would have turned down the TV so I could hear what they said. In the end, the nods and the lingering hug told me more than I wanted to know.

The beast howled. Only her anger allowed me to choke down the tears that wanted to fall.

"Elle, talk to me."

"About what?" I swung into the maple tree and waited for her to join me as gentle flakes of snow began drifting down. "The house was locked up tight. The story Jax heard about Kris and his family checks out. Maybe he didn't go hunting, but we have no way to track him now. He's not there." Sliding open the window, I climbed back inside with her close at my heels.

"That isn't what I meant, and you know it," she whispered, closing the window. It squealed a little as it slid home and I jotted down a mental note to hit it with some oil before tomorrow night.

I threw off my clothes, put back on my pajamas, and climbed into bed before answering. "You know what. Here's the thing, if you've got some brilliant insight into the case, I'd love to hear it. But if this is some 'we're sisters and we should share' crap, I'm really not interested tonight." I turned to the wall, trying to meditate on the glossy patterns in the wallpaper.

She stood right by the head of my bed and sighed deeply. "Whatever. But sooner or later, you're going to have to deal with your issues and get a grip. Goodnight." Next thing I knew, she'd climbed into her bunk, leaving me alone. Again.

So much for meditating.

The beast had been restless all night, prowling and pacing inside me. Now I felt the same, unable to relax. Trapped, like the walls were closing in and locking me in a cage, like the animal I knew I was deep down.

Cass's gentle snoring grated on my frayed nerves. It didn't help that the sound also drove home the fact that *she* could settle down. I watched the minutes on the clock tick away. Maybe the monotonous blinking would lull me to sleep. One-thirteen. One-fourteen. One-fifteen. By twenty after, I'd had more than enough. I flung off the covers, dashed the window, threw it open, and leaped to the tree.

I had already shimmied to the ground and stripped by the time the icy air woke Cass. The change had me in its grip when I heard her hiss, "Elle, don't."

The sound pushed the change. Before she could do anything to stop me, I was off. I ran. And ran. I didn't care where we went, so I let the beast take the reins. I didn't want to worry about control. I just wanted to get lost in the glory of the run. In the feel of the earth beneath my toes, yielding and gentle. The harsh transition when she bounded across a street. The exquisite ripple of the wind through my fur.

The cold front had brought early lake effect snow with it, and giant flakes of brilliant white eddied around me and coated the ground. They glowed in the moonlight for my wolf eyes, shining like earthbound stars. With the air brisk and clean and full of promise, I sank into the bliss of the run—for the moment wild and free.

An animal at my core. Just as I'd admitted.

I hadn't paid much attention to the beast's path, other than to notice we seemed to be circling. It wasn't until she stopped that I realized she'd had a destination in mind the moment we'd left the shelter of the maple tree outside my bedroom window. We stood outside a different window, our paws on the ledge, nose pressed to the icy glass. Every time we breathed, a fog obscured our vision. Between exhales, our friend the wind blew through, clearing the condensation away. We stared at Jax, lying asleep in his bed, a pile of books on the floor next to him.

Pain clawed at my heart. I knew I shouldn't be here. He wasn't a suspect anymore. What I was doing was wrong in so many ways. I should leave. I thanked the heavens for the snow; it would cover my tracks. Jaxson would never know I'd been here. But the beast didn't want to go. Truthfully, neither did I. So we lingered.

Just one more minute.

The shrill jangling of a phone ringing inside the house pierced my ears—and Jaxson's. His eyes opened drowsily, whereas mine went as wide as my wolf face would allow. I froze, afraid movement would draw his attention. If he saw me like this, I hoped his brain would chalk it up to a dream.

Recognition lit his eyes. *Will my luck never change?* He sat up, swinging his legs off the bed. I dropped away from the window and ran.

Stupid...stupid...stupid...

My brain was too busy berating me to control my movements. The beast took over, striving to distance us from the "threat" of Jaxson Espisito. Our frantic retreat brought us to a familiar path toward an all too familiar destination. The wind whipped its scent toward my nose. Taunting me. Indian Fields lay just across the road—waiting. The urge to do something reckless, something dangerous, rushed through my blood, flooding my system with adrenaline.

I can catch him. I can end this. All I have to do is go over there and wait.

The beast wanted it. She wanted the fight, and the part of me that ached wanted it, too. More though, I wanted to be a hero.

A little bit of Cass's logical nature had rubbed off on me, and it started to argue. Its voice was squashed the instant I caught a whiff of blood blowing from across Milham Road. Blood that smelled like burning metal dipped in musk, rosemary, and cinnamon. He was there, right now, performing whatever twisted ritual called for all that blood.

No thought other than stopping him crossed the synapses of my brain. I dove headlong onto the road. I didn't look; I just leaped.

My feet had barely hit the pavement when I felt a crushing blow as something far bigger than me impacted my body. Bones crunched in agonizing pain. For a moment as I soared through the air, more adrenaline coursed through me and the pain disappeared. Rational thought vanished, and I had the fleeting idea I'd magically developed the power of flight.

The respite from pain didn't last long. I hit the pavement and skidded across the rough concrete. It tore at the flesh beneath my fur. I tried to howl, to scream, but nothing came out. My head swam, the only part of me capable of movement. I faded in and out, seeing the headlights of the van that had run into me, then blackness, and then the lights again.

If I die here, will I die a wolf? Will anyone even know that's what happened? Or will they think I just left?

New pain ripped through me as I thought of my family. Of how my disappearance would destroy Jen and Eric. Cass might figure it out, but she'd never be able to explain. There was nothing I could do. My insides were broken. No one would put in the time, money, or effort to save a wolf, not beat up like this, and I wouldn't survive long enough to heal. The faces of my family flashed through my mind, and I tried to decide which was the lesser of the two evils before me. Die a wolf? Or expose myself and probably die anyway?

Hands brushed at my fur and voices whispered soft, soothing words that I couldn't comprehend. They seemed so far away. So much less important than my decision.

Then a sharp pain pierced my thigh, and I managed to whimper. I felt two pairs of hands slip under my body and hoist me into the air. After that, I didn't notice anything other than the darkness that opened its arms and embraced me.

Chapter Twenty-Five

Saturday, October 29 - early morning

A loud chittering sounded from overhead. *Damn it, Cass, if you moved the alarm up to your bed, the least you could do is shut it off.* "Just a few more minutes. Please," I groaned.

The noise stopped for all of about twenty seconds. Then it started all over again, and I swear to God it was louder. I reached down to grab my blanket and pull it over my head. Slime slid through my fingers and across my face. "Ahhh!"

Sitting up, I batted it away. Then I finally opened my eyes, taking in the sodden leaves clinging to my fingers and the snow that coated the ground. It was only then that the first shiver ran through my body. I was lying in the woods stark naked.

For a minute, I couldn't remember anything about how I'd ended up here. So, I focused on the last image that came to mind—Jax. Standing outside his window. The rest came rushing back, like someone flipping through a bunch of old snapshots. Everything froze on the picture of the headlights.

I should be dead. And even if I'm not dead, I should still be broken in a hundred places.

But I wasn't. Parts of me ached, nothing more. Scratch that, I was freezing, too. The icy dampness chilled me to the bone and made it hard to even think.

I couldn't exactly run home with no clothes on. Kneeling in the soggy leaves, I begged for the beast to come. The bitch took her sweet time waking up, and then she plowed forward like she thought I might take back the invite.

The parts of me that hadn't hurt when I woke up screamed to life during the shift. I don't know what exactly had the beast in such a tizzy, but she battered her way out. As soon as I caught my breath, I ran from the slowly lightening sky toward home.

Running helped clear some of the pain, as all the muscles that had clenched up while I slept in the snow finally loosened. I could take the cold easier in wolf form, but somehow while my body came alive, my brain still felt fuzzy. In the end, I concentrated on the thing growling for my attention: the beast. Something was a little off in my gait. Then I felt what she had sensed. In all the other hurts, the little pinprick at the top of my leg had escaped notice. Now I couldn't stop feeling it. The spot throbbed weakly, just like when I used to get shots there as a kid.

No wonder the beast was so fired up. Someone had injected us full of drugs.

৶

"Where the hell have you been all night?" A fully dressed Cassidy yanked me through the bedroom window.

The extra force shifted my balance, and I stumbled to the floor. "Gee, thanks for that, Cass." I stood up and brushed off my pajamas.

She didn't give me the chance to actually answer her question. "I put your uniform in the bathroom already. I'll beg you a portable breakfast. Just go." She shoved me out of room, shaking her head in disgust.

The meet. Ugh. I stripped and climbed into the shower, scrubbing myself with as much speed as I could manage. One of these days I'd get a nice long shower again. I just had no clue when that might happen.

I stepped out and wiped the steam from the mirror. Twisting back and forth, I examined every inch of my body I could see without the use of multiple mirrors or removable eyeballs. My skin was flawless. Hell, it looked better than it had before I went out last night, never mind my run-in with the van.

My blood ran cold as I traced my fingers across ribs I knew had been broken. "Does this make the people that hit me bad guys or good guys?" I whispered the question, but my reflection had no answer.

I whipped my wet hair up into a ponytail and ran downstairs.

We barely made it to school in time to catch the bus, and this time my portable breakfast wasn't nearly as tasty. I only bothered choking it down because if I didn't, I risked wolfing out as I ran.

Cass leaned against the bus window and eyed me. "You went running alone in the middle of the night again. This is turning into a really bad habit of yours."

I took a swig of the soda I'd snuck out of the fridge before answering her with the most emotionless voice I could muster. "I couldn't sleep. My brain wouldn't shut down." I shrugged, refusing to look at her. "I figured running would help."

"What were you dwelling on so hard? Anything"— Cassidy cast a covert glance around the bus—"helpful?"

"The PRT was definitely first and foremost in my mind." I looked at her, took a bite, and chewed thoughtfully. "But no, I didn't come up with any brilliant plans."

Cass twisted around to lean her back against the seat in front of us and narrowed her eyes at me. "So what happened? You ran to Battle Creek and back without managing to relax? Or did you decide to crawl under a tree somewhere and sleep there?"

The waffle lodged itself in my throat, and I took a long drink to wash it down. I had to tell her sooner or later. "Yeah, I slept under a tree, right after I got hit by a car." Unable to handle her unblinking gaze any more, I turned back to my breakfast.

"Seriously? You handled it well, I guess." She chuckled, but the sound dried up when I turned back to her.

I wasn't laughing. "Maybe I should rephrase a little bit

then. A big white van plowed into me hard enough that I felt most of my body break. When I woke up, I was in the middle of the woods, human, and naked, without a scratch on me."

"But...but..." Cass at a loss for words was one to go down in the record books.

I crumpled up the bag. It didn't matter how hungry I was, I couldn't choke down any more of the spongy waffles. "Whatever happened to me wasn't an accident. It wasn't just a tap on the butt either. Even with my healing, I should at best be lying in a hospital barely clinging to life right now, not on a bus getting ready to run in regionals. I'm ninety percent sure I was drugged."

"I...I don't know what to say." Cass speechless lasted as long as I expected—about five seconds. "Do you think they're connected to the altar-builder? "

I shook my head and drained the rest of my soda. "I don't think so, but we aren't going to worry about them right now, whoever they are."

The bus pulled up to the stadium and stopped just as Cass's mouth gaped open. "What do you mean? Of course we worry about them—they ran you over and..."

"And healed me." My arms wrapped around my not-broken ribs. "Assuming I'm not wrong and this wasn't some weird werewolf thing, we don't know what their agenda might be. It's less important than going after the person who attacked Jen. Our priority has to be the one who is hurting people. Fighting evil trumps whatever curiosity we might have."

I bent down and grabbed my duffel bag, my body raring to go. Too bad I'd have to hold back when I ran. With the energy zinging through me, I wanted to show them what I could really do. Yeah, yeah. Bad idea.

⁂

Jax and I stood outside the bookstore, debating what to do. "Where the hell is Cass?" he asked, rubbing his hands up and down his arms.

"Some fire demon you are." I raised a brow toward his hands. "She's probably still studying with Corbin. We could always wait in the car."

His fists dropped to his sides and he scowled. "I figured it would be easier if she saw us when she got here."

I felt my own lips twisting into a sneer. *Cass is with Corbin. Cass wants to be with Corbin. Jax will just have to deal. Kind of like I have to deal with this.* "You know, you can stop being pissy with me any time. It wasn't my fault the fire alarm went off in the bookstore."

He reached up and raked his hair back, searching the outskirts of the parking lot. Looking for Cass or too embarrassed to look at me? "Sorry. What happened to you last night spooked me more than a little. I don't think any of us should be out alone. Not when there's a chance someone's targeting you, er, us."

"Look, like I told Cass, I refuse to worry about it." I laid my hand on his arm and forced my lips to turn up at the corners.

Jax shifted his eyes from the parking lot to my fingers, some unknown emotion playing across his face. "Then I guess I'll do the worrying for you." He sighed. "Let's drive over to the café and wait for her there."

We pulled into the same spot we'd parked in the day before, and Jax let the Chevelle idle. He'd done something to quiet the engine a bit. With the muffled engine noise, we could have talked, but we didn't. Jaxson fiddled with a piece of door trim, and I fidgeted. "Maybe I should go let Cass know we're here."

He still didn't look at me.

I wasn't sure what his issue was or if it was just leftover animosity from when I yelled at him last night. Either way, I wanted out of the car.

"Yeah, that's probably a good idea. I'll keep the car warm." He turned on the radio, freeing me from the silence and the car.

When I stepped out into the air, the scent of him drifted away. I felt emptier but calmer. Without him right next to me, it didn't hurt so much that he'd decided to ignore me. Determined to let it go once and for all, I squared my shoulders and strode up to the door of the café.

Through the window, I saw them—sitting huddled in two armchairs in the corner. No table today—they didn't need the extra space for us. Cass's face lit up with something Corbin said. She looked so happy; jealousy stabbed my heart. She didn't really want anyone, yet all the guys loved her. Trey. Jaxson. Maybe even Corbin. Wouldn't that complicate her plan? If the guy she pretended to fall for actually reciprocated? My lips twitched as I thought of her face if he told her he wanted to go out regardless of the age difference.

I shook off the reverie and pulled the door open. For a moment when I stepped inside, I thought maybe Jax had followed me. Just like yesterday, the scent almost bowled me over. It was all here: the hot metal, the rosemary, the cinnamon. Then, as I sucked in a deep breath with my eyes closed, trying to find the source of the odor, garlic mingled with the other scents, and I almost gagged. My eyes flashed open to see a short woman in a baker's apron bringing out trays of bagels.

It wasn't Jax. It wasn't even the altar-builder. It was food.

No wonder I thought Jax's smell was so strong yesterday. All the scents that I associated with him, and by association, the altar-builder were here, too. I'd have to be careful in our hunting to separate out food smells.

I twisted toward Cass and Corbin and saw her wave as she packed up her things. Still reeling from the odor, I decided to wait in the alcove with at least one set of doors protecting my senses. The two of them joined me a minute later, once again letting in the smell that reminded me so much of the altar-builder.

"Elle, lovely to see you again." Corbin held the door open for us. "Cassidy tells me you blew away the competition at your meet today. Congratulations."

"I wouldn't say I blew them away. I won. Second place was right on my heels at the finish line." I stood by the door to the Chevelle, waiting for them to say their goodbyes before opening it. Sure Jax could warm up the inside in no time, but he'd have to act put out if I held it open. I wasn't sure he would do it, and it was better to be safe than sorry.

Corbin brushed his lips across Cassidy's fingers again.

The door creaked open, and she pulled her hand from his in one of those moves you only really see in the movies—the one where the couple holds on until the last possible second. Jealousy played its little stabbing game with my heart again.

I nodded to Corbin and started to climb into the car when he stopped me, plucking a couple hairs from my jacket. It took every inch of willpower I had to keep my eyes from widening. The hairs didn't belong to me—they were far too short. They belonged to the beast.

Corbin's eyebrows pulled together as he stared at them. "Cass never mentioned that you had a dog. I love dogs."

I swallowed hard and forced a smile. "We don't. It must be from my friend Bailey's dog. Her parents brought Cookie to the meet today."

"Ah, too bad." After releasing the hairs to the wind, he looked back at me, all trace of consternation gone, replaced with his perfect smile. "Enjoy the rest of your weekend, Elle. I'm sure I'll see you again soon."

Chapter Twenty-Six

Saturday, October 29 - late afternoon

"There's no way we can always be with someone else," I argued once we were safely in our bedroom.

"Why the hell not? I'm just thinking about everyone's safety." Jax tossed his backpack near the door as he shut it.

Cass plucked at the rug. Nice of her to leave this one to me.

I twisted up to my knees, looking him squarely in the eyes. "Because there are too many problems with the idea. If, or more likely when, I have to go back into Indian Fields, Cass can't go. So either you stay with her or with me. Sorry to say, but if we have to chase after someone, you can't keep up with Cass and me unless you have the motorcycle with you."

His lips pressed into a tight line, and he thumped his fist on the floor. "Damn it, I don't want to see you…either of you get hurt." His face flushed, and he turned away from me.

Cass still hadn't said a word, but for some reason, she seemed entirely too entertained by the argument.

I refused to let her frustrate me. "Look"—I stared Jax, my voice low again—"how about we make a deal?" He cocked his eyebrow, and my insides turned to mush, making me wish for a split second that I didn't have a sister. I shook the thought away. *I love Cass. I need Cass. Cass is more important than any boy.* "It's mathematically impossible for the three of us to divide up

197

evenly. One thing we *can* do though is agree to stick to populated areas as much as possible, especially if we're flying solo."

Cass rolled her eyes at me, and Jax tipped his head sideways. They didn't believe me.

"Really, no more late night solo runs. I'll behave." I raised my hands in surrender, and then stared Jaxson down. "Will that satisfy your masculine need to protect the women?"

"Look, it isn't that I don't think the two of you can take care of yourselves. It's just…" He avoided looking at us, staring instead at his fingers as he ran them through the threads of the rug. "…I like you, and I don't want you to get hurt because you think you're tougher than you are. No matter how strong or fast you might be, the guy waiting around the corner could be stronger and faster."

Cass leaned back against the wall, twirling a finger in her hair. "Jax is right. We've got a known bad guy and some unknown threat that might grab us and pump us full of drugs. It's better to be safe than sorry."

"I agree. I just want us safe *and* functional. There's a big difference between that and tying our hands so we can't do anything." I pressed my fingers against my spine and arched my back. This floor thing was for the birds.

I waited, but no one said anything else. We'd either reached an agreement or an impasse. I liked to think it was the former. "So, Jax, did you find anything helpful during last night's research?"

His amber eyes searched mine—for what, I didn't have a clue. "Yeah. I think I did." He rolled onto his side and propped himself up on one arm. "Elle, you asked last night if I was evil."

I winced. *Did he have to bring that up?*

"I thought about it," he continued, "and from what I can tell, the power isn't good or evil, it's just power. Sort of like a gun. Guns can be used for all sorts of things, from paperweights to killing machines. Demon blood is kind of like that, but just like a person with a gun, the power can be corrupting."

"Following you so far." Cass tugged her finger from her hair.

I just nodded, still trying to get over feeling guilty about the "evil" thing.

"For instance, I could decide the only way I would use my power was to start campfires. I'd be nothing more than the coolest counselor at summer camp." He opened his free hand and a tiny blaze lit the center of it. "Or I could use it to incinerate teachers who gave me crappy grades. Or I could randomly burn down day care centers in the middle of the day. There are all sorts of things I could do. It's about making choices."

It wasn't hard to see what he was getting at. "So you figure the guy we're after is a half-demon gone to the dark side?"

"Yes and no. Yes, I think he made that choice, but I don't think that's all there is to it. Starting campfires would teach me to control my power. The bigger things? The awful things? They'd show me just how much power I have. It'd be like a drug, always needing a bigger hit."

"He's high on his power," Cass whispered. "Like I get sometimes."

I reached out and squeezed her hand, trying not to remember what it felt like to have her teeth at my neck. "A half-demon power addict. That's something we can deal with."

Jax cleared his throat, dragging my attention away from Cass. "Um, yeah. I think there might still be more to it."

Slumping against the desk, I closed my eyes. "What else?" He cleared his throat, and I could feel him staring at me. It made my stomach flutter and my pulse skip beats here and there. Life could beat me in the head with the reality of him liking Cass, but I still couldn't get over him. I waved a hand so he'd keep talking and give me something else to focus on.

"You said the smell of his blood was different than mine, had more components to it."

"So?" Cass asked.

"So, I think that maybe the scents Elle picked up on have to do with our supernatural abilities."

My eyes flashed open, and I jerked up. "Wait a minute.

How is that possible?" The air in our bedroom felt heavy and oppressive, like something in the atmosphere had shifted—and not for the better.

Jax laid his hand on my arm, the touch warming me instantly. "I'm not sure. If you'll humor me though, I'd like to perform a tiny experiment." He arched a black eyebrow over one glittering amber eye, turning the request into a dare.

As the fearless leader, what choice did I have?

Two minutes later, sitting blindfolded in the desk chair and holding my nose, I wished I'd thought of a way out. "This is stupid. And where is Cass?"

Jaxson's voice came from my right. "She's in the bathroom. We figured it would be safest considering there's blood involved."

Even though Cass and I had come to the unspoken agreement that we trusted him, the situation made me uncomfortable. "It's not that much blood. She'd be okay."

"It was her idea, so let it go." He pulled my hand away from my nose. "Take a sniff."

"Wouldn't this be easier in wolf…?" Something passed beneath my nostrils. I inhaled the unmistakable odor of rosemary and cinnamon. *Wolf form be damned, I can do this.* "That's yours." My lips twisted into an awkward frown, and I shifted in my seat. I might be able to smell clearly without her help, but the beast still reacted. She rolled inside me, wanting to bathe herself in Jax's scent. "Next please."

"Okay, try this one."

A new odor assaulted me, this one less pleasing to the beast. Still rosemary but with a heavy dose of something metallic. It was almost a taste, like putting pennies in your mouth—lots of pennies. I pulled away from it. "Okay, that one's different. Some parts are the same, but not all of them."

Someone knocked on the door. I reached up to yank off the blindfold, but Jax's hand fell on mine. "Relax." His boots echoed across the floor and the door creaked open. "You didn't need to do this."

The wood muffled Cass's voice. "Yes, I did. You know it as well as I do."

The door clicked shut again. "Okay, just two more."

"Two?" I asked as he shuffled around. Then another scent: rosemary, pine, dirt, grass. The beast settled down inside me and curled up, ready to sleep once more. Not me though. I was strung tighter than a piano wire. "Where's the last one?"

A new sample passed beneath my nose, and I inhaled deeply. *What the…?* "Can I smell that one again?" This time Jax held the sample steady. It smelled like blood—nothing more.

"Done?"

I nodded.

Jax deftly untied the scarf from my eyes. "Be right back." Cass came back in when he left. A few seconds later I heard the evidence of our little game flush down the toilet.

Once Jax returned and shut the door, Cass pounced. "Well?"

"They were all different." I gripped the sides of the chair while my eyes darted from one face to the other. I swear I'd never felt more like an animal than I did in those few minutes. "Jax was easy; I've paid attention to his scent for too long not to recognize it. The second one had a lot of heavy metal in it, almost like blood inside of blood. Guessing that was Cass."

Jax nodded.

"The third had to be me—it reminded me of the forest. All of them had one thing in common though: rosemary."

"And the last one?" Cass stared at me intently.

I fidgeted under her scrutiny. "Nothing. No defining scents at all." Sick of being under the microscope, I shifted the questions away from me. "Where'd you get it?"

"From downstairs. Jen cut herself chopping up vegetables for dinner. I brought up the towel." Cass said it like it didn't matter.

"At least that gives us something to go on." Jax settled back onto the floor. "Rosemary identifies us as supernaturals."

They weren't getting out of it that easily. "Why Jen?" They looked at me with blank faces. "Why did you make me test her blood?"

Cass snorted and rolled her eyes. "Because we had to know if regular people smell different. There might have been some odor in blood you needed to ignore." She settled back into her seat against the wall.

"And what if Jen had turned out to be one of us?"

Cass's mouth formed a small "o". "I hadn't thought of that."

I gave my head an angry shake. Maybe Corbin wasn't good for her after all; she was slipping.

"It doesn't make a difference." Jax kept his voice calm, trying to soothe me. "Because you said her blood didn't smell special at all. She's normal. What about the rosemary thing? Do you agree?" His gripped my chin gently and turned my face to his, forcing me to break eye contact with Cass.

I jerked my head from his grasp. "Yeah. It makes sense." Between feeling like an animal and feeling like I was on trial, all I wanted was to get out of the bedroom. I settled for ditching the chair and sliding back to the floor.

Jax sank down, balancing on the balls of his feet rather than sitting. "Okay, that means the differences between our scents might indicate what kind of power we have."

"Okay, but I fail to see your point."

Cass shifted forward. "The cinnamon is fire demon."

"Yeah. I got that, Cass, thanks for your help." I wondered if I should just go. They had what they needed from me, and the two of them seemed to be on the same page. I pushed up from the floor.

Jax put his hand on my leg, not to pull me down, but just enough pressure to keep me from getting up. "So the other stuff you smelled in his blood means he's something else, too."

No.

This was too much. I sat down again resting my head on my knees. "And we don't have any way of knowing what else he is."

Cass's hand fell on my shoulder. "You said before you smelled metal in his blood. Could he be like me?"

I couldn't tell if the odd tone to her voice was hope or fear. I shook my head, rubbing my forehead against my jeans. "No. It was different. The metal in your blood is…cold. In his, it's hot, burning hot, like metal in a forge." After a couple deep breaths, I looked up at Jax. "You wouldn't have brought this up if you couldn't explain it."

"I have a theory, but that's all I've got." He reached out like he was going to smooth my hair back but dropped his hand before he touched me.

He held my gaze another moment before diving into his explanation. "From what I've found, half-demons are the result of demons taking human form and having sex with a human. At this point, we assume the genetics work the same as with people—half my DNA comes from my mom, half from daddy-demon. Since I look human, I'm going to guess that most demon genes are recessive, only the abilities are dominant."

I laid my head back, resting it on the chair. It was Saturday; I didn't want to deal with bio on the weekend. "Jax, I'm in biology, too, but I fail to see your point."

"My point is what happens on the rare occasion a pair of half-demons hook up and have a kid?"

Chapter Twenty-Seven

Saturday, October 29 - early evening

Jax waited as his words sunk in, then it hit me—there was going to be homework. I could really learn to hate this job.

He grabbed a piece of paper and a pen from the desk and drew a Punnett square. "We'll use D for the demon power trait and, it's a little unorthodox but, 0 for the...lack of a demon power." He added notations for both parents as D0 then filled in the square. "The offspring will fall into one of four categories. There's the possibility the baby inherits neither demon trait—00. Or they could inherit either mom *or* dad's— D0. But there is also the possibility of DD."

"Both traits," I whispered.

He nodded, tapping the paper.

I stared at the marks on the paper. "You think that's what he is, don't you?" Pulling my gaze away, I met his eyes. "You think we're dealing with a DD."

He lowered his eyes from mine for a second and his lips twitched as if he was trying not to smile.

"Jax, her eyes are up a few inches." Cass gave a snort of disgust, shaking her head.

"Sorry." He winked at me, as I crossed my arms over my chest.

"Besides, she's a D at best."

My face must have gone crimson with how much heat rose into my cheeks.

Even Jax blushed as he went back to the lesson. "Elle's right. I think whoever this is, he got demon power from both parents, and based on his blood, I'm guessing the powers are co-dominant."

"Great, so if we're right, he can throw fire and do something else. Which means we're right back where we started—how the hell is he zombifying people?" I wanted to pull my hair out. Every time we figured something out it just opened up more questions.

Cass pointed at the diagram. "This covers the demon powers, but what about the other demon genes? How much of this guy is human and how much is demon?" she asked.

"I don't know. It could just be the powers or he could be all demon inside a human skin. He could be something in between. I'm not even sure what to call it. He's not a half-demon, he's not a demon…"

"Demon spawn."

I turned toward Cass, her voice had been little more that words exhaled with her breath. "What?"

She tipped her head up. Cass looked like she had aged a couple years in the few hours we'd been upstairs. She actually looked fifteen now. "I said demon spawn. Maybe this is the reason demons breed with humans in the first place. So they can have perfect little minions running around topside."

"Cass, I don't…"

Jax interrupted and laid his hand softly on her arm. "Cassidy, this happening is so improbable that if we weren't confronted with it, I'd have never even considered the possibility."

She placed her hand over his and held it a little longer than was really necessary for a girl who didn't, you know, like him. "Okay, sorry. I'm a little stressed what with Jen…and my inability to help out at the cemetery."

"I'll work on that. We'll figure something out." He gave her one of his heart-melting smiles before he lowered his hand. He turned to me, and I averted my eyes, not wanting him to see the jealousy brewing there.

A knock on the door saved us from the awkward moment. Jen popped her head in a second later. "I'm sorry to interrupt, but Jaxson, I have to ask you to leave."

"What?"

"Why?" Cass's question overlapped with mine.

Jen shook her head, her hair waving about her face in a slow, sad dance. "It isn't anything personal, really." She looked at Jax and added, "You can come back over tomorrow or something. I'm not trying to be awful, really, I'm not."

Jaxson stood up and smiled at her, all politeness in the face of being kicked out on his ass. I really wasn't sure how he pulled it off. "It's all right, Mrs. Smith. I don't want to get on the mom's bad side or anything. Is it okay for me to call, or are they grounded?"

Cass pressed her lips together, looking all sorts of indignant, but Jen just choked out a tense laugh. "No, nothing like that. You can certainly call."

"All right then, if it's cool, I'll just let myself out." He turned around and winked at us. "I'll talk to you later tonight." He grabbed his jacket from where he had casually tossed it on my bed and squeezed past Jen.

The instant we heard the front door shut, Cass and I jumped to our feet. "What the heck was that all about?"

Jen held up a trembling hand. For the first time, I noticed the dark circles ringing her red eyes. "I'm sorry, girls. Eric just called with some awful news. Os...I mean, Uncle Oscar is in a bad way and the two of us need to go see him. We won't be back until tomorrow. Jaxson can come over then, but I'm just not comfortable leaving you at home alone with a boy." Her body stiffened as if she expected a fight, but she leaned against the door like she could fall over any minute from exhaustion.

Cass started to protest, but I covered her mouth with my hand. "It's cool, Jen. We'll be fine. Just go do what you need to do."

She came in and pulled both of us into a fierce hug. "Thank you. I hate leaving you alone after what happened the other night, but we really have no choice. We'll be home before noon, maybe even before you wake up."

I hugged her back. "No worries."

The garage door rumbled, and Jen stepped back. "That's Eric. I have to throw together some clothes and stuff. Do you want him to pick you up some...?"

"We'll take care of dinner, Jen." Cass gave her a weak smile.

Fifteen minutes later, after hugs goodbye and promises that we wouldn't let any boys into the house, our foster parents were out the door and down the driveway. Another five minutes passed before the phone rang.

I found the handset on the second ring. "Hello?"

"So, are they gone for a while or what?"

"Jax?" I pulled back the curtains in the den and looked out the window. Just as I'd expected, the driveway was empty. "Where are you?"

"Down the street. Waiting."

"Why?" How could he have known they were leaving? We hadn't.

I could almost see him snickering on the other end of the line. "Call it intuition. Jen looked upset and you two seemed confused. So I waited and watched. Eric tore into the drive like his tail was on fire, and they peeled out a minute later the same way."

"You're good."

"You have no idea." I heard his engine catch, starting the noisy machine once more. "So, back to the original question, are they gone for a while?"

Cass noticed I was still on the phone and wandered over.

"Yes." I sighed, wishing I could have given him a different response. "But you can't come over."

"Um, any particular reason?"

"Because we promised."

"You're kidding, right?" he asked. That didn't deserve an answer. "You're not kidding."

Cass mimed putting on coats and walking out the door.

"Hang on a second, Jax." I covered the mouthpiece with my hand and whispered, "You want to go out?"

"Sure; we didn't promise we'd stay in. Besides, we *never*

stay in. Safety in numbers and all that." She raced upstairs to get our jackets.

Sometimes, especially at night, Cass acted like this whole thing was one big adventure. Standing in the glow of the oak kitchen with our parents gone for the night, I had to agree the thought of staying put like innocent little girls bordered on the far side of ridiculous. I uncovered the phone. "Change of plans. Care to join us for dinner?"

Fifteen minutes later, we pulled up in front of a pizza buffet. The place teemed with students from Western. I was still wondering why so many of them were here when Jax answered my unasked question with a wave of his hand. "Welcome to the post-football-game drunken eating extravaganza that takes place prior to the Saturday night Bacchanalian frat parties."

I walked through the door he held open. "Wow, and to think for thousands of dollars of debt, this too can be ours in just a couple years." I sighed deeply, taking in the sorry sight of wasted co-eds. "On a high note, I doubt anyone will recognize us here."

Cass glided through the buffet line. "And who knows, maybe Corbin will pop in."

While I groaned, Jax muttered, "Great. Corbin."

I wasn't sure whether to be happy Jax and I were on the same side or upset that he was upset about her bringing him up in the first place. Thinking about it made my head hurt, and with my stomach already roaring, I needed to dull at least one ache. "Who cares? Can we have food now?"

Eating here had one added benefit. The people fell into one of three categories: drunk, self-absorbed, or dealing with their drunk or self-absorbed friends. Everyone in the restaurant was far too busy to take any notice of how much food I packed away.

"Slow down, Elle, the pizza isn't going anywhere." Jax winked.

Of course, *he* would notice. "They say all you can eat. I'm a firm believer in getting my money's worth." I stuffed another bite of pepperoni, sausage, bread, and cheese into my mouth.

Cass dropped the pizza crust she'd nibbled right to the edge and piped up. "So, with all night ahead of us, where should we start?" She peeled tiny pieces from a cinnamon roll and popped them in her mouth.

Jax wiped at his lips with a napkin. "I've got a few things to research still and I want to hit some books since the internet has me going in circles. I suppose you could join me at the library." A groan from Cass had him changing his tactic. "Or you can follow another lead and call me when you want a pick-up."

"Great. You go hole up in the library. We'll just wander campus or something." The lack of a plan ruined my appetite and I pushed away my plate.

Cassidy must have sensed my irritation. Either that or my voice hadn't been quite as perky as I'd planned. She leaned in close and spoke in a loud whisper. "When I went up for food earlier, I heard a couple girls talking about some guy who's been frequenting a bar around here. She said he hung out with her roommate one night last weekend and that she's been acting strange ever since." Cass shrugged. "Might be worth at least sniffing out the parking lot."

It sounded like another dead end to me. Our options all sounded crappy, and I wondered why we hadn't stayed home after all.

"Doesn't sound like a bad idea." Jax stacked our plates at the end of the table. Of course he'd agree with her. "I've been thinking that maybe the problem started here. Former Northern High student goes to Western. He'd still have connections at the high school to could account for the attacks there. Plus, most of the other people we know about have ties to either the college or the area."

It did make sense. "But what about Kris?"

Jaxson leaned back in his chair, balancing it on two legs. "The way I see it, he's a big guy. With a good fake ID, he could fake it. Of course, there's still the possibility that it's someone else."

I buried my head in my hands. It still hurt. I'd known all along the knife was a flimsy lead, but if it wasn't Kris, then all

Jax had done was narrow down our search area from anyone in a town of over a hundred thousand people to WMU's student body, which accounted for somewhere around twenty-five thousand of that. Our haystack was shrinking, but we were still looking for a really small needle.

"We've got our plans for later, but what should we do now?" Cass asked, resting her chin on her hand. "Unless I miss my guess, we're a bit early to check out the bar." She raised her eyebrows at Jax, giving him what I could only translate as a suggestive look.

What is she doing? Flirting? She doesn't even like him!

"Yeah, a few hours too early. We could wander around campus for a bit. There's sure to be some rooms at Bernhard Center that are open." He tipped his head to the side in a sort of half-shrug.

"That would work, I suppose." At least he hadn't glommed on to her bizarre come-hither stare or whatever that was.

We drove through campus talking about how stupid people could be, like the drunks at the pizza place. "Maybe it's just because they haven't seen the really bad things that are out there. If they did, they might step up and protect themselves when they can. And maybe even stop jumping at shadows."

"Jumping at shadows?"

"Yeah, like irrational fears and the idiotic behavior that comes with them."

Jax pulled into a parking garage, where real shadows leaped from behind vehicles at every turn. "Like being afraid of the dark?"

I rolled my eyes at him. "I am not afraid of the dark."

He laughed nervously as he slammed the car into park and climbed out of the car. I could barely make out his face in the blackness of the parking garage. "Who said I was talking about you? And having a torch handy all the time makes me a lot braver in places like this than I would be otherwise."

I stared at him as we made our way to the stairwell. Odors poured off him in waves, and not just his normal, natural scent. Sweat. Fear. Had I been in wolf form, they'd have overwhelmed me. He was first inside the well-lit alcove and leaned against the wall, breathing an audible sigh of relief.

Cass didn't bother stopping, she just bounded down the stairs.

Jaxson's breathing evened out, and he started to follow her. I grabbed his arm and pulled him back. "You were serious."

He swallowed hard and tried to force a smile, but it wouldn't hold. "Yeah." He turned from me and started down the stairs, trying to hide his embarrassment. "In my oh-so-humble opinion, it's in our best interests to know as much as we can about each other, especially our strengths and weaknesses."

"But...the dark?" I clomped down the steps after him, trying to make sense of it. Jax was the tough guy, the loner, the...well, not the guy who slept with a night-light, that's for sure.

He didn't turn around to talk to me, but he slowed enough so I trailed him by only a step. "I think I knew early on there really were things in the dark. Things that hunted you. I'm pretty sure in her heart, my mom knew, too. She never said the word demon, but she also never told me there was nothing to be afraid of. When I would wake up in the night screaming, she would just hold me and sing songs in Italian until I fell asleep."

I didn't say anything for a while, and our slow steps rang against the metal, echoing eerily up the stairwell. Jax had calmed down, but now my heart raced. I kept craning my neck around, expecting to see someone following us. *You're only paranoid if there is no one out to get you.* Considering someone had run me down and drugged me, and there was a power-crazed demon spawn on the loose, I figured paranoia was healthy.

Even after my last glance back verified we were alone, my nerves still screamed for me to fill the air with something besides reverberating footfalls. "Italian?"

Jax jerked to a stop, a curious expression on his face. "Espisito didn't give that part away?"

I let out a strangled laugh, sure the lights didn't help to hide my blushing. "Yeah, I guess it did."

"It's okay. I'm actually a bit of a mutt, Italian and a bunch of other things." It was his turn to wince and go crimson. "I'm sorry. Mutt isn't an insult or anything, is it?"

My lips twitched, but I couldn't smile. He didn't know how much I hated the beast. "Hell, I'm just a crazy lone wolf, I wouldn't know if it's a foul term in the world of lycanthropes or not." I rubbed my arms, fighting off a chill that had little to do with the night air. "Sorry I'm so out of it, I'm just really on edge tonight." My eyes darted over my shoulder again. "Silence isn't my friend right now."

He brushed his fingers against my chin, turning my gaze back to his face. Then he reached up and held my hand. "I'll protect you from the boogey-man behind us if you promise to fight the werewolves and other things lurking in the dark for me."

"It's a deal." I stepped onto the stair with him. "But what if I'm the werewolf waiting for you in the dark." *Oh my God, why did I say that?*

Jax gave a crooked grin and squeezed my fingers. "In that case, I don't think I'd want saving." He started down the steps again, tugging me along. "After all, I didn't call for help when you were outside my bedroom window last night."

Chapter Twenty-Eight

Saturday, October 29 - late evening

Uh uh. Not happening. We weren't having this conversation in the echoing stairwell. He could deal with the dark outside. Once the door had closed behind us, I sucked in a breath and asked, "You saw me?"

He laughed, and the sound reverberated off the sides of nearby buildings, filling the night with mirth. "Saw you? Hell, I took my robe and slippers outside for you in case you'd come over to talk. But after about ten minutes outside, I gave up. I would have thought I'd dreamed the whole thing, but your paw prints were still in the snow outside my window." His voice sounded hopeful, but I really had no idea what he was hoping for.

There was no way it could be what he'd made it sound like. Was there?

I still saw his hand on her arm and the lingering glances. "As much as Cass might like you as a friend, I really don't think she will ever think of you as more than that."

A befuddled expression ghosted over his features, disappearing as he broke into gales of laughter. Cass turned around to glance at us, but he waved to her. She must have decided it wasn't worth walking back for, since she wandered to a bench and took a seat to wait.

I felt stupid, standing there staring at him while he cracked up. "What's so funny?"

His laughter tapered off when he looked at me. "You think I like Cass?"

"I...uh...I've seen the way you look at her. Since the moment you came into our house, you've been buddying up with her. So it hasn't exactly been outside the realm of possibility." Though the low lighting here wasn't beneficial to co-eds wandering around at night, I was glad of it. I was getting damn sick and tired of him seeing me embarrassed.

"Wow, and here I thought I'd done everything I could without just blurting it out, but Cass was right."

My turn to be thoroughly confused. *Did I miss a memo somewhere?* "She was right about what?"

Only when he pulled me closer did I realize he still held my hand—had been holding my hand since he took it in the parking garage. "Cass was right you didn't have a clue that I've been chasing after you since the night of the Homecoming game. She actually warned me off at one point because she thought I was being too stalkerish."

"B-but you look at her like...like..."

He shook his head and reached up to brush hair out of my face, his fingers lingering on my neck. "Elle, didn't you ever notice that the only times I ever 'looked at Cass' you were standing next to her?" He ran a finger down my cheek. "I never looked at her. It was always you. And the only reason I tried to get on her good side is because she's your sister and the two of you are tight."

Jax liked me? Me? "I'm dumbfounded."

"Well, at least you've got that half right." I felt my face turning even redder and tried to lower my gaze, but he raised my chin with the gentle touch of his fingertips. His expression had lost all traces of humor and taken on a very serious air. "Hey, it was a joke; I don't really think you're dumb. That would cause all sorts of problems, considering I refuse to date stupid girls." He let go of my chin, and his lips twitched as if he was holding back a smile. "Of course, that is assuming you don't have issues with my type, or with me on a personal level, or—"

"You know better than that though," I interrupted. "Cass told you, didn't she?"

The smile broke through as he shrugged.

It was answer enough, and neither of us saw my response coming. When my fist met Jaxson's abdomen, a look of shock crossed his face and the air rushed out of his lungs. He staggered back a few feet, released my fingers and fell on his ass. *I hit Jax.* My mouth dropped open and I stared at my fist. I was mad but not *that* mad. Why would I have…? The beast. I was losing control over her completely. Damn her and her stupid freaking temper. I could only hope he'd forgive me and understand as I tried to rein her in better. "I'm sorry. I was…a little mad that you let me go on thinking you had a thing for my sister, and the beast just…I'm sorry." I winced and held out my hand. "But if you're still interested…"

He grabbed my wrist and let me pull him up. "I suppose as long as you promise to keep me on my toes and not let things get boring, I'm still interested."

I twined my fingers with his. "I'll do my best. And I'll try not to knock you on your butt next time you get out of line."

Jax pulled me close, and the nearness of him woke the beast and sent her rolling about inside me. He leaned over and breathed along my neck, whispering, "You can try it, but you wouldn't get rid of me that easily anyway."

I met his amber gaze and wanted to lose myself in those eyes, in the comfort they promised. His hands slid under my coat, taking up position just above my waist, his fingertips finding the spots he had burned into my memory only a week earlier. I didn't know if the warmth that flooded through me came from his hands or if being so close to him brought a heat that had nothing to do with demon blood.

I inhaled his scent, the glorious combination of rosemary and cinnamon—forest and home. For a moment I couldn't tell who wanted to rub up against him more, me or the beast. Then I realized I didn't care and inched nearer. I ran my hands up his chest, remembering the day I'd seen him stepping out from the locker room. His skin was hot to the touch and made me think of summer and days at the beach where he would have no need for a shirt. The beast gave a dreamy growl and I moved even closer.

Jaxson arched his eyebrow in the way that drove me crazy, and the growl escaped my lips. He smirked and moved one hand from the small of my back to behind my neck. "Down, girl." The words were meaningless. His body told a different story. A better one.

I felt gentle pressure on my neck, but I didn't need any encouragement. I tipped my head up the tiniest bit and found his lips with mine. I closed my eyes and savored the softness of his lips, the taste of him—the cinnamon and rosemary flooding my senses. His fingers pressed into my skin, heating it, and I knew there would be small burns on my back and neck, but I didn't care. In that instant, I didn't care about anything in the world except him. Except the soft pressure of his mouth on mine. His tongue gently caressed my lips, and I parted them willingly—eagerly.

He pushed his tongue into my mouth, tentatively stroking mine. The touch sent shivers through me and I wound my arms around his neck and tangled in his hair, pulling him tighter against my body.

"Ahem."

Jax pulled back. I turned toward the sound with a snarl on my lips for whoever interrupted us, compliments of the beast.

It was Cass, still sitting on the bench, yards away. "Look, I'm happy for the two of you and all, but I'm feeling a bit weird sitting here watching this. So, any chance you might, you know, go out on a date or something—*without me*—to make out?"

I shoved the beast back down—Cass didn't deserve her irritation. "Um, yeah. Sorry." Jax moved his hand from my back and started to shove it in his pocket. That wasn't happening; I grabbed hold of it before he got that far. I was willing to stop kissing him for now, but I'd be damned if I couldn't hold his hand. Now that I had him, I didn't have any intention of letting him go.

Wandering around campus at eight o'clock on a Saturday

night proved fruitless as far as sniffing out suspects. The people who weren't going out had already holed up somewhere doing whatever it was they did. And the ones who were going out were busy getting ready. Or something. Whatever the case, campus was more or less deserted.

Which was fine by me. I spent the time reveling in Jaxson. He liked me. Really really liked me. Every time he glanced my way and smiled, or gave my hand a squeeze, I wanted to melt and I'd shift a little closer to him. After about an hour, we strode into Bernhard Center, walking almost hip to hip, and found a place to hole up for a while.

We hunted through the building, searching for something to do. "What do you mean they don't have a bowling alley or pool tables?" Cass whined. "No wonder this place isn't in the big ten."

I leaned my head back, resisting the urge to bang it against the wall behind me. *A busy Cass is a happy Cass. Or at least as happy as she gets.* "They do have a big old bank of computers. You could see what kind of trouble you can find hacking into the student database."

Her eyes lit up. "Now *that* sounds like fun." Without another word, she tore off down the stairs.

Jax smiled. "How about that coffee now? There is a Biggby's near the computer stations."

I froze. "Wait a minute? You mean when you moved our tutoring sessions to the bookstore and offered to buy me a coffee or something that was actually you asking me out?"

He nodded like it should have been obvious.

Resisting the head-banging just got harder. "Cass was right. Again. I hate it when that happens."

Jax laughed as he tugged on my hand and led our way to our first sort-of date. At the coffee shop. In the basement of the student union. At a college neither of us attended. Before we went our separate ways for the night. To hunt for a demon spawn who was terrorizing the town.

As messed up as our situation was, I couldn't help the giddy feeling that filled my heart. Jax liked me. Smart, sexy, fire demon Jax with the heart-stopping smile knew my deepest secret and he still liked me. If it was possible to get used to feeling as happy as I did in that instant, I didn't want to know. I wanted it to feel this special every time he looked at me.

Chapter Twenty-Nine

Saturday, October 29 - night

"ID please?" The bouncer stood six feet tall and based on his build, he could've played tight end for the college football team. I could probably take him in a fair fight, but out in public like this, I'd have to roll over and play dead like a good little puppy.

Cass turned on her vamp charm. "Oh, come on, we're with our friends, you already saw our ID."

"No, I didn't."

She didn't try the vamp mind tricks very often, mainly because the results were iffy at best. Based on this guy, I figured the recipient's IQ helped determine if it worked or not. Apparently people weren't susceptible to her skills unless they had two brain cells to rub together. The only thing this guy rubbed together were his hands, squeezing them and flexing every visible muscle.

Cass turned to me.

What? Did she expect me to fix this somehow? I could barely suppress the urge to do a partial shift and make the idiot piss his pants. We needed to get inside though. The scent of the demon spawn *had* come through here. Two hundred plus pounds of brawn was all that separated us from the ability to match a face to the smell. I strode up to the bouncer and tried to shoulder past, but he grabbed my arm.

"I need to see some ID."

The touch of the bouncer's fingers on my biceps was an annoyance I didn't have time or patience for—not with our quarry this close. "Is this enough identification for you?" I spun on him with a snarl. I hadn't actually shifted at all. I just let the beast take control of my face for a second.

It must have been pretty ugly, because Cass gripped my hand in her own and pulled me away from my position next to Mr. Intimidating. "Look, we'll just go check the car and see if we left our licenses in there."

We weren't getting into the bar. That much was clear. I grinned at the bouncer as Cass tugged on my hand. The dim lighting and dark denim may have hidden it from view, but my nose caught a whiff of his fear. And the urine that now stained the front of his indigo jeans.

Sometimes I just had to settle for finding joy in the little things.

An hour later, I hid behind a copse of trees in the northwest corner of the parking lot and slipped back into my clothes. I wanted to rant and scream, and quite frankly, to go kick the ever-loving shit out of the bouncer for not letting us in. Human and dressed once more, I stalked back to Cass.

"You're lucky Stadium Drive is so busy, otherwise everyone would have heard you howling." She'd been watching the entrance to the Wayside ever since she'd taken up her current position, but now she gave me a brief glance. "I take it things didn't go well."

I growled and started pacing. "Let's see, I've got a wolf inside me who is all pissy because I didn't let her run. Oh, and our buddy the demon spawn crisscrossed the damn parking lot like some messed up piece of abstract art. I don't know if he was meeting friends, trying to confuse anyone—like say, us—who might be following, or looking for his next victim." I kicked at a clod of dirt, sending it toward a cute little black sports car. On my way past, I caught the model: 370Z, a Nissan. It looked like the kind of car a guy drove in hopes of getting laid. I kicked another hunk of dirt at it for good measure. "The only thing I know for sure is the scent dissipates outside the parking lot. He came here in a car, but I can't tell you which one. We'd have been better off doing research at the library with Jax."

Cass leaned against a tree, looking a lot calmer than I felt. "Will you be able to smell the guy from here when he comes out?"

"No. I'll just have to move in and check people as they start to leave."

"Stop pacing. You look like an animal trapped in a cage at the zoo." Cass waved a hand at the spot next to her. "Want to talk while we wait?"

Great. All I wanted was to hunt something big, bad, and ugly, and my little sister wanted to have a heart to heart in the parking lot. I didn't have a better idea though, so I slogged over to the tree and leaned against the other side of it. "Fine."

I'd never realized how little Cass and I actually talked about life. Sure, we talked about patrols, and we talked about people at school. But honest *real* conversations? We never really had those until tonight. We leaned against the tree talking about all sorts of things, mainly about Jen and Eric and the great life we had with them. Protecting it at all costs. Cass kept dancing around something. I didn't know what. Then she finally spilled.

"I played out so many ways to say this in my head." She picked at a piece of bark on the tree, looking anywhere but at me. "First, I need you to know, I'm happy about you and Jax. Really. I'm just...afraid."

The retort I'd readied to throw at her died on my lips. "Afraid? Of what? You're one of the things that go bump in the night, remember? Other creatures of darkness fear you. What could you possibly have to be afraid of?"

"Of him taking you away from me." She was turned the other way, and if it had been anyone but Cass, I would have thought she was crying. But Cass didn't cry. Then again, Cass didn't get scared either. "I hate the idea of losing the Smiths, and the demon spawn's attack has really brought that home. But most of all, since the day we found out about each other,

I've been terrified of losing you.

"All my life, I've felt alone, Elle. I'm a freak of nature. I shouldn't exist. Then somehow, by one of those weird cosmic twists of fate that some people call miracles, I end up in a foster home with another freak. And even crazier—as different as we are—the two of us actually kind of like each other. Now, freak number three enters the picture, and sure he likes me, too, but he wants to be with you. Which leaves me alone. Again."

She stared at some fascinating dot on the horizon, and I tried to pick my jaw up off the ground. Once I managed that feat, I reached out and touched her lightly on the shoulder. "Cass, I had siblings. Before...well, before. You're more than a sister to me. You are my best friend, but we've always had other friends. They've never pulled us apart. Jax—"

"Is different. He isn't going to be just a friend, Elle, he's more to you than that. I see it in your eyes when you talk about him, and I saw it tonight. Plus he's part of the team now." Her shoulders trembled.

She's not crying. Cass doesn't cry. She...

She turned around at last. If it weren't for the fact that the lights in the parking lot made her eyes glow blue, I'd have thought she'd vamped out on me. The expression on her face was fierce, just this side of anger.

Thank goodness. This was the Cass I knew. I shook my head, turning back on my sarcasm. "He isn't going to come between us. Any guy who asks me to choose between him and you will find his butt kicked to the curb." I punched her in the arm. "We're sisters, Cass. Sisters are for life. Boyfriends? They might lead to a life sentence via marriage, but I don't believe in counting chickens that far in advance."

She snorted a laugh and I caught the ghost of a smile on her face.

"We good?"

"Yeah, Elle, we're good. Sorry for being such a dork."

I smirked. "Hey, we're all entitled to moments of crystal clear stupidity. They make life entertaining for the people around us. Otherwise what stories would they have to tell us when we're old and gray?"

"Oh, sweetie, I've seen your fur. You shouldn't talk about gray like it's a future color."

"Yeah, and I've noticed your preference for older dogs. Remind me to wear a spiked collar to bed for protection." We shared a brief laugh, and then both of us went rigid.

The door had opened. Music rushed out into the night—the bass much higher than necessary, and the beat altered in odd ways that were supposed to make the song easier to dance too. Instead it just made it sound strange and distorted. I caught a whiff of stale beer, but nothing more. We needed to be closer. A quick nod to Cass, and she followed at my heels until we stood in the shadow of the building about five yards from the door—close enough for smell, but not so close as to get chased off by bouncer pee-pee pants.

The first couple stumbled out amid shouted goodbyes. They smelled like sex, but not like the product of demon sex. The second pair smelled of marijuana dusted clothing and sweat, infused with other unnamable, but most likely illegal, forms of pharmaceutical entertainment.

I shook my head, giving Cass all the information she needed. The time for idle chitchat had ended. The college bar witching hour had begun as some people left and others took their places inside. This was our post for the rest of the night. Anywhere farther away and we might miss the demon spawn leaving.

So, we ignored thirst.

We ignored other biological urges.

We waited.

We watched.

And time after time, I passed the same message to Cass. "Nope, not our guy."

Shortly before two, larger groups of people started to leave the building, and it was all I could do to keep up with smelling them all. For a while, I managed. Then, a group of about fifty exited together, and while I was busy trying to catch the scent of those in the front, the unmistakable odor wafted past my nose.

"He's here."

"Now? Where?" Cass pushed off from the wall.

I pointed. "Somewhere in there. Time for us to blend in with the crowd." But just as we left the security of the shadows, even more people stumbled out of the bar, impeding our progress. We managed to merge with the group, but we couldn't make any headway.

Finally the crowd broke up enough that the odors of so many people so close stopped overpowering my nose, and I picked up the trail. We strode through the parking lot with purpose. Past the designated drivers struggling to get their friends into cars. Past the people arguing to get their keys back, because of course they were okay to drive. Past the one who definitely wasn't okay to drive struggling to figure out why his cell phone wouldn't unlock the car no matter how many times he pushed the send button.

The scent trail led us directly to the northwest corner of the lot. To a spot right next the "screw me" car I'd kicked dirt on. I hadn't given the car next to it a second glance because when we searched the lot, the trail hadn't come near here. And now the car was gone.

"Damn it!" I kicked at the concrete edging the lot.

"How did we miss this? We were *right here*. How did we miss his car?"

I gritted my teeth and shook my head. Why didn't we split up? She couldn't smell him. She could have watched and waited for a signal. "Do you remember anything about the cars that were here?"

"No, we picked this spot so the old smells wouldn't distract you if he came out. You said it was clean over here, so I didn't pay attention." She paused, and I continued pacing between the empty white lines. "How did he cover his scent?"

I bent over and grabbed a chunk of broken concrete. A scream of rage and frustration threatened to burst from my body. Instead, I released the emotions by hurling the manmade rock as hard as I could. It gave a satisfying *thunk* as it impacted a tree several yards away. "He didn't cover his scent."

"What do you mean?"

"I mean he came in one of the cars I checked out earlier. I

don't know which one, but one of them. He didn't leave in the same car. He left in this car," I sniffed at the air, "with a girl wearing Obsession. A girl who probably isn't going to be quite her normal self by tomorrow, all because I missed catching the freaking bastard when he came out here."

Cass tried to console me, but I didn't want to hear it. We couldn't save the girl who'd taken him home. We couldn't track her. We couldn't even hunt for her car. Once again, we'd lost the demon spawn.

Cass called Jax because I was apparently too angry to scroll through my contact list with any accuracy—I passed his name three times before she took the phone from my shaking hands. After we piled into his rumbling hunk of metal, she said the five words I least wanted to hear, "We'll try again tomorrow night."

I punched the dash and the door to the glove compartment fell to the floorboards with a clatter.

Jax flinched, but I had to give the guy fabulous boyfriend points—he didn't bitch. He just sighed. "I guess the dashboard might need to come before a paint job."

Cass leaned over the seat and patted him on the shoulder. "If you are going to continue letting Elle ride shotgun, you might want to hold off fixing anything she can touch."

"Shut up, Cass," I said.

"Lighten up. We'll just keep hunting. We'll get the guy eventually."

I twisted around in the seat, rage contorting my face. "How can you be so calm about this? Every day we screw up, he gets to more people. Hell, he tried to take out Jen. Our *mom.* Doesn't that mean anything to you?"

"Yeah, Elle, it does. It means we have to keep our heads. It means we have to be smarter than he is. It means we can't just react because overreacting could be as dangerous as doing nothing. So we keep hunting. There are two..." She glanced at Jax. "I mean three, of us. There's only one of him. As long as we keep each other on track, all we have to do is wait for him to screw up."

I slumped against the passenger door, silently praying it

didn't fly open beneath my weight. "And what if he doesn't screw up?"

She smiled, and for a moment it looked like wings and a halo would appear any second. "He's the bad guy. They always screw up."

Chapter Thirty

Morning, as usual, came too early, and regardless of what Jen had said about noon, she and Eric walked through the door at seven forty-five. I could've slept through them coming in, but the stuffed animal assault that rained on me from Cass's bunk was another story.

"For crying out loud—what?" I chucked teddy bears off my bed.

"They're arguing again, but I can't quite make it out."

I couldn't wait 'til the day Cass finally managed to rid herself of this obsession with hearing every little word uttered by our foster parents. "Fine. Just shut up and I'll do my best."

Jen's voice, rough with worry came first. "It's spreading. No one knows what to do."

"One of them will figure it out. It's what they do, Jennifer, we have to trust in that," Eric replied, but his voice was tight, like his own emotions were a runaway steed and the only hope he had of not falling off was to keep a death grip on the reins.

I was ready to tell Cass to go back to sleep, that they were just worried about Uncle Oscar. Then Jen spoke again. "What about the girls?"

What the hell?

"Eric, what about the girls? Do you think they're at risk?"

Of what? Catching a disease from someone we've never met? I ignored Cass's expectant look and concentrated on hearing everything.

"As far as I can tell we're all at risk." Eric sounded completely wiped out. "But I don't think they're in any more danger than anyone else."

"So what do we do? Hire a sitter?"

"We can't do that; they'll think we don't trust them."

"But we have to go back tonight; there are decisions that need to be made." Jen started clattering dishes around in preparation for breakfast.

The noises stopped, and I could just imagine Eric walking up and wrapping his arms around her tightly. "Then we do what we've tried to do all along—we rely on them to use their judgment. They won't let us down."

"I hope you're right."

They stopped talking, and the only sounds that reached my ears from the kitchen were of Jen cooking. Doing what she always did, as if nothing was wrong. But from what I'd just heard, there was more to their problems than met the eye.

I whispered the gist of the conversation to Cassidy, and then feigned sleep for another hour. Jen and Eric would be suspicious if we came downstairs too early, but even as late as we had gotten in this morning, I couldn't fall back to sleep.

Finally, Cass rolled out of bed and made enough noise to get me up. Breakfast was a quiet affair. Regardless of their attempts at making life seem normal with food, neither Jen nor Eric seemed inclined to talk. Even their responses to innocent inquiries about the mysterious sick relative were short. They answered politely, but with tones that indicated they didn't want to discuss it.

Doing dishes came as a relief for the simple reason we no longer felt trapped at the table in forced silence. The phone rang just as we were putting the last of the plates away. Jen answered with a curt "Hello?" Then she stood there and listened for a few moments. "Yes. That would be fine. I'll ask them." She held the phone towards us. "Your friend Jaxson wants to know if the two of you are interested in going to the pumpkin patch."

Cass covered her surprise better than I did. "Yeah, that'd be fun. We could get a pumpkin for tomorrow…unless you aren't up to trick-or-treaters."

I groaned; I'd completely forgotten about Halloween. I took the phone from Jen's outstretched hand.

"No," Jen said, "a pumpkin would be lovely. Even if we have to go back to the hospital, we'll set out some candy." She left the kitchen and returned to her computer, shuffling her feet, shoulders slumped. Jen needed rest, but normalcy was her rock, and it wouldn't be normal for her to go to bed at almost ten o'clock on a Sunday morning.

I raised the phone to my mouth. "Hey, Jax, yeah, we'd love to go. What time are you coming over?"

"With that deep a sigh, I'm wondering if you really want me to."

Hearing his voice sent a tingle of happiness through me, and I gave a short laugh. "No, it's not that." I glanced into the other room. "We'll talk later. Cass and I just need to know what time to be ready."

"In that case, beautiful, how's eleven sound?"

My stomach fluttered at the endearment. "Sounds fine. We'll see you then."

Jax arrived a little early in a car that ran a lot louder than it had the night before. "Sorry, I tried making some adjustments."

Cass yelled from the backseat, "Might want to try the other direction."

"Thanks, I'll give that a go later." Jaxson laughed as he pulled onto Portage Road. "We'll just wait 'til we get there to talk."

I nodded and tried to shut out the noise for the thirty-minute drive.

When we parked at last, Cass announced, "You *will* make some other adjustments before we leave, or I may just have to kill you in your sleep tonight."

I climbed out of the car and turned exhausted eyes to Jax. "If that's what happens when you make adjustments on something, remind me to never ask you for a backrub. If I wasn't made of such stern stuff, I'd puke on your shoes right now."

Cass snorted. "That isn't because you're tough, Elle. It's just because you wouldn't waste food like that."

Jaxson held up his hands. "Okay, ladies, I surrender. I was working on the car when all the puzzle pieces clicked, and I thought it was better if we talked right away." He glanced from one of us to the other, his face falling when our expressions didn't change. "I promise to fix the noise issue before we take off, fair enough?"

We nodded and let him lead the way into the office where he purchased tickets for the corn maze, earning back the great boyfriend points the noisy car had lost him by paying for both of us.

The man behind the counter eyed us warily. "You're the only people we've seen so far today. Word is an early winter storm might be rollin' in. You sure you want to try the maze?"

"Yes, sir." Jax grinned. "We've been waiting for this all fall; it's the first chance we've had to come out."

"All right, just remember to give a holler if you need help. Pay attention to the people on the bridges. If the weather looks like it's gonna turn ugly, they'll tell you to haul your butts out."

"We will. Thanks." Jax ushered us outside. "Come on, let's get ourselves lost."

We followed Jax into the maze. The benefits of dating a guy who knew what I was had to include the fact that it wouldn't surprise him when I could find our way out of this mess blindfolded. With the way he twisted and turned our path through the rows of cornstalks, I got the feeling he actually counted on it.

"So, in all my reading, I've had the whats and whys going through my head. This morning, it hit me. What could a demon spawn want?"

I glanced at Cass who looked at me with a blank expression. "Okay, I'll bite, Jax, what?"

"Save the biting for later." He winked, and I felt my face turn crimson. "The same thing I do on the rare occasions when my mom and I fight really bad: I wish I could see my dad."

Cass shook her head, running her fingers along the cornstalks. "But based on what you said before, the demon spawn has two half-demon parents."

"Yeah, but he is still missing that whole 'where do I come from' thing." Jax glanced from Cass to me. Neither of us must have given the oh-my-God expression he was looking for. "Isn't it obvious? He's looking for access to the pit."

"Isn't that a little extreme?" Cass asked, breaking off part of the cornstalk she held.

Attempting entry to Hell actually fit into the Worse-than-anything-I-had-imagined-so-far category. And as much as I wanted to agree with Cass, it made sense: the altar, the ritual, the blood, the zombies. Still I didn't want to believe it. "You have got to be shitting me."

"Hey, I'm research guy, remember? And while the Internet didn't help much, I did some digging in the old books I found at Western's library and found a few links to satanic ritual type stuff." We'd reached a dead end in the maze, and Jax stopped so he could turn and look at us. "I'll need to look into some more tonight, but I think we're close to an answer on how to stop him."

"What kind of rituals?" I asked, sniffing discretely to make sure no one was in the maze near enough to us to hear.

"Something about offering souls." He raked his fingers roughly through his hair. "I don't know Latin, and I have to translate a lot of stuff word by word. It's pretty much a given that I'm getting some of it wrong."

"Okay." Cass bounced around to keep warm. "Let's assume for a minute that our demon spawn is taking people's souls. It makes sense, given what we've seen. If that's all he needs, why isn't he burning in Hell and out of our hair yet?"

Jax pulled off his scarf and held it for a few seconds, his hands glowing red, before giving it to Cass. "As best as I can figure, he doesn't have enough. Almost like the offering isn't a worthy one."

Cass wrapped the scarf around her neck and tucked the ends into her jacket. "Okay, with us living in the great frozen north, your power rocks."

I didn't care about the scarf or the cold. I'd watched Jaxson closely as he talked, and something about the squareness of his shoulders seemed off—tense. "What aren't you telling us?" He turned and opened his mouth to say something, but he couldn't meet my gaze and turned away again. I put my hand on his arm and felt the heat radiating from his body through the leather. "Jax, we're a team, remember? What is it?"

His eyes reflected a pain in his heart I would never understand. "The translation might be wrong. I don't want to…"

"Tell us." I refused to let him look away again. "Jax, if it has you this worried, we need to know."

He gave a resigned sigh and nodded. "One of the texts made reference to abilities granted to those who enter the pit and return to the land of the living."

I waved for him to continue, knowing in my heart we didn't want to hear what came next, but that we needed to anyway.

"It said a successful journey to the underworld and back would give the traveler unlimited power over both the living and the dead. They would become a puppet master over all human existence."

Did I mention we didn't really want to know?

Chapter Thirty-One

Sunday, October 30 - early afternoon

I found our way out of the maze in half the time that it had taken Jax to get us lost in the first place. Cass and I wandered around to choose pumpkins while he fixed the car. The fence surrounding the patch groaned as the wind picked up, and a nearby scarecrow started to writhe in the breeze. The farm that had seemed so festive and happy such a short time ago had taken on an air of menace with the news Jax had delivered. I picked my way through the pumpkins, taking no joy in the thought of carving one into a jack-o-lantern.

"So what do you think?" Cass asked.

"About the pumpkins? I don't care; just grab a couple so Jen doesn't ask why we didn't bring any home." I couldn't focus. All I could think about were all those people. With their souls ripped from their bodies. And other than us, no one even seemed to notice. What did that say about humanity?

"Hello? Earth to Ellery…" Cass waved her white-gloved hand in front of my face. "Are you even listening to me?" She put her hands on her hips and for a brief second, her facial expression made her look like Tinkerbell, albeit in a puffy pink parka.

"No. Sorry, I was lost off in my own pessimism. What did you say?"

"I said, what do you think about what Jax said?"

"Oh." My mood sobered again. For a second there, I'd actually managed *not* to think about it. "I think we're screwed."

Cass shrugged, hefted a pumpkin, and thrust it into my arms. Then she bent down and grabbed a second, smaller one. "I'm interested in a little more detailed thought on today's news. Do you think it's even possible?"

I stared at the scarecrow, watching its legs flop around as a raven clung desperately to its perch on the arm. "Do I think it's possible the demon spawn is stealing souls? Oh yeah, as soon as Jax mentioned it, I knew it fit."

"And the rest?"

As we walked toward the store to pay for our pumpkins, Jax slammed the hood and caught my eye, giving me a wink and a crooked smile. I returned the smile, but in my mind, I saw him as the puppet of some demon madman, and the grin melted from my face. "The rest? I think we have to assume it's real. Because if we choose to pretend otherwise, and the bastard makes it to hell and back, it'll be too late for us to do a damn thing about it."

❧

Jax and I stood in the driveway alone; Cass had already taken the pumpkins to the porch and gone inside. "You want to what?" I stared, incredulous, sure I had misheard.

Jax cleared his throat before speaking again. "I…want…to…take…you…to…the…movies."

"The movies?" I stared at him blankly, my mouth gaping a bit until I realized it was open and snapped it shut.

"Uh huh. It's this crazy new invention. They have people moving around and talking on a big screen. It's kind of like a book, but it's almost…" he paused and waved his hands dramatically, "alive."

"I know what a movie is, Jax. I'm just confused about the why. If you wanted to talk more, we could have stayed out longer. It's going to be odd asking if Cass and I can go out again when we just got home. Besides the movie theater isn't exactly the prime place for a secret chat."

Jax leaned against the car and stuffed his hands in his

pockets. He stared at me for a minute until it finally got to me, and I started shifting under his gaze. Then he snorted. "You really don't get it do you?" Jax pushed off from the side of the car, closed the distance between us and rested his hands on my hips. He waited until I lifted my eyes to meet his before speaking. "I'm asking you out on a date. Just you and me. No Cass. No demon spawn. No plotting. No planning. Just us."

A date? We had work to do. "We can't go on a date."

Jax gave a crooked grin and kissed me gently. "Of course we can."

None of my arguments changed his mind though. Then he pulled out the "You are so strung out you can't even follow a simple conversation. You need a break." I couldn't fight him because he was right. All I could think about was the altar-builder and stolen souls. I was rapidly developing tunnel vision, which meant I'd miss seeing things sneaking up on us.

And of course, Cass had known Jaxson would ask. I didn't doubt she had Jen watching out the window the whole time. The instant I walked inside to see if I could leave again, Jennifer waved me out with the first genuine smile I'd seen on her face since Saturday morning.

Standing at the concession stand while Jaxson purchased a huge tub of popcorn and drinks, I realized that at least one good thing had come of the date. For one fleeting moment, Jen had been happy again. Then I caught sight of the grin on Jax's face, and I had to admit that this had several things going for it, even if I couldn't stop thinking we should be working instead.

With his hand heating up the small of my back, Jax ushered me to the theater, and the ideal spot in the back row. He handed me the popcorn. "Here, eat. I know that quick sandwich we grabbed at your place couldn't have been enough for you." He pulled two small packages from his pocket—protein bars. "I managed to procure these from Cassidy before leaving the house."

It must be love, or at least serious like. Most guys just thought about getting a girl alone in the dark when they went to a movie. Jax cared enough to worry about my stomach first.

"Thanks." I started munching on the kernels, trying my best not to appear greedy, even though he clearly knew how hungry I was. I glanced around and couldn't help laughing.

Jax cocked an eyebrow at me. "What's so funny?"

"This is just so weird."

"What do you mean?"

"Last night we hunted a soul-sucking demon spawn, and today we're at a movie."

"Yeah, that means today is normal. Last night was weird."

"Well, my life has more strange than it has normal. So the simple fact that this is normal makes it weird."

He raised his hands. "Okay, I give up, you win." When Jax lowered his hands, he took the opportunity to settle the one nearest me along the top of the seat behind my neck.

I leaned back, laying my head on his outstretched arm. "So, I heard this movie kind of sucked. Any particular reason we're watching it?"

Jax turned his body towards mine. "Because supposedly it sucks. Which means we should have the place all to ourselves." He inched forward until our lips met.

Apparently he was enough like other guys that he had planned on getting me alone. His fingers ran through my hair and pressed softly on the back of my head, drawing me closer to him. We kissed slowly, savoring the gentle caresses of lips and tongues as the popcorn bucket sat wedged between our bodies. He tried to move it once, before he noticed the death grip I had on its rim.

Hey, a girl has to have her priorities.

We actually watched the movie. Or at least we watched enough of it to confirm that it did, indeed, suck. I left the theater feeling really and truly human for the first time in years. We'd laughed at how badly written the dialog was. How the male lead couldn't act his way out of a box, even if it'd been left open. How stupid it was for the hero to stop mid-fight to kiss the girl. During *every* fight.

And we'd kissed.

And cuddled.

And it had been blissfully normal.

The realization that my life could be something other than the colossal mess it felt like on a daily basis elated me. Normal life stood within my grasp. I looked at Jaxson and decided that, for me at least, it was love.

Through it all, the beast slept.

Chapter Thirty-Two

Sunday, October 30 - afternoon

After the movie, we went on a walk near the house, holding hands like regular people and everything. The wind blew, and leaves fell from the trees around us in cascades of reds, golds, and oranges. It was magical.

Until we stumbled on the family of deer eating.

And the beast stirred.

"Jax?" My voice sounded so small, I feared he might not have heard me. So I said it louder, "Jaxson?"

He gave a very contented, "Hmmmm?"

His hand felt warmer than usual. Probably because mine had gone cold. "Can you take me home, please?" My voice sounded panicky, and I struggled to control my breathing. To control her.

Jaxson turned toward me. "I thought you were having a good…"

"I was. I am. Just, can we go back?" She wanted out. She wanted to chase the deer. And I wanted this time just for Jaxson and me. It wasn't hers to steal. "Please," I whispered.

Without another peep, he turned around, and we walked away from the deer. Scratch that, he tried to be civil and walk; I grabbed his hand and tried to run. I needed distance. I needed her to go back to sleep.

Jax ran alongside me for about half a mile then he tugged

me back to a walk. "If you need to run, you'll have to do it without me, Elle. I'm not the track star, remember?" His breath came in gasps.

I'd set a quicker pace than I'd intended. But we were away from the prey, and though the beast snarled and snapped, she couldn't grab hold of me as easily. "I'm sorry. The deer…"

He laughed until he started coughing. "What? You don't want to be in the position to choose between me and hunting?"

My eyes widened, and I was so mortified I wanted to throw up. "You knew?"

Jaxson leaned against a tree for support and gave me a quizzical glance as he tried to catch his breath. "Elle, you're a werewolf. Hunting's in your blood. I get it. It's okay."

I dropped his hand and backed away. "Is that how you think of me? That I really am some sort of animal?" The joy I'd felt earlier started blowing away like the leaves from the trees, falling to the ground to be crushed underfoot.

Stepping forward, Jaxson raised his hand and touched my face tenderly; I cringed away. "No, I don't think of you as an animal. I think of you as Elle." He caressed my cheek. "And Elle just happens to have some animalistic urges upon occasion."

No.

No, no, no. He couldn't think of me like that. I wanted what we had at the movies. I wanted normal. "That isn't me! It's her! I try to control her, but sometimes she's just too strong. It's like trying to tame a wild animal without having any sort of training or anything. I don't understand her, and she…she…"

Balking must have become the name of the game Jax and I played, because his mouth dropped open, and he stared at me. "Are you nuts? You can't tame her. She isn't a pet, Elle, she's part of you. That's like putting a choke chain on yourself."

He didn't understand. How could he? "Jax, I can't let her control me. I just can't…I can't become an animal. I'm a human being. I need to stay a human being." Tears sprang into my eyes and streamed down my face.

Jaxson's arms curled around me, pulling me against his

strong chest.

I tried to push away.

He thought I was an animal. He thought I was some sort of monster. I didn't want him holding me.

But he refused to let go; I would have to hurt him to put distance between us. "It isn't about you controlling her, or her controlling you," he whispered into my hair. "It's about learning to live with all the parts of you intact. And like it or not, she is part of you."

The scent of him filled the air I breathed. I wanted to cry because the beast loved it so much. I didn't want her happy. I wanted to feel normal again. I wanted her gone. "You don't understand."

"Probably not, but hear me out." For a minute he just held me and didn't say a word. "When I was a kid, I went to visit my great grandfather. He was a wonderful man, except for one thing. He was a hunter and kept dogs."

I bristled.

Jax ran his fingers through my hair, soothing away a bit of my ire. "He kept them locked up. He only let them out for hunting and training. He believed showing them affection would make them soft. When I was there, I snuck out of the house one night and into one of the kennels. That poor dog didn't know what to make of a little boy stroking its fur and offering it stolen table scraps." A painful lump formed in my throat at the image, and tears filled my eyes as Jaxson continued talking, "I refused to go back to his house after that visit. Even as a little boy, what he did made me sick. I knew it was wrong. He always said he had wonderful hunting dogs, but to this day I wonder how great they could have been if only he'd loved them just a little bit."

He kept his hold on my arm but stepped back so he could look at me. Jax tipped my tear-streaked face up to his. "Don't do that to her, Elle. Don't cage her like a tool you can just pull out and use whenever you feel like it. She's alive and she's part of you. Embrace her. Love her. Let her be part of you so both of you can be stronger."

Tremors shook my body as I struggled to understand the

emotions that surged through me. "I don't know how."

He leaned toward me and kissed the tears from my cheeks. "Then we'll figure it out. I won't make you do it alone."

I bit my lip hard enough to draw blood, but I nodded and burrowed my face against his chest again. Here, close to Jax like this, the beast and I both found contentment. With him, I could almost understand what he meant.

☙

"Are you sure? One of us could stay here." Jen wrung her hands. The last few days had taken their toll. Dark circles ringed her eyes, and her hands trembled all the time. She was aging before our eyes. "Uncle Oscar will understand if Eric shows up alone."

I exchanged a look with Cass while we gathered dishes from the table. "We'll be okay, Jen. It's Sunday night; both of us will be busy finishing homework. Do what you have to do."

Cass gave a firm nod. "She's right. Go take care of Uncle Oscar." Jen made a strange face at the name. "I'll make sure Elle is up in time for the bus if you aren't home yet."

Eric wrapped an arm around Cass but directed his words at me. "Girls, if you need us here, we'll stay. You're more important than…"

I interrupted with a shake of my head. "Eric, he's family. It's cool. Cass and I are pretty resourceful; we can manage another night alone and get up for school." I smiled at Jen, trying to appear as strong and capable as possible, without looking like I was shoving them out the door. Which was precisely what I was doing. "Go. Take care of your uncle."

Jen stood up, brushing her hands on the front of her apron. "If you're sure…"

"Positive."

"I'll go get my things then." Jen hung up the apron and left the kitchen.

I turned to put dishes in the dishwasher, fully aware that Eric still sat at the kitchen table. And that his narrowed eyes tracked my every move.

Jen and Eric's car pulled out of the drive, and before the garage door had even finished closing, the phone rang. "Hi,

Jax." I hadn't even heard his voice yet, but knowing he waited on the other end of the line brought a smile to my face.

The rich laughter that burst from his mouth sent a shiver up my spine. "Have I become predictable already? I'll have to work on that, otherwise you might get bored with me."

Cass sat with a book in her lap, staring out the window. She waved at me.

"Not likely." I smiled, knowing it would take an awful lot to make me bored with him. "But you're going to have to wait for a bit. I'm not sure they bought our innocent act. We need to hang out for a while, just to be on the safe side."

The tone of his voice shifted, and I could just see his lips twisting into a sarcastic smirk. "And no guys in the house while they are gone."

"Yeah, I'm sorry. It's just…"

The Chevelle roared to life. "Don't stress about it. I'll take off and give you a call from home in about, what? An hour?"

"Okay, that works." An hour would give us enough time one way or the other. "Thanks for understanding."

"No worries, beautiful."

❧

"So, did you finish all your work?"

I slammed the door shut. "Yes, Mister 'I'll call back in an hour'. Giving us twice as much time let us finish our homework." I paused and glared at him as Cass snickered from the backseat. "Of course, it also gave me ample time to wonder if you were okay. Especially since you didn't answer your phone and…" Then I saw the small box on the seat between us and blinked to clear my vision. *Nope, it was still there.*

Jax started the engine, and I caught him looking my way from the corner of my eye. I tried to tear my gaze from the box, but he'd noticed. "Sorry, I was a little…busy." He nudged the box toward me.

My mouth went dry, and I glanced from Cass smirking in the back to Jaxson nervously fiddling with the radio. My hands inched toward the box then I pulled them back.

"Oh for crying out loud, Elle." Cass kicked my seat. "Just

open the damn box so Jax can drive."

I looked at him, and he gave me the shyest smile I'd ever seen cross his face. Then he placed the box in my hands. I opened the lid and my breath caught. Nestled against the lining lay a thin rope necklace that glistened white under the glow from the streetlamps. And dangling from the chain was a charm in the shape of a wolf's head howling at an unseen moon. My hands shook as I sat the box back on the seat. I leaned over and kissed Jax on the cheek, whispering, "Thank you, it's gorgeous, but I don't think I can wear silver..."

He turned his head and pecked me discretely on the lips. "That's okay," he whispered back. "It isn't silver."

My eyes turned to the box and the chain that shone too brightly to be steel, then back to him. "Jax...it's too much. I can't..."

He reached over and squeezed my hand. "Hey, I am part Italian. Sometimes it pays to have connections." He winked at me and threw the car into reverse.

Cass couldn't let that one slide. "You got her a gift from the mob? Nice."

Jax pulled out of the drive and headed out of our neighborhood. "Maybe, but I know him as Jim, the same second cousin that gave me the car. He happens to be a jeweler." He glanced at me, and his face fell when he the gift still lying between us. "If you don't want to wear it..."

He left the sentence hanging there, waiting for me to do something with it. "I do, but I never wear jewelry. If I shift with it on I might lose it." And the last thing I wanted was to lose the first gift he ever gave me.

"I'm two steps ahead of you. I made sure the chain is long enough to still fit your neck in wolf form. It shouldn't cause a problem." He turned his hope-filled eyes to my face for a second. "Unless you don't want it, that is."

I shook my head as I lifted the necklace from the box. The chain shimmered as we passed streetlights, but the wolf held my attention. He'd given me a reminder of the beast. A reminder of her beauty and her solitude. I found it hard to swallow the lump in my throat enough to talk. "Of course I want it." I threaded the chain around my neck. "Thank you."

Jax pulled to a stop at a red light and turned to me again. I'm sure he saw the tears glistening in my eyes, and I'm equally sure he knew what they meant. He reached out and caressed my cheek. "Anytime."

Cass cleared her throat. "This is wonderful and sweet and all, but the light is green. Can we go?"

It seemed like the light wasn't the only thing that was green.

Chapter Thirty-Three

Sunday, October 30 - late evening

Cass plucked a leaf that clung tenaciously to its branch. "So when you two were having your little goodbye kiss, did Jax happen to say what he was doing tonight?" Her fingers ripped at the dried fibers, letting them float away in the gentle breeze.

"He said he wanted to do more research on the ritual. There might be a way to wreck it with the altar or something. Or a simple method of releasing the souls back to the bodies they belong in." I stopped talking as a group of revelers passed by us, my nose twitching for any hint of familiar scent.

Cass's duster billowed out behind her as she walked. If we had to prowl campus again, she would need to dress differently. Tonight she was drawing way more attention than I was comfortable with, but she seemed to soak it up.

"Why did you have to wear that? You look like a reject from the set of some futuristic thriller."

She preened. "It's the night before Halloween; lighten up. People are noticing, but not in a weird way." She eyed my jeans, boucle sweater and short leather jacket with disdain. "At least I fit in. What the hell are you dressed as?"

"A college student on a Sunday night." A quick look around proved she was right; most of the students out and about tonight had on costumes. Outfits ranged from what someone might find on a street corner in a seedy area of town to nuns in full habits. There were a bunch of people whose only effort at dressing up took the form of make-up. I lost count of the zombies in one group that walked by us. Sadly, more than one of them looked like they might have actually been zombies of the soulless variety.

On the plus side, I did find a certain amusement in the fact that the vampires tended toward frilled collars and tuxedo jackets, especially when I saw the way Cass glared at them. Apparently she didn't find it quite so funny, because from that point on, she made an effort to point out every werewolf we ran across. "Oh, now that one." She waved a hand toward a guy standing next to a woman in a bunny costume that would give her frostbite all over if she didn't get inside soon. "That one looks just like you after you change."

A few days before, being compared to the…thing…he was dressed as would have left me fuming. The mask had more leather on it than fur; people probably only called the costume a werewolf because they had no idea what else it could be. Tonight though, I was riding high on the date, Jaxson's gift, and the feeling we were close to stopping the demon spawn. So, I looked at the guy hunting the Playboy Bunny and said, "His tail is gorgeous. I hope mine looks that good after tromping through the woods."

"Wow, you've got it bad."

"Yeah, and you wish you had it." I stuck my tongue out at her. "Let's get back to work."

She laughed, and I think she sensed it, too—things were looking up for us. "All right, but I do have to say I think this is a lost cause."

I snorted. "What? You don't think randomly wandering around campus with my incomparable nose on the job will seal the deal?"

She tilted her head to the side and shot me a look.

My cell chose that exact second to burst to life. I jerked it out of my pocket and flipped it open.

"Oh. My. God." Cass gaped at me for half a second before she burst out laughing. "Please tell me that isn't the song that was playing at Homecoming when you and Jax danced together."

My cheeks burned, and I pressed the phone against my ear. "Hey, Jax, what's up?"

"I've got something. Meet me in front of the library. I think I know how to stop him." His voice was alive with excitement. "Don't run or anything. You don't...want to...attract attention."

I frowned at the way his last comment had broken up. "All right, all right, we'll walk." When he didn't respond, I asked, "Jaxson, is everything okay?"

"Huh?" He paused like he had to register what I'd said. "Yeah. There's just some guy out here having car trouble. I think I'll see if I can help while I wait for you."

An icy chill ran down my spine, waking the beast. "I'm not sure that's such a good idea."

"Lots of light here and tons of people out tonight."

"Okay, just be careful."

"Of course. Always. But to be fair, what are the odds of me finding trouble under the hood of a car?" He chuckled, but rather than making me smile, the sound had the beast's fur bristling.

"Are you kidding? I've seen your car. We'll be there in a few minutes."

"Sounds perfect. We'll find a place to grab some grub and talk." His end disconnected.

Cass bounced alongside me. "So? What's the word? Other than 'walk', I got that one."

I bit my lip nervously and turned to her. Then my mouth dropped open at the sight of a group of those zombies we'd noticed earlier moving toward us—a few holding weapons that gleamed too much to be plastic. "Wrong word." I pointed behind her. "Walk just changed to run."

I don't know if she looked or if she just trusted me, but she was on my heels as I dove into a patch of trees. Something about the way the zombies moved told me they wouldn't really care whether or not we were around a bunch of people if they caught us.

"Elle." Cass tried to grab my arm.

I jerked away. "Just run."

"Damn it, Elle, look out!"

The tunnel vision I'd worried about had come back full force. I'd never seen the zombie coming at us from the side. He plowed into me, and we landed on the ground hard, leaves erupting into the air from the impact of our bodies. I rolled, but he kept a grip on my ankle, yanking me back.

With a snarl, Cass flung herself at him. Her eyes vamp-black, she grabbed a handful of his hair and jerked his head back. Her fangs flashed as she dove at his neck.

"No!" I'd known what she was going to do the instant she jumped on him, but it wasn't until I saw Diego's face that it hit me how wrong it was. Cass paused. "They're people, Cass. People with families. People we know. We can't kill them."

Diego bucked in her grip, and the sound of our pursuit grew louder.

"And what do you suggest we do? Let them kill us instead?" Cass asked, grinding her teeth together. Then she opened her mouth and screamed as a pair of meaty hands grabbed her and pulled her off Diego. Bill. Big, burly Bill. Unless she bit him, Cass was out-matched.

Shit. "Sorry, Diego." I shifted under him, pushing against his chest as he tried to find a grip on my neck. "But you should really stop using this part of you so much anyway." As soon as I had enough space, I jerked my knee up, driving hard into his balls. The beast enjoyed the feeling way more than was healthy, but Diego rolled off me without resistance when I pushed.

I leaped to my feet and, casting a glance at the approaching group of zombies. Pain shot through my arm as my nails shifted briefly to claws and I grabbed Bill's arm, jerking it from Cass's waist. He tried to grab for me, but as soon as she dropped from his grasp, I spun and kicked at his kneecap. He crumbled to the ground in a moaning heap.

Cass and I didn't wait around for the others to overtake us; we bolted.

"I thought he wasn't supposed to be able to control the living and the dead until *after* he entered hell." Cass thrust a branch out of our way.

I ducked as it snapped back in place. "Guessing Jax translated that bit wrong or the zombies are a special case. Let's just grab him and get the hell out of here."

The library came into view a couple minutes later, and I breathed a sigh of relief when Jaxson's form shadowed the ground in front of the steps. Even though the beast remained on high alert, a smile lit up my face as we approached him from behind. I would definitely need to teach him a thing or two about covering his back. I wrapped my arms around his waist. "Hey, stranger. Love to stay here and chat but we really need to leave now."

Jax pulled my arms away and spun in a languid circle. My breath caught in my throat and my heart sank into my gut. I backed away from him, refusing to believe what my eyes couldn't deny.

Jaxson stared at us blankly for a moment and then blinked his wide vacant eyes at me twice before opening his mouth and forcing out a single word. "Hello."

Chapter Thirty-Four

Monday, October 31 - just after midnight

"No." I trembled and backed away from him. "No. No. No. No!"

Cass grabbed me by the arms and shook me until my head rattled. "Get a grip, Elle. The zombies are still coming. We need to get him into the car and get out of here. He can't drive. I don't have my license yet. You need to drive him home." I must not have responded because she slapped me hard across the face. "Damn it, he needs you."

I wanted to throw up. "It's not him."

"Yes it is. He's still Jax. He's still our friend. And we still need to help him." She picked up the backpack at his feet and slung it over her shoulder. Then she fished the keys out of the pocket of his leather jacket and plunked them into my hand. "So pull yourself together and go get the car."

The metal bit into my palm as I made a fist, and I closed my eyes, relishing the pain. It gave me a focus other than Jax and his empty stare. If I could avoid looking at him, avoid thinking about it, I could get us home. I could manage that much. I had to.

As long as he didn't try to attack us, too. *No.* I shoved the thought away by squeezing the key harder and striding into the parking lot. Tears stung my eyes when I found the Chevelle. I almost wished he drove a normal nondescript car like all the other guys at school. That way I could have looked at it and just seen a car. Looking at the Chevelle, it was all Jax.

Just get in and drive. Just get in and drive. I slid behind the wheel and twisted the key. *You can do this on autopilot.* The engine roared to life. I yanked on the gearshift and pulled cleanly from the parking space.

The car idled against the curb as Cass loaded...him...into the backseat and climbed in beside me. "Go."

I drove without seeing anything. My eyes stayed glued to the road. King Kong could have been playing baseball with a tree and a boulder on the side of the highway and I wouldn't have noticed. When I pulled into Jax's driveway, my hands had a death grip on the steering wheel. Cass reached over, put the car into park, and slipped the keys from the ignition.

"Get out of the car, Elle."

I didn't move. I couldn't. My knuckles were white and my shoulders had started cramping, but letting go wasn't an option.

Cass reached over and laid a hand on my arm. "It's his car. You have to leave it here. And you can't stay. So you need to get out." She began gently prying my fingers from the wheel.

She was right. It didn't matter though; my muscles still wouldn't obey. I tried to open my hands, but the instant my fingers loosened their grip, my arms fell limply at my side. Staring at my traitorous limbs, I tried to feel my heart beating. It seemed like it had stopped completely. The only noise inside my skull was the keening whine of the beast. For the first time, I wished I could reach out and hold her; she was the only one who understood what I felt.

Cass reached across my body and pushed the creaking door open. When I didn't climb out, she shoved me with what supernatural strength she had. I landed on all fours on the driveway. The irony of the position was enough to make me cackle. A door slammed on the other side of the car, and before I could stop my frantic laughing long enough to catch a breath, Cass hauled me to my feet and shoved my body against the side of the Chevelle, rattling the entire vehicle.

"Damn it, Elle, you need to get hold of yourself. Jaxson

needs to get into his house. You can either help me do the job or not, but if you bring neighbors to their windows with your screeching we'll have a whole other mess on our hands." Choking on the laugh turned it into a sob, and tears began to stream from my eyes. "Tears suck, but at least they're quieter. Are you going to help or not?"

Silent sobs wracked my body. "I can't, Cass, I just can't..."

"Fine." She walked up to the house and unlocked it. Back at the car, I heard her lure Jaxson out. When they came into view, she was dragging him. The concrete grated against his knees and the toes of his boots as he followed her, stumbling.

The sight was too much for me to bear. "Stop. I'll help." My breathing was quick and shallow, but I made it to her side and got Jax to his feet. I wrapped a shaking arm around his waist and started walking toward the door; he stumbled along beside me like a drunk.

Inside, Cass whispered, "We need to get him to his room without waking his mother."

I shook my head, my ponytail whipping about behind me. "She works nights this week. I know where his room is, I'll take him."

Cass stopped me with a worried look. "Are you sure? I can come with you."

I pressed my lips together, trying to ward off a fresh set of tears. "No. I need to do this."

She nodded curtly, and I ushered Jax down the hallway and into his room. After pushing him to a seat on his bed, I pulled off his boots and jacket, laying them neatly by his desk. I turned to find him staring at me. His hair had fallen over his eyes again, and the urge to reach out and brush it back seized my heart until I thought it would burst.

The tears came once more. I fell to my knees at his feet and took his hands in mine. "Jax, if any part of you is in there, please remember. I just found you. I can't lose you. Please remember me." I pressed one of his hands to my heart and the other to my cheek and squeezed my eyes shut as I willed him to come back.

When my eyes opened at last, his head was tilted to the

side, but still he only stared. My lips trembled, and I tried to hold back the cries threatening to escape my mouth. Releasing his hands, I pushed him back on the bed and lifted his feet onto the mattress. I kissed my fingertips and pressed them to his mouth. "I'm so sorry, Jaxson. I should have warned you people don't usually survive caring about me."

I caught my lower lip between my teeth and bit down; it was the only way I made it out of the room without sobbing.

Cass shut the door behind us. "We'll fix this. He'll be okay, Elle." In her hands she carried his backpack filled with the research he'd done at the library.

The books didn't matter. Without Jax they were meaningless. I shook my head. "No he won't, none of us will."

After the words had left my mouth, I lost it. Cass had to lead me home like I was newly blind and, considering how badly the tears blurred my vision, the image was apt. She helped me into bed, and as she yanked off my shoes, I had an image of me doing the same thing to Jax and my keening started again.

I hadn't even realized she'd left until Cass strode into the room carrying a steaming cup. She handed it over and, like a drill sergeant, snapped, "Drink it."

I glanced at the mug. I didn't know what was in it. I didn't care. I just raised it to my lips and tipped it up. The liquid burned all the way down and I knew it would hurt for a long time. I wanted it to hurt. I wanted to feel something...anything...other than the empty place in my heart.

Cass took the cup from my fingers and threw my legs on the bed. She pulled the comforter up to my neck before pulling on her own nightgown and climbing into her bunk.

The beast curled up in a tight ball, and I felt my head start to spin. "Cass, what did you give me?"

"It doesn't matter. You needed it."

In moments, I felt the tug of sleep. Spying the blissful emptiness before me, I realized she was right—I did need it.

꒰ঌ

"Stay home," Cass said. "I'll tell them you're sick."

The Smiths had come home sometime in the night; I could hear Jen fussing in the kitchen below us.

I stumbled from my bed and flopped into the desk chair, resting my head in my hands. "I can't sit here all day. Thinking about it by myself would be worse." I couldn't voice how it would be worse, I just knew what I'd said was the truth. I pushed to my feet and staggered out the door before Cass started arguing again.

The water pressure in the shower that always blissfully needled my skin felt dull. Though my flesh was red when I stepped out, the water had felt like a gentle rain. Downstairs, breakfast turned my stomach. I didn't want food.

Cass kicked me under the table and hissed, "Eat something."

Jen glanced at me, concern in her dark-circled eyes. "Elle, are you feeling okay?" She reached out and placed her hand on my forehead. "You don't have a fever."

I forced a wan smile. "I'm good, really." I stabbed a piece of French toast with my fork and shoveled it into my mouth as proof. It tasted like ash, but Jen seemed appeased, or at least distracted.

School passed in a haze. Every time I thought I should have stayed home in bed, the memory of the night before would stab at my heart, and only focusing on schoolwork pulled me past the hurt. The demon spawn knew we were the ones after him, and the attack on Jaxson felt like another personal blow. Until school ended, I wandered around looking and feeling entirely too much like I'd been one of his victims myself.

Cass leaned against the locker next to mine and wordlessly handed me a backpack. Only when I blinked at her did she bother to talk. "It's Jaxson's; you left it in our room this morning. I took his research out and figured you could return the bag when you see him after school."

I balked. "Cass, I'm not going to the bookstore." Seeing the unfilled backpack sagging against itself made me feel empty all over again.

"Don't be stupid. You have to go. We need to act like everything is normal. So you will go meet Jax and I'll spend the hour with Corbin."

I spun on her, my fear and rage finally finding an outlet. "That's what this is about? You don't want to pass up your time with Corbin?" My gorge rose and what little I'd managed to eat threatened to escape my stomach. "You selfish little…"

She slapped me—again. "Yeah, Elle, you're a wreck, and all I can think about is spending time with my tutor. Nice to know what you really think of me." Tears welled up in my eyes again, and she squeezed my hand. "We'll go through the research when we get home. We'll figure this out. We'll save him. But in the meantime, we have to pretend nothing is different."

I choked down the hurt and nodded, not trusting my voice.

"I'll see you in an hour. I'll meet you at the bookstore like we did last week." She gave my hand one last squeeze and strode down the hall toward the library, her golden glow making her the one ray of sunshine in the dreary gray of the building.

Glancing down at the weight in my hand, I swallowed hard and gathered the canvas into my fists. Jax needed me. If I couldn't do this much for him, I might as well go home and bathe in liquid silver before the demon spawn claimed me, too.

Chapter Thirty-Five

Monday, October 31 - afternoon

Jax didn't even look up when I walked in. I sat on the couch next to him, our legs almost touching, and he still didn't react. Tears welled in my eyes, but I forced them down with my mantra: *normal…normal…normal…*

I lifted his backpack and held it out. "You left this at my place."

Jax raised his head and blinked at the canvas. Finally, he reached out and grabbed it. "Thank you very much."

Who was I kidding? Anyone who had seen Jax and me together would know this wasn't normal, even if they had no clue we'd hooked up over the weekend. Instead of dwelling, I yanked out my history book and tried to pretend he was a new tutor. Someone other than Jax. Anyone other than Jax.

We made it through the hour. Barely. He seemed to know he should be there, but couldn't figure out why. I decided to pretend our roles had reversed for the day and did most of the talking. He nodded and took notes as if this was how things were supposed to be. I, on the other hand, managed to finish my assignment while wishing I could curl up in a ball and cry until the broken heart finally finished me off.

I glanced at my watch and started packing up. "It's time to go, Jaxson." He looked at me with his empty stare. "You need to drive me and my sister home."

"Oh." He stood up and gathered his things. The familiar stretching of his T-shirt across the muscles of his arms sent a physical pain through me, and I had to look away. At least he remembered his car and walked toward it without needing me to give him directions.

Outside, Cass was nowhere to be seen, and I silently cursed her. I couldn't handle being around this shell of Jaxson by myself. I swung my head toward the street, hunting for her familiar halo of blonde hair to come into view.

"Would you like to wait in the car?"

His voice startled me. I had no idea how to respond, but when the cold air bit through my jacket, I nodded. There was no way he would hold me and let his unnatural warmth seep into my skin. Not today. Maybe not ever again.

Jaxson wandered to the driver's side, opened the door, and climbed in. I bit my lip and closed my eyes, steeling myself. Then I yanked on the handle and jumped into the seat before I thought better of it. The door groaned when I pulled it shut. I sat there, my breath coming in shallow bursts, pleading mentally for Cass to show up soon, and hoping the demon spawn couldn't make Jax turn on me from afar.

"What should we do now?" he asked.

The phrase sounded like something Jax would say to flirt with me, but this time it was just a question. I leaned my head against the back of the seat and shut my eyes against the tears that threatened once more. "We wait," I whispered. He didn't speak again, and the silence soon became oppressive. I bit my lip and glanced his way to find him staring at me. "You don't remember me at all, do you?"

"Of course I do. You're Ellery Jameson."

"Yeah. Of course I am." I turned to the window. Images from the night before flashed through my head. *If only we'd been just a minute or two quicker. We'd have seen him. We'd know...* I jerked upright so quickly I almost hit my forehead on the upper edge of the window. "Jaxson?"

"Yes, Ellery?"

I swallowed the retort about my name. This wasn't the time. "What did you do last night?"

"I went to the library."

My heart started beating faster. "Did you see anyone while you were there?"

"Yes."

Damn the Jaxson-shell and his one sentence, or worse, one word, answers. "Who did you see?"

"You and your sister were there."

"Okay, Jax, did you see anyone else? Maybe before we showed up to take you home?" I tried to will him to remember, to force at least that part of his brain awake.

His brow crinkled, and I could see him trying to recall something. Then he shook his head. "There was no one else. Only the two of you."

My shoulders slumped against the seat. I had to remind myself it wasn't his fault, because all I wanted to do was shake him. "It's okay, Jax. Thanks."

"You are most welcome."

It felt like talking to a robot, and I couldn't handle it anymore. "Drive to the school. If we see Cass on the way, we'll pick her up."

"All right, Ellery."

But we didn't see Cass walking. Nor did we find her in the parking lot. Jaxson pulled up in front of the door nearest the library.

"I'm going inside to find Cass. Keep an eye out; if she happens to leave through the front door or something, lay on the horn." My gaze traveled over the Chevelle. "She'll hear it." *Assuming the horn works at least.* As soon as he nodded, I stepped from the car and slammed the creaking door.

The wind whipped up, swirling my hair about my head in a tornado of honeyed strands. For a moment, it obscured my vision, but I had no patience left, for my hair or anything else. I wanted to go home, to curl up on my bed, and block out everything. I reached up with a clawed hand, tearing the hair from in front of my eyes and ripping out a sizable chunk in the process. The pain felt glorious.

For a second I managed to not think about Jax—until the school door clicked shut behind me. The silence of the empty halls pressed on my raw nerves. Without people, without noise, without distractions, the quiet left too much room for thinking. I reached out and punched the nearest locker. My fist left a serious dent in the metal, but the echo that resounded through the hall was worth it. The noise released the hold my mind had on my legs and allowed me to move them. The heels of my boots made a sharp tapping noise with every step, helping to keep my thoughts at bay.

A glance through the doors to the library confirmed what I'd suspected. Cass stood there talking to Corbin, running her hand along a bandage on his forearm. He smiled down at her and brushed the fingers of his other hand through her hair. On some other day, seeing Cass so happy would have made me ecstatic. Today, it made me more than a little pissed.

I jerked open the door. "Cass, we waited for you at the bookstore. What…" I stopped midsentence as the acrid stench hit my nose and stared wide-eyed at Corbin. All-American, boy-next-door handsome Corbin, the math whiz.

Cass turned to me. "Oh, crap, Elle, I'm sorry, I didn't realize it was so late. Corbin hurt his arm over the weekend and was just telling me about it."

I swallowed hard and tried not to breathe. "I'm sure he was, but Jaxson is outside waiting. Can the story wait 'til tomorrow?"

Her eyes twinkled, and Cass gazed at me quizzically. "Um, yeah, sure. I'll see you tomorrow, Corbin."

He flashed Cass a grin, showing off the whitest, straightest teeth I'd seen outside of a toothpaste commercial. "Sure thing, Cassidy." He turned his hazel eyes to me. "Lovely seeing you again, Elle, and please give Jaxson my regards."

"I'll make sure to do that," I said through teeth clenched into a smile.

Cass threw on her jacket and picked up her backpack. The instant she reached the door, I nodded at Corbin and spun around. Leaving the library behind us, along with the unmistakable combination of odors.

Rosemary, cinnamon, hot metal—and charred flesh.

I waited until we got home to tell Cass about the scent of

demon spawn in the library. "Every time I was around him, Jax was there. One scent mixed with the other, I couldn't tell the difference."

"No way, Elle, you're wrong."

I slammed my fist against the dense wood of the bunk beds. "No, I'm not. The smell was fresh. It came from someone in the room, and we both know it wasn't you."

"Then someone else must have been in there." She spun on me. "This is just your emotions about Jax taking over. You want to blame someone. If you really thought Corbin was the demon spawn, you would have shifted in the library and taken him out." Her blue eyes glowed with anger.

It took less than a second for me to cross the room and grab her by the arms. I wanted to shake her. I wanted to smash her into the wall. Whatever it took to make her listen. "I couldn't shift there, and you know it. That would have put us at risk. Not to even mention the fact that if I killed him there, we'd never know what he did with the souls he took." My fingers squeezed her arms so tightly I feared her bones might snap, and I forced myself to relax. "Cass, you've always trusted my nose before. I wouldn't make up something like this. Not now. Not ever."

She shook her head fiercely. "But you can't be sure." She knew I was though, I could see it in her eyes.

"What did he say about his arm?"

"What?"

"You heard me. The arm."

She stared at me for a full minute before wrenching her own arms from my grasp and responding. "Corbin said his neighbor's cat got itself stuck in a tree. Being the nice guy he is, he climbed up to get it, and the damn thing ended up scratching him really bad. He thought he was going to need stitches in a couple spots."

I pursed my lips and gave her a tight nod. "Okay, then tell me this: why did his arm reek of charred flesh?" Cass gaped at me. "And even more than that, charred flesh on top of smoldering meat?"

She raised a hand to her mouth, probably imagining

exactly what I had—our friend the fire-demon lashing out when he was attacked. "Oh my God. Jax."

"Yeah. He fought back." The pain on Cass's face pierced my heart. I hated having to tell her that her golden boy was anything but perfect. Too bad our situation left no room for subtleties. She had to know.

"So what now?" she whispered.

I pointed to the stack of books resting inconspicuously next to the closet. "Now we figure out what Jaxson found last night." I took her hand in mine and squeezed it gently. "And we figure out how to use it to stop that sweet-faced liar from hurting anyone else ever again."

Chapter Thirty-Six

Monday, October 31 - late evening

Jen and Eric had gone off to deal with Uncle Oscar again. This time we practically did shove them out the door. We poured over the books Jax had in his backpack. He'd taken notes, but in some cases, the Latin made more sense.

Cass slammed the tome she was reading shut. "That's it, we either have it or we don't; I don't think I'm going to figure out anything else from these books."

"Yeah, you're probably right. We don't have the time to worry about translating more gibberish." Cass had already spent hours plugging things into online language translators. Some of it helped us understand the written notes, but the rest came back as incomprehensible as the original language. We'd figured out almost all of Jaxson's scribblings, but my lips twitched in consternation as I stared at one last piece of his chicken-scratch handwriting.

"What is it?" Cass peered over my shoulder.

I pointed to the paper. "This. I can make out your name, so I don't think it has anything to do with the Latin stuff."

She cocked her head to the side and tucked an errant strand of hair behind her ear. "Does that say morgue?" Her finger touched a word.

"Maybe, but what would a morgue have to do with you?"

Cass shrugged. "Damned if I know. Unless he wants me

dead."

"Doubtful." Something tickled my brain. On our date, Jax and I had talked movies for a bit. Everything from animated to horror. The tickle turned into an itch. We'd compared our favorite movies of all time…his was *Silence of the Lambs*. The itch became a pinch, grabbing hold of me and yanking the memory from my brain. Me mentioning the goofy scene in the morgue where everyone put something under their noses, and him explaining why they did it. "The smell. He figured out how to get you inside the cemetery."

"Really? That rocks." Her face brightened, but when I didn't go on, the smile faded. "You plan on sharing anytime soon?"

"You aren't going to like it."

Cass snorted. "I don't like the idea of you dealing with that piece of hell-spawned filth alone either. I'll deal. What is it?"

I stood, strode out the door, and down the hall to the bathroom. I returned holding a small blue jar in my hand. "Menthol rub. Wear enough of it under your nose and you shouldn't smell anything else."

She gagged and her lip curled in disgust. "Please tell me there's something else."

I shook my head. "Sorry, Sis, it's basically what they use to block the smell of decomposing bodies, anything less might not be enough."

"Have I mentioned how much I hate Corbin?"

My lips curled into the first real smile I'd felt since the night before. It was a slightly evil one, but genuine nonetheless. "Not until now." I tossed the jar, and she caught it deftly. "Make sure to visit one of your canine companions before we leave. I want you well fed, just in case that doesn't work."

"Are you sure you don't want to shift right away?"

The cold lanced through the coat I wore, piercing my skin. We'd tucked the rest of my clothes safely inside a duffle bag. "No. We need to destroy the altar. We'll have an easier time doing that with me in human form. I'll shift when Corbin shows."

Cass fidgeted as we loped through the trees. "What if he can sense the altar somehow and knows that we've destroyed it? He might not come at all."

We neared the edge of the trees, and the full orb of the moon showed Cass's eyes bleeding to black.

"Then we hunt him down and deal with it," I said. "For now, put on your party make-up before you decide I look like a tasty late night snack."

She twisted the cap off the jar and smeared a glob of the jelly under her nose. Then she retched, quickly turned away, and vomited up a stream of dark liquid.

"So much for you not being hungry for this," I muttered.

She wiped her mouth with the back of her hand, leaving a smear of blood on her cheek. "No worries, my friend was in a giving mood tonight. There's more where that came from." She spread another liberal application of menthol under her nose.

"You killed the neighbor's dog?" That seemed extreme, even for Cass.

"I didn't kill Rex. He's going to need a nice recovery period before I feed on him again, but he's fine." She winced away from the odor she couldn't escape, but her eyes had returned to the perfect blue pools nature had meant them to be. "Let's get in there and get this over with."

I nodded, and we turned as one toward the cemetery. We crossed the street without incident, but as we made our way to the altar, it became obvious we didn't have to worry about tracking down Corbin. He was already there. Waiting for us.

His handsome, angular face took on an evil cast as fire flared in his palm. "Welcome to the party, ladies." With a sneer, Corbin thrust out his hand, the flames flying toward us.

Cass and I dove away from each other in order to avoid the oncoming fireball. I jumped to my feet, but before I had the chance to do anything more, the ground around me erupted in towering flames, the heat licking at my skin and threatening to set my coat ablaze. He had trapped me in a narrow prison of fire—there wasn't even room for me to shift. The beast snarled, enraged by the flaming cage, and a growl escaped my own lips.

Corbin grinned and shouted, "It'll be your turn soon enough." He turned his gaze to Cass. "Right now I have plans for your sister."

As if he had summoned her, Cass leaped up and charged at Corbin. He didn't bother with fire. He didn't have to. Cass had vampire speed and strength on her side, but Corbin had something, too—his other demon power. Cassidy reached him and pounced at his throat with her fangs bared. He grabbed her with one hand, and flung her straight up as if she weighed nothing. She screamed in rage, and he yelled over the sound, "Bet you didn't see that one coming, did you?"

Corbin caught Cass in one hand with as much ease as he had thrown her. "You stupid. Little. Girl." He held her by the neck as far as his arm would allow, and her attempts to kick him were futile. She couldn't get the leverage she needed to do any damage. Her fingers flailed at his arm, hitting and clawing, but all he did was release an evil laugh that cut through the heat of the fire and chilled me to the bone.

I could just see Cassidy's eyes. The blackness that she pushed to the surface had begun to bleed away. Corbin squeezed her neck tight enough she was on the verge of passing out.

"Fight it, Cass!" I screamed, but she was too far gone to hear me. And as the sound of my voice faded, I heard something else: the sound of feet shuffling through the dead leaves. A whole lot of feet.

Zombies were closing in on me from every side. Slowly though, not attacking like last night. I wasn't planning to run off, so I tried to ignore them and focus on my objective…and my sister.

Corbin pulled her sagging form toward him. "You are pathetic. I played you like a toy, teasing your emotions day after day." He scowled at me. "If it wasn't for your sister over there, this would have all happened so much nicer. But now, the two of you have screwed with things and left me no choice but to take what I want by force. And I'm sure you both have such innocent, pretty little souls. Adding you to my collection should be more than enough for the gatekeepers. They'll have to let me in now."

He started chanting and waving his free hand through the air in a dizzying pattern. I froze as soon as it hit me that I had a front row seat to watch him turn my sister into the living dead.

I crumbled to the ground. I couldn't help her. The fire burned so thick around me I couldn't see a way out. So close I couldn't shift inside the circle. If I moved at all, it would burn me. There was nothing I could do but watch.

Desperation had me ready to risk running through the flames anyway when I caught a good look at the zombie closest to me. The one that wore Jaxson's face.

First Jax. Now Cass. I'd failed them both.

In the moonlight, the chain around my neck glittered. The beast clawed at my aching heart, struggling to get out. Then I remembered what Jax had said, "Let her be part of you so both of you can be stronger." A smile probably more reminiscent of an animal than a person crossed my face.

This may kill us both, but at least we aren't going to just lie down and die.

I stood up and flung the coat off my back; the blaze incinerated it almost instantly. Lifting my nose to the air, I let the beast take me. The two of us issued a brief howl. Then I jumped and soared through the flames. They licked my skin, and I felt it begin to bubble. The stench of burning flesh assaulted my sensitive nose even as I felt the layers of skin sear away. The fire ate the oxygen, and I gasped for air.

I cleared the flames at last, and in those final milliseconds as I soared through the air, my body contorted. When I hit Jaxson and knocked him to the ground, it was with paws that took off at a run. I still hurt, I could still feel the burns, but my new body didn't have a mark on it. It was whole. It was strong. I let the beast and her instincts take over. The man in front of us was attacking our pack. And that was not allowed.

We bared our teeth and snarled, vaulting over the cut fence and flying toward him. Cass dangled in his grip with her mouth slightly agape, and a faint pearlescent mist hung in the air before her. We leaped at the arm he held Cass with, our canines puncturing the skin and tearing the flesh away. Our sister fell from his fingers and we pounced at her, shoving her out of his reach.

"Bitch, you'll pay for that!"

We spun on our prey as he issued a command. We didn't need to hear it. He spoke to the zombies, and we only cared about him. He held something shiny in the arm that still functioned. "Knife," the human part of our brain supplied. Our lips pulled back and adrenaline coursed through us. Many things we'd hunted were dangerous. But we'd tasted him. He was food.

The knife ripped through the air. We had just enough time to move so we caught it in our flank rather than our chest. Blood leaked from the wound around the blade and we howled in pain. The brief distraction was all he needed. He was on top of us, muscling us to the ground with inhuman strength, grabbing the blade and twisting.

We snapped at him through the pain. He might be strong, but so were we, and his flesh was even more vulnerable than ours. Our teeth found purchase on his abdomen and we bit down. Jerking our head back and forth, we tore the mass of flesh and muscle away.

He screamed and drove the blade through the thin flesh behind our hock and embedded it in a tree root. We were pinned to the ground. If we pulled from the knife, it would slice through the tendon—crippling us. He stood and kicked us in the head.

Our world spun in a dizzying array of light and pain. At last our vision cleared, and we saw him standing before his altar as the zombies closed in on us. His eyes were closed and he'd started chanting again. The ground beneath us trembled and steam rose into the air.

He was doing it—he was opening the way.

A familiar face swam into view, devoid of the life we'd so come to love. Jaxson. We had to save him. Had to save them all. Even as a zombie, he gave us strength.

We reached our muzzle around, and gripping the handle of the knife in our teeth, yanked it free. The blade nicked the tendon, but didn't sever it. In one movement, we were on our paws and airborne. Corbin opened his eyes just in time to see our forepaws hit him in the chest with all the momentum a hundred and thirty pounds of wolf could pack. He flew backward, his feet scrambling for purchase on the rough ground. His heel caught on a rock and he fell onto his altar. The impact of his body splintered the wood and the altar bent in two, broken through the middle.

The tremors below our paws ceased. We jumped at him from solid ground, landing on his chest, our ears ringing with his scream of rage. A thin line of drool trailed from our gaping mouth, a grim reminder that we were there. His eyes met ours, and the stink of fear filled our nostrils. Our jaws snapped shut on his neck and we wrenched our head back, tearing his throat from his body in a gushing spray of blood. Silencing him forever.

Epilogue

Monday, October 31 - nearing midnight

We had our muzzle buried deep in the still warm entrails of our prey when we felt a gentle tap on our back. Without bothering to raise our head from dinner, we issued a warning growl. This was our kill. The scavenger could feast once we'd eaten.

"Elle?" The quiet voice had a familiar ring, and we paused in our binging. "Elle? You need to stop. You're eating a person."

I pulled back mentally from the beast and yanked our head from Corbin's remains. The beast wanted to keep eating, and it was all I could do to rein her in and remind her that at our heart, we were human.

"Good girl, Elle." Cass's voice was calm, soothing, like she feared I'd turn on her next. The thought made me sick. "We need to get rid of the body somehow."

We snorted and blood sprayed from our nostrils. The stench of menthol assaulted our nose, and I wondered how much Cass had put on when she'd recovered her senses. A quick examination of the corpse told us she was mistaken though. Corbin's body showed no evidence of foul play. He looked precisely like the victim of a wild animal attack. Ignoring Cass and her sputtering, we wandered into the cemetery and dug a small hole in some loosely packed dirt.

She followed closely behind. "We can't just leave him, Elle."

It's time.

The beast whined, but she knew I was right. The shift happened in seconds and without pain. We were partners now, the beast and I; while the balance still fluxed, we'd never again battle for control as we had. I stood wobbling on my two very red, very tender, and still very warm, human legs. Then I promptly dropped to all fours and vomited up everything my stomach felt willing to release. I wiped my mouth with the back of my hand and started shoving dirt into the hole.

"Yes we can, Cass. If his body goes missing, there'll be an investigation. If we bury or burn the remains it just proves people were involved in his death." I glanced back in the direction of the altar. "We leave him as is—the unlucky dinner of a pack of hungry dogs."

Cass's brow wrinkled, but she gave a mute nod and handed me the bag containing my clothes. "Thank you," she whispered, "for saving me. I couldn't stop him and…"

"No worries." I winced as I tugged rough denim over my burnt limbs. The shift had helped dramatically, but they would still hurt for a day or so. "I'm just glad I got to him in time." I stepped forward and staggered. The nick in my Achilles would take more than a few days—good thing there was almost a week before I had to run in state finals.

She picked up the bag and started toward the cemetery gate, turning around when she noticed I wasn't behind her. "If we aren't getting rid of his corpse, we probably shouldn't hang around."

I jerked my head toward the altar. "I want out of here, too, but we aren't done." I waved a hand at the group of zombies. "I know a few people who might like to have their souls back, and we can't leave them." I picked my way through the cut in the fence.

Once inside, I addressed the silent group. "Go home. All of you. Forget you were here. Sleep." As one, they turned their blank gazes on me, and I suppressed a shudder. My voice quavered as I said again, "Go home. Now."

The zombies did as I'd ordered and stumbled from the field. So much for no evidence of people. It couldn't be helped though. I stepped toward the altar again.

Cass caught up to me just as I reached the circle on the ground. The cold night air had made the blood on the ground slick and my good foot flew from beneath me. The weak ankle couldn't support my weight. Cass reached out to help, but I ended up taking her down.

We lay in the dirt for a moment, manic laughter coming from both our mouths. Then I reached up and, grabbing the edge of the altar, tried to pull myself to my feet. Corbin's weight had shifted and no longer held the wood stationary. In using it to lever myself up, I yanked the altar toward us, and the jar on it soared through the air, crashing against my head, and dousing both of us with blood. Cass and I stopped laughing.

"And how are we supposed to explain this?" she asked, wide-eyed.

"It's Halloween—we don't have to…as long as you'll be okay." She waved my concern away, her eyes swirling, but still mostly blue. "I'm just glad it wasn't the other jar."

"Other jar?"

I pointed at the opposite side of the broken altar. A large piece of stoppered pottery rested against the wood. "I saw it when I was trapped by the fire." Stepping around Corbin's body, I picked up the earthenware jar, and carried it over to Cass. "Here's hoping this is all it takes." I tugged out the stopper and we peered inside. Pale mists of every color of the rainbow swirled and writhed within the jar, emanating an unearthly glow.

"Is that them? The souls?" Cass's voice was quiet, reverent.

I bit my lip and nodded.

"Why are they still in there?"

Shoving the stopper back in place, I scowled. "Because nothing is ever that easy." I cocked an eyebrow at her. "Ready to learn Latin?"

Cass groaned.

I put my arm around her shoulder, and without another

word we walked out of the cemetery and headed home. No one gave us a second glance. Even splattered with blood as we were, people assumed we were just another pair of Halloween partiers. Their nice, normal world was still safe.

And I was content to let them keep believing it. I wanted nothing more than to get home, get cleaned up, and get to bed. Our lives were complicated enough without a bunch of questions. I slid my key into the door and twisted the handle. We slipped inside the glow of the foyer light, and I slumped against the door as it latched closed behind me. We'd made it. We were home. Now all we had to do was figure out…

"Girls?" My eyes shot open to see Jen and Eric step into the tiny room. I didn't have a chance to think of an explanation before Eric spoke again. "I think we need to talk."

~ABOUT THE AUTHOR~

Teenagers are greatly under-appreciated. Until one of her students read a piece she wrote and told her she should become an author, Julie never seriously considered it. To this day, she still appreciates the wisdom and council of teenagers.

No longer teaching, now she splits her time between raising her own kids and living in the world of her imagination (where her children occasionally visit). They reside in southwest Michigan with her wonderful (and very patient) husband and the faithful German Shepherd mix they're all convinced is a person trapped in a dog's body by some sort of curse. She doesn't want to change him back though - it'd be too hard for him to lie on her feet under the desk if he was human.

You can visit Julie at: www.julieparticka.com

Immerse Yourself in Fantasy

with

Decadent Publishing

☙

www.decadentpublishing.com

CPSIA information can be obtained at www.ICGtesting.com
Printed in the USA
267346BV00001B/7/P